Present Fears

'Taylor mingles the elegant with the grotesque, as if seating Flaubert next to William S. Burroughs at dinner' – *Publishers Weekly*

'Elegant, polished surfaces . . . deftly turned and easily read'
– *Literary Review*

'Very funny . . . much about Bad Gentiles — and, alas, Bad Jews — but its cool cruelties do deserve a wide readership'
– Amanda Craig, *Jewish Chronicle*

'She writes brilliantly of emptiness, and the need for love'
– Elaine Feinstein, *The Times*

'Elisabeth Taylor writes beautifully, every word neatly chosen, every sentence clear as a bell' – *The Tablet*

'Elegant and witty surfaces break open to reveal the darkness at the heart of these cosmopolitan tales' – Georgina Hammick

Present Fears

Elisabeth Russell Taylor

ARCADIA BOOKS
LONDON

Arcadia Books Limited
6-9 Cynthia Street
Islington
London N1 9JF

First published in Great Britain 1997
Reprinted 1997

A catalogue record for this book is available
from the British Library.

ISBN 1-900850-04-4

Typeset in Monotype Bembo by
Discript, London WC2N 4BL
Printed in Great Britain by
Biddles Limited, Guildford and King's Lynn

Arcadia Books are distributed in the USA
by Dufour Editions, Chester Springs, PA 19425-0007

Published with financial support from
The London Arts Board

CONTENTS

ELISABETH RUSSELL TAYLOR

was educated at the Sorbonne and at King's College, London.
She has received numerous awards, including a
Wingate scholarship and grants from the Arts Council and the
Authors' Foundation. As well as six highly acclaimed novels,
Russell Taylor has published literary criticism, journalism and
children's literature, and has written for film and radio.
She is married to the painter Tom Fairs and lives in London.

The Sin of the Father

'Put me through to the doctor.'

'I'm afraid the doctor's still with a patient.'

'Do you know to whom you are speaking? This is Mrs Grossman! Put me through at once!' Dr Grossman's secretary knew better than to demur.

'Joseph! I want you home at once! Portia is out of control. She's been rude to me!'

'Sybil, I'm with a patient. I shall be at home at the usual time.'

The doctor put down the receiver carefully and turned back to the young woman who lay on the examination couch in the foetal position, her face to the wall. She was fully clothed but for her French knickers that were pulled down round her knees exposing her naked bottom. The doctor drew on a pair of gossamer-thin rubber gloves and as he gently explored the woman's rectum for a possible growth Dr Grossman found his solace. Here was something with which he could cope: a physical diagnosis. He felt well pleased with himself. Only that morning Sir Barnes Fitzpatrick, the royal physician, had rung him, Joseph Grossman, a mere South African Jew twenty years his junior, for a second opinion. And only last week the organizing secretary of the London Cancer Convention had written asking him to elaborate on his article in the *Lancet* on varieties of rectal carcinoma. As Joseph's fingers probed the diseased cavern, somewhere from the back of his mind the thought seeped into his consciousness: some varieties of birds shit over their feet to keep cool.

Joseph Grossman had not wanted to be a doctor. He had wanted to be a geologist.

'And what sort of a profession is that for a nice Jewish boy?' his father had bawled, adding that it was sheer lack of gratitude on his son's part so much as to suggest such a thing. He would be made a laughing stock at his Lodge.

'What am I to say? "Joseph? Oh he's studying stones." Stones, my boy, we Jews know enough about stones without studying them. We've been the target of stones for two thousand years: big stones, small stones, sharp stones, blunt stones....' Baruch developed the theme with all its variations until he was satisfied he had exhausted its range.

'So, go ahead, my boy, break your old father's heart.' And when that

elicited no opposition he delivered the *coup de grâce*:
'There'll be no money for studying stones!'

Joseph studied medicine. But to spite his father he failed his first MB. He regarded the humiliation his father suffered as worth the personal inconvenience of having to resit his second year.

Baruch Grossman's pride would have been best served had his only son stayed in Johannesburg, bought an architect-designed house in Houghton, recruited a minimum of six servants, put in a larger swimming pool and a tennis court, married Baruch's partner's 'lovely' daughter, and become a brain surgeon. In the event he settled for Joseph's removal to London, England, to take up a houseman's job at Barts, to prepare for his Membership. Baruch was still in something of a dilemma, however. Should he give Joseph all the material assistance his son expected, or keep him short, show him who was master and thereby lure him back to South Africa and the prospects of wealth? The compromise he settled on was like most compromises, a disaster.

Things might have been different for Joseph had his mother lived but she died when he was an adolescent. His father raised him, taking good care that Joseph never became attached to a surrogate mother. Indeed, it seemed that Joseph became suspicious of women after his mother died. When invited to parties he tended to search out the younger children of the household and, rather than dance, he played with them or read to them. He never mentioned his mother's name. She was lodged in his heart and he did not dare dislodge her to examine his feelings.

In 1927 Joseph and his fellow examinees sat for their Memberships. On receiving news of his success Joseph put in a call to his father, and Baruch, over an admittedly faulty line, was predisposed to understand that, out of sixteen examinees, his son alone had been successful. Drawing himself up to his full five feet and three inches he looked down at his personal servant who had been polishing his master's shoes under his office desk, and communicated the news. The bemused African, realizing his pay-master was expressing extreme pleasure, and knowing which side his mealy-meal was seasoned, rose from under the desk, plastered a smile from ear to ear across his face, and jumped from his left to his right foot and back several times.

'Masser Joseph right fine man, baas!'

Joseph had met Sybil Young at a dance given in Bayswater by a pollarded branch of the Rothschild family. By making astute enquiries he had been able, throughout the London season, to weave his way in and out of dances and dinners to which Sybil had been invited. His relations with the haughty young woman were straightforward enough – he placed her on a pedestal and sat at its feet, an attitude she approved – and worshipped her. Sybil had one London season behind her, and had had to come to terms with the unpalatable realization that no member of the Rothschilds, the Sebag-Montefiores or the Waley-Cohens had shown serious interest in her. English Jewry knew her provenance. Whilst unanimous in their agreement that she was as beautiful as she was accomplished, they were as snobbish as their hosts, the English, and Sybil's father was a travelling salesman. For her part, Sybil was determined not to marry out, however persuasive Sir Avon Smythe, and she was certainly not making herself available to trade, and although a South African cut no figure in London society, a rich doctor of South African extraction (she would do something about the terrible accent in due course) *was* a possibility.

Sybil had been blessed with an abundance of auburn curls, a straight back, a slim figure and somewhat above average height. She had cold grey eyes and thin lips and unless she remembered to appear interested in what she was being told, or at what she was required to direct her gaze, her mien was expressionless. She had been taught at dancing class that it was *comme il faut* to eschew enthusiasm. And so it was she affected indifference and a languid pose towards life, and directed her gaze, particularly towards men, from lowered eyelids. Within the family circle no one ever crossed Sybil. Her very presence was regarded as a privilege; she performed as it was deemed correct to perform and was gracious in accepting praise for so doing. Her mother and father were aware of her coldness but interpreted it as a sign of good breeding and therefore an essential ingredient for social success – and a good marriage. It had been their greatest pleasure to indulge her.

Sybil had to contend with the none too agreeable fact that her family originated in central Europe ('thank God not from Poland, though'), and was neither rich nor educated. Fortunately, her parents had had the good sense to send her for a year to Aunt Rosie in Paris to 'finish' her. 'Finishing' expressed itself in the acquisition of a variety of accomplishments with which Jane Austen's heroines would have felt well satisfied. Sybil sang sweetly to her own skilled accompaniment, embroidered exquisitely, and was able to reproduce a likeness from nature. 'Tante' had married for love and notwithstanding achieved an enviable position in French society by judicious dealing on the Bourse. Sybil's cousins were generous in sharing with her the benefits they had reaped. Sybil's finely tuned ear helped her with her French pronunciation and her eye, assisted by her cousins' fashion sense, led her to dress more stylishly than her English rivals. Her doting parents mortgaged themselves to the hilt to

9

equip her with the extensive wardrobe 'Tante' indicated was the minimum required by a young woman looking for a husband more privileged than herself.

Not long after his return from Paris Joseph's cup was to overflow. He
was in Sulka, poring over swatches of shirt materials, when he bumped
into Sir Avon Smythe, a young man whose father was one of the direc-
tors of the Bank of England.

'So sorry you won't be at the Applebys' on the 14th, old man,' Sir
Avon mumbled over an adjacent swatch. 'And I hear the beautiful Miss
Young is otherwise engaged! I've got tickets for a show – Naunton
Wayne and Millie Sim – I'm sure she'd love it but when shall I see her?'
Sir Avon whined theatrically. But Joseph was not listening to that part
of the conversation. The word 'engaged' had startled him and he saw no
reason to account for his own absence from the Applebys' to Sir Avon,
who attended many of the same parties as he and Sybil and was a rival
for her attentions. But should he be relieved that Sybil would not be
there? At least Sir Avon would not be sitting at her feet. Would someone
else, however? And where? Joseph would not be at the Applebys' because he would be in synagogue observing the Eve of the Day of Atone-
ment. Could it possibly be that Sybil would be likewise engaged? His
pulse raced; he selected an unsuitable silk, and in a loud voice ordered a
shirt to be charged to his account. He almost ran up Bond Street back to
his flat in Portland Place; he went straight to the telephone.

'Lenny, will you do something for me? Ring Sybil Young and ask
her to dine with you on the 14th.'

'My dear Jo, it's the Eve of Yom Kippur.'

'Precisely!'

'I don't get you.'

'It'll establish her credentials.' With the help of Lenny, whose call to
Sybil concluded with some embarrassment and not a little colonial ineptitude and did not convince *him* of her religious affiliation, but only that
she did not want to dine with him, Joseph satisfied himself that Sybil's
background was remarkably like his own. While his family had been
leaping on a boat in the Baltic to avoid the attentions of the murderous
Cossacks, hers had been jumping on an ox-cart somewhere south of
Sophia.

Joseph asked Sybil for her hand in marriage and Sybil, her eyes lowered and her expression impenetrable, nodded her assent. It had never
crossed her mind to marry for love.

For the first two years, Sybil enjoyed the status marriage to a doctor assured her. For his part, Joseph enjoyed the unexpected achievement of having acquired an accomplished and elegant wife who did not remotely resemble the vulgar South African girls with whom he had been raised and with whom Baruch had expected him to share his life. Sybil's taste led her to furnish the Nash house in Regent's Park strictly in period. She disdained the fashionable Art Deco, feeling much safer with style that had been long accepted. Joseph never tired of listening to the compliments showered on his wife by everyone who entered the house. When Rubinstein came to entertain some dinner guests and Gerhardt to sing, Sybil was so overjoyed by her conquests that she came to Joseph when the guests had gone and told him that without him she could never have achieved such heights. Sybil had traded love for power and found it deeply fulfilling.

Had either known, Joseph was no more than head-over-heels in awe of Sybil and Sybil no more than satisfied to have added to her accomplishments that of wedlock. But neither did know.

And this was the climate into which their daughter Portia was shortly born. Sybil's pregnancy started as a pleasure – her latest accomplishment – but its inevitability and tendency to disfigure made it unpalatable after three months, when Sybil was overwhelmed by the sense that with the swelling of her abdomen came the withering of her youth. Unable to accept or offer social entertainments, Sybil was entirely dependent upon Joseph's attentions, which were absorbed by his patients. It was during her pregnancy that Sybil started her monthly letters to her father-in-law. She described the house to him; she elaborated on Joseph's remarkable career; she sent him photographs taken on holidays they took abroad. And the result of her regular and long letters was another conquest.

In her mother's estimation, Portia was born six weeks later than nature intended, thus incommoding her from her conception. Unlikely though this reckoning was, Joseph knew better than to question Sybil on the matter. The baby was certainly advanced; she emerged into the world pearly-pink and unwrinkled, with a head of golden curls and ten perfect finger nails. The midwife remarked on the baby's first cry; it was one of sheer joy to be alive, she said to the gynaecologist. Joseph, who counted his relations with little girls the most satisfactory of all, was delighted to have a daughter.

'She's exquisite!' he murmured to Sybil on first sight of Portia.

'And me? Am I not exquisite?'

Sybil was shocked to discover that the nanny she had engaged to look after Portia expected to take a day off a week as well as every Sunday afternoon; she solved this inconvenience by asking an infertile friend to take over on Tuesdays, explaining that she was not going to entrust her own flesh and blood to any of the maids. On Sunday afternoons, when Sybil habitually attended a concert at the Queen's Hall, Joseph cared for the baby.

In the early stages of her life, when Portia was confined to pen, cot or pram, she presented few problems and Sybil was able, largely, to ignore her. But by the time she was three, Sybil found her presence all too burdensome. The joyful baby metamorphosed into a sad, disturbed little girl with straight hair, bitten finger-nails and a nervous stutter. Furthermore, she was obsessed with the vision of a night visitor; an old wizened woman who, she insisted, stole into her nursery dressed from head to foot in a green cloak that concealed all but half of her decomposed face. She sat bent forward on the wicker chair (that creaked), until Portia went to sleep, and then slid over to the child's bed and strangled her. Because both Sybil and Nanny dismissed the visitor, 'there's no such person, Portia', because each responded, 'you're imagining things', frustration and fury against Sybil and Nanny were added to her terror. The child often woke from her trauma at two in the morning and screamed until dawn. Sybil's reaction was to buy herself ear plugs, banish Portia to the room over the garage and give Nanny a bedroom in the attic.

It was late 1935. Baruch signalled his intention of visiting Europe the following summer. He would stay with Joseph and Sybil before going on to Germany where he would try to persuade two of his deceased partner's relatives to get out while they still could. Storm clouds were gathering. Perhaps they were easier to see from afar. Joseph wondered whether Sybil would manage a measure of warmth towards his father who had in the past been disorientated by her manner; his father mistook her elegant letters for a greater interest in him than Sybil felt.

At the same time as Baruch was making his plans Hitler was making his. Joseph and Sybil were sitting in the dressing-room, Sybil working a tapestry and Joseph reading *The Times*. Most uncharacteristically, for she could not bear being read to, Joseph quoted out loud: 'Nothing like the complete disinheritance and segregation of Jewish citizens now announced has been heard since medieval times.' Sybil replied that she had been approached to lend the house for a fund-raising luncheon to bring out from Germany (she thought) some Jewish children but had not really wished to get herself involved: 'I've enough on my plate with the musicians' charity,' she added by way of explanation. Joseph stopped reading out loud. It was not that his wife had silenced him but that a

lump had risen in his throat and he was incapable of speech. He was reading a report about a Jewish doctor in Berlin who had been sent to a con-
centration camp for 'race defilement'; in order to save the life of a non-
Jewish patient he had given the man a transfusion of his own blood. The
lump in Joseph's throat was the first he had experienced since the death
of his mother. Unless he was careful his mind was going to flood with
memories and pains. He rose quickly from his chair and said in an unexpectedly loud voice,

'I'm not having Father visit Europe. We'll go out to Jo'burg.'

'Oh, must we? I'd far rather drive down to Nice.'

'There's going to be a war,' Joseph told his wife.

'Really?' she asked, dipping her needle in and out of a bunch of flowers, 'and when will that be?'

It was Tuesday afternoon. Sybil's infertile friend had been called to her
mother's sick-bed and Sybil found herself in the alien and unwelcome
position of having to supervise her daughter. On reflection, she judged it
would be less of a strain to take Portia shopping with her than to entertain the child in the nursery; and so it was mother and daughter found
themselves together in Cattlaya, the florist's shop owned by Miss Pym.
Miss Pym invariably remarked on Portia's beauty. On this occasion she
did so not only because it struck her but because she judged it would flat-
ter the mother, and she accompanied her words with a bunch of violets
she pressed into the hands of the little girl.

'How kind! Say thank you to Miss Pym,' Sybil murmured, as un-
enthusiastically as her grasp of graciousness demanded. Portia looked at
Miss Pym, snatched the violets and in a loud voice said,

'Ta!'

Sybil was stunned: where did the child pick up that sort of language?
She must impress upon Nanny that Portia was to be kept out of the
kitchen. Meanwhile Portia disappeared under the eucalyptus foliage,
into a corner where she sat concealed on an upturned box.

Sybil took it for granted that Miss Pym would always come forward
to serve her personally, and would not delegate her assistant, Valerie, to
receive her. Miss Pym judged that Valerie might not treat Mrs Grossman
with the servility owed to so healthy a bank balance. Whereas Valerie
knew a species rose from a hybrid, she did not have an equal talent for
distinguishing between the highly valued and the less valued customer.
Sybil was gratified to be served by the same Miss Pym who had served
Clarissa Dalloway with flowers for her celebrated party in the days when
Miss Pym was merely an assistant in Bond Street, saving to open her
own premises. Sybil identified with Clarissa; she too liked to give

parties, bring people together. She too, after seven years of marriage to Joseph, wondered whether she might not have achieved more by marrying out, by marrying Sir Avon Smythe. He might have made a more stimulating husband and assured her of the central position in his life and not insisted upon parenthood. And now there was all this trouble in Europe in which she was going to be involved. Joseph was clever, at least in his professional life. But he was not commanding in his private life, and would never show the panache and social ease Sybil regarded as a necessary accompaniment to her own gifts.

'Yes, Miss Pym, white lilacs; masses of them, if you please. I want a white May in all my rooms!'

Miss Pym said she would have the delivery boy cycle over with the flowers that evening. With a piece of white chalk she deftly marked three green jugs containing lilac with the letter 'G'. Sybil watched Miss Pym lean humped-back over the book as she wrote out the order with her left hand. Sybil was suffused with a desire to be particularly solicitous to poor Miss Pym, a woman who not only had that nasty disadvantage of left-handedness but many others too. Who would ever marry a stick insect with so pasty a complexion, so flat a chest, so curved a spine, and hands wrinkled and red as if they had been stood in cold water with the flowers?

'We must go now, Portia. We mustn't keep Miss Pym; she has work to do.' A rustle in the eucalyptus leaves heralded the re-emergence of Portia, clutching her violets.

'Say goodbye to Miss Pym. And thank her – nicely this time – for the violets.'

'I don't want to!'

The two women looked at one another. Miss Pym indicated by her expression that 'children will be children' and that it was quite natural for a child of Portia's age to behave as she was behaving. Sybil indicated by her expression that children were a mystery to her, that she despaired of Portia, and that somehow it was seemly for a woman in her position not to be able to control a child; it was an expression that indicated, moreover, how exhausting child rearing was and what efforts she had to make to conceal the fact. And as the two women exchanged their unspoken points a green tin jug filled with madonna lilies fell from its perch, bringing down in its wake several other green tin jugs crammed with roses, carnations, stocks, and branches of viburnum and deutzia. The child watched fascinated as water cascaded down the plinths and over the floor.

Miss Pym's sensible shoes and overall were some protection against the flood; Sybil's chiffon ensemble, white silk stockings and shoes were not; her soaked dress and jacket clung to her body as if in fright. She wondered whether she should apologize to Miss Pym but quickly dismissed the idea as being unfitting. Miss Pym wondered whether she should comment upon the incident but dismissed the idea as being unfitting. Meanwhile, Portia slopped happily on the stone floor, kicking up the pools of water, and murmuring over the scattered blooms,

'Poor fflowers! They're swimming Mummy! Poor fflowers!'

It was half a mile from Cattlaya to the Grossmans' house. Sybil led Portia back through the park by the scruff of her neck. She dragged the child upstairs and threw her into the nursery and locked the door behind her.

'You'll stay there until Daddy comes home. And then he'll give you a thoroughly good hiding.' Portia sat down at the child-size table on a child-size chair and had a tea-party with Edward, her bear.

'Do you take Chchina tea, Mr Bear, or would you befer Indian?' Leaning toward the bear, who was seated in a second child-size chair opposite her, Portia placed the bunch of violets between his paws,

'I bought you these from the jjungle, Edward Bear!'

No sooner had Joseph put the key in the lock than Sybil appeared in the hall ready to launch into the drama in which she would play the victimized heroine seeking justifiable redress from one who owed his all to her.

In the early months of their marriage the ice-princess had melted just sufficiently to permit her husband's admiration to express itself in occasional acts of desire. But following the birth of Portia, Sybil's narcissism and her determination to avoid further children combined to reinstate her frozen image more impermeably than ever. Although determined to keep Joseph's admiration at arm's length, she calculated that she might have to submit to his desire from time to time. But the intervals had lengthened and Joseph had sought out Cissy.

It was only when her husband became physically incapable of making love that Sybil started to reflect on her marriage and Joseph's love for her. She judged that the two matters were independent of one another. The marriage was a social contract and, as such, worked well. Joseph's love for her, on the other hand, was wanting. According to conventional wisdom, admiration on the part of the husband for the wife should find its expression in acts of passion. It was not enough for Joseph to say he admired her, he should demonstrate the fact. She did not wish to subject herself regularly to his sexual appetite but, she felt, he should show gallantry, and impotence fell short of that. He had no problem expressing his love for Portia; he positively slobbered over the little girl, and spoilt her outrageously. She could do nought wrong in his eyes. There was something obscene – unnatural – in his love for Portia.

And it was only when Joseph realized that he was physically impotent with his wife that he reviewed his marriage and his relationship with Sybil. So far as the outward form of the marriage was concerned he was well satisfied. He was proud of Sybil, she was beautiful, she dressed elegantly and it was a joy to load her with jewellery. He could confidently lay claim to the most scrupulously maintained house, presided over by the most gracious hostess in London. Sibyl gathered illustrious company to her dinner table; she served impeccable food, faultlessly cooked, and kept an exceptional cellar. As a couple, they enjoyed the same plays and the same classical music – a recent visit to *Glamorous Nights* at Drury Lane, in which their friend Ivor Novello appeared, had been a particular success. And now that the purchase of modern art was becoming so fashionable, he enjoyed as much as Sybil being courted by the art dealers. He might not have chosen the Picasso drawing himself but the Eddy Woolf portrait pleased him; he liked knowing the artist personally. Joseph thought back to Baruch and Johannesburg: he had come a long way in a short time. It did not enter his thoughts that he might, en route, have stubbed his toe on the pedestal he had made for his wife. However, it was somewhat embarrassing to find oneself impotent with one's wife even if, over the years, she had shown precious little enthusiasm for sexual congress. Perhaps his problem was actually a relief to her? But if that were the case, why did she pout and look forlorn as if offended? He made a note to pop into Boucheron and buy the sapphires he had noticed in the window when last he ordered shirts at Sulka. And he resolved to show more interest in Sybil's fund-raising for the Home for Aged Musicians.

On the whole Joseph was well pleased with himself. He had a successful practice, a consultancy at a teaching hospital; he had been made President of the British Cancer Committee. The wives of his colleagues were flattering in their attentions and so too were his women patients; they made him feel entirely desirable. Given half the chance, he was confident that he would be well able to satisfy them all. From time to time he had been the butt of some anti-Semitism but he could honestly say that it had never affected him emotionally. Meanwhile, Cissy never complained – unless to regret that he only found two hours a week to spend with her. Perhaps he would organize a surprise for Sybil: drop everything, take a week off to motor up to Scotland. Soon there would be war and no question of holidays.... Meanwhile, there were queues of young doctors waiting to do a locum for him. Sybil liked that vast

Edwardian hotel ... and the soft air in Scotland in summer was particularly suited to her constitution, being neither too hot nor too cold and always moist for her complexion. Yes, that was what he would do. And he would astonish her with the sapphires there, in the moonlight, on the terrace....

'The child's impossible! She's uncontrollable and she's insolent. She takes not one iota of notice of any instruction I give her. She's wilful. She does these things to test me, to annoy me and to humiliate me. You've got to show her once and for all, you won't put up with me being treated in this way!'

'Sybil! She's five!'

'She may well be five but she knows perfectly well what she's up to. And if you don't make it clear now who's who and what's what, you'll have a little criminal on your hands by the time she's seven. She's no respect for authority, that's her trouble. She'll end up with no friends and no school'll keep her. I'll wager that before long we'll find ourselves with a so-called "difficult" child on our hands and I'll be spending three afternoons a week at the Tavistock Clinic!'

'I'll have a word with her.'

'No you won't! Words are not what are needed: you'll give her a sound thrashing! That's what she deserves and that's the only language she understands!'

Sibyl unlocked the nursery door. Portia was on her bed, asleep; she had her right thumb locked in her mouth and her left arm round Edward. Without warning, Sybil pulled the child's arm free of the bear and dragged her off the bed. Portia was still with fear.

'You're hurting! You're hurting, Mummy!' she screamed.

'Nothing like the hurting you're going to get, you little beast. Daddy's here.'

What was intended as a threat spelt relief. Portia tore herself free from Sybil's grasp and rushed towards her father's outstretched arms and kissed him:

'Ddaddy! Ddaddy! Ddaddy!' Joseph caught his daughter in his arms and hugged her to him.

'Mummy tells me you've been a very naughty little girl, my darling,' he said, kissing her face.

'Yes, I bbeen very naughty, I sssplashed Miss Pymy and Mmummy in the jungle.'

'Did you do that on purpose?'

'The water did it on purpose. It just jumped out of the jugs', Portia waved her arms about to illustrate her point, 'and made a pond.' Joseph was entranced by his child. Sybil stood by, silently observing his seduction. She could bear it no longer and stamped her foot.

'Joseph, this child is incorrigible. She may be only five but she understands perfectly well what she's up to, and she's got to be disciplined.'

'Ddaddy, I'm hungry.'

'How's that my darling? Didn't you have your tea?'

'She most certainly did not and she won't be having her bedtime drink.' Joseph took a bar of chocolate from his pocket.

'Green peppermint cream. Your favourite! And don't forget to give Mr Bear a piece,' he whispered in Portia's ear. Portia turned to retrieve her bear from where he lay on the floor; he was lying face down where he had fallen when Sybil had pulled him off the bed. Portia picked him up and kissed him and said 'I love you Edward Bear' three times, and pressed chocolate against his leather lips.

'You're such a good bear, Edward,' she added emphatically.

And while she was absorbed in play, Joseph ushered Sybil into the drawing-room. But he left the nursery door wide open; he made a point of doing so.

'You'll do it tomorrow morning, first thing, before you leave the house!'

'No child of that age would remember what she's being beaten for by then. She almost certainly wouldn't know if I did it *now*!'

'The trouble with Portia is that she knows she can get away with murder with you. She believes you love her so much that you don't mind how she behaves – particularly to me.'

'When she's with me she behaves quite beautifully.'

'That's because you spoil her.'

'If spoiling leads to good behaviour I would prescribe overdoses of it. And if she murdered Mr Bear I'd still love her.'

'Don't be frivolous, Joseph! One of your troubles is that you won't take a firm stand.' Sybil had not chosen her words with conscious care; nor were they ones she would ever utter in another context. They had risen unbidden, but encapsulated her resentment with uncanny precision.

That evening, while Sybil talked at length to Boris Tchernickov about the charity ball he was to design and she was to organize as a fund-raising occasion for the old musicians' home, Joseph bathed Portia. He blew soap bubbles and promised not to use soap on the child's face, as Nanny always did, getting it up her nose and into her eyes where it stung. And as he lifted her into bed Portia begged him to stay, seated in the wicker chair so that the ghost wouldn't have room to sit down.

'I've told that ghost that she must never, never come again, my darling, so you won't have to worry about her. But now I've got to go and change for dinner. I'll leave the little light on. . . .'

When Joseph had changed and descended to the dining-room, he noticed that Sybil had left a note for Nanny on the silver salver on the hall table. He unfolded the note and read the instructions: Nanny was to bring Portia to the door of their bedroom suite at 7.30 next morning, and leave her in the corner until the doctor fetched her.

Sybil was seated before the looking-glass in her négligé giving her auburn curls their one hundred strokes when she caught sight of Joseph, sitting in bed, admiringly watching her. She turned to face him:

'Boris says he's sure you'll get a knighthood. I'd like that,' she murmured. 'Sir Joseph and Lady Grossman! It sounds right, somehow. You're so clever, Joseph, and I was so right to marry you.' She let her négligé fall to the ground, and in her slinky nightdress she approached her husband and kissed him tenderly on the face and ran her hand round his neck before slipping into the twin bed by the side of his. He really must find ways to please her, he thought.

Portia was dressed in a flowered Liberty print smock. In her arms she clutched her teddy bear. She stood in the corner, her face to the wall. She was shaking. When Sybil threw open the door she stood so near to the child that Portia had to throw back her head to get her mother and now father in view. Sybil was resplendent in her satin négligé trimmed with ostrich feathers. Joseph was immaculate in his grey pinstripe suit.

Joseph crouched on his haunches and took his child's hands in one of his. He looked into her eyes.

'I'm going to punish you, Portia, for being rude to Mummy, yesterday, in the flower shop.' He spoke slowly, quietly, 'You were a very naughty little girl, you know that, don't you? You upset Mummy. I'm going to smack you very hard so that you remember in future that it is a thoroughly wicked thing ever to upset Mummy.' He felt the bile of treachery rise in his throat. 'You mustn't upset Mummy,' he repeated more firmly as he felt increasingly uncomfortable. Portia gazed, bewildered, at her father. But as he looked into the child's face he started to see what was a condensed version of Sybil's. He turned into his dressing-room. Sybil followed, dragging Portia behind her.

'Lean over Daddy's lap,' Sybil ordered. Silently, obediently, the child did as she was told. Sybil drew down the frilly knickers that matched Portia's dress and exposed her pink buttocks. With his eyes fixed on his wife's face Joseph took the ivory-handled hairbrush Sybil held out to him and landed five blows across his daughter's bottom. Portia was so stunned by the first two blows that she did not react, on the third and fourth she screamed deafeningly in pain and terror, and on the fifth blow her sphincter gave way and Joseph's immaculate Savile Row suit received the contents of his daughter's bowels.

The Dancing Partners

If the suspicion that she was a 'woman of easy virtue' – a phrase in general use at the time, but most particularly in ecclesiastical circles – if such a thought drifted into the minds of those who knew Amalia Braun, it was quickly dispelled. Those who knew the girl knew her father, the Lutheran minister, and the respect and devotion in which they held him embraced his family. It was a fact, however, observed by members of the minister's congregation and even picked over by them, that since the age of thirteen Amalia had been peculiarly free with her attentions to members of the opposite sex. But if her attentions were unfettered, so was her heart: she had no one particular boy-friend.

Amalia Braun had been born to serve; she passed her childhood in the sick-room of her bedridden mother, nursing her with every appearance of filial affection. Her devotion persisted until the final, terrible stages of illness robbed her of the privileged duty.

Shortly after the demise of his wife, the minister offered the master bedroom to an elderly widow, and moved himself and his frugal belongings into the spare room. He put it to an unconvinced Amalia that the widow, reared to fulfil the demands of *kinde, kuche, kirche*, would lighten Amalia's domestic load and leave her free, for the first time, to give her undivided attention to her job.

Amalia worked for the Society for the Welfare of Lutheran Gentlefolk. The job had been her first and now, after five years, at the age of twenty-three, she was running the charity. She did the books, taking in donations and apportioning them as she saw fit; she interviewed the needy, most tactfully, and her recommendations to the small committee, whose members signed the cheques, were adopted unquestioningly.

Her salary being a modest one and her devotion to her father something upon which the latter had learnt to depend, the minister showed just a suspicion of hurt when Amalia floated the idea of taking a small flat on her own – 'well, bed-sit really' – over the launderette.

'Mrs Hegerman will take your moving out as a personal slight.'

'Oh, I don't think so, Father. Mrs Hegerman is a sensible woman. She'll understand.' And Mrs Hegerman *did* understand: Amalia was redundant.

But the truth is rarely monolithic.

From her early teens Amalia had led a double life: beige from nine to five and scarlet from eight to midnight twice a week. While still at school she discovered the Palais de Danse; and together with this discovery another: she had a taste for duplicity. On Tuesdays and Fridays she would take a plastic bag – apparently filled with dirty washing – to the launderette, and leave it there in the care of the assistant until she came out of school, or finished work. Under a sheet and towel she concealed a saucy dress and shoes, and a box of make-up, and these she applied with the flourish of a diva in the 'Ladies' at the Palais.

Her success with men at the Palais was the result of the balance of signals she operated. Her expression was demure, her figure slight and unprovocative. But her make-up was dramatic, and her dress so clung to the gentle nursery slopes of her body that her partners, as grateful as they were willing, were effortlessly led downhill. Lured by the signals flashed by Amalia's dress and make-up, they were nevertheless reassured by her passivity of expression in face and body; she was no threat.

Rapturously Amalia tangoed and rumbaed and waltzed the evenings away. While she was a schoolgirl her parents had no reason to suspect she was not with a friend, poring over her books. Later, they had no reason to suspect she was not detained by work.

Her taste for dancing might have been acceptable to her parents had it taken the form of Greek dancing, or Eurhythmics. Had Amalia found the need in her soul to express in her limbs the elm and the willow and the breeze blowing through her leaves her parents might not have demurred; nor would they have objected if she had joined the Scottish dance club and found satisfaction in their flings. In the event, Amalia's predilection for South American music and motion made her deception as much a sensible precaution as an exciting subterfuge.

She was free from prejudice as far as her partners were concerned. So long as they had rhythm in their blood and care in the placing of their feet she barely noticed whether they were Eastern potentates or Western bank clerks. Over the months she accumulated a phalanx of regular partners. Accustomed by day to bend her ear to confidences regarding deprivation and social injustice, and to hand out compensation for both, she found herself by night attending to other areas of need. Her Eastern partners – unmarried – rehearsed their problem, a cultural one, resulting in a woeful condition of permanent frustration that only she, with her unique understanding and generosity, might allay. Her Western partners – married – rehearsed theirs: rejection by wives who judged their appetites excessive, who starved them of the nourishment to which their marital status entitled them, and upon which their very sanity depended.

Amalia found herself providing her dance partners with the relief their circumstances denied them. In return, her dancing partners provided her with the means to little luxuries she might otherwise have had to forego. And when the light of consciousness dawned on her situation Amalia judged the exchange appropriate. Needs must be met.

The Reverend Braun died a few months following his marriage to Mrs Hegerman and Mrs Hegerman (as she remained in the mind of Amalia) followed him to his final destination within weeks. Amalia pondered the significance of that marriage; its example only reinforced her determination to avoid the sacrament. She preferred to put her caring skills at the disposal of many, rather than one.

As the frugal fifties gave way to the swinging sixties, Amalia adjusted to the needs of older men, men prohibited by personal habit and social custom from enjoying the more open relationships that were now the fashion. But these partners did not turn up regularly and Amalia found herself more frequently than she chose waiting alone at the bar consuming tonic water. And by the time her fortieth birthday had come and gone the Palais had been monopolized by very mixed groups of young people – the girls wearing skirts like pelmets and the men shoulder-length hair. And instead of dancing in close embrace to the strains of 'Jealousy', they hurled themselves about at arm's length to something called the 'Twist' that involved a display of knickers. Not only was the so-called permissive society inimical to her taste, Amalia observed it was robbing her of her supplementary benefit.

But as dire as the loss of income was the loss of excitement. Amalia relied on scarlet evenings to propel her through grey days. Working on her tapestry before the gas fire, with only a canary for company, did not foster in her a sense of desirability or make her feel needed. She had emerged from a well-ordered regime that had lasted twenty-five years to find herself superfluous and lonely. Her once trim figure sagged; her once fresh complexion sallowed.

'I'm socially superannuated,' she confided to her bird, 'I'm past "it", and being past "it" means I'm going to have to marry! My blessings are taking too short a time to count, my reverses too long.'

Ten days prior to her appointment with the Professional Person's Marriage Bureau, Mr Horace Braithwaite entered Amalia's field of vision through the glass door of the Society for the Welfare of Lutheran Gentlefolk. He arrived with a donation. His mother had, in her youth, fallen on hard times and received assistance from the society – a matter she had regulated in her will. She'd left instructions to her son to deliver the gift personally, when the sad day arrived.

Sitting on the hard straight-backed chair, in an attitude of penance, Mr Braithwaite communicated both his mother's gratitude and his own feelings of loss and inadequacy. As a bachelor who had always lived with his widowed mother, he was emotionally and physically helpless without her. Amalia recognized a challenge and determined to confront it.

It was a quiet wedding. Four ancients from the late Reverend Braun's congregation and two couples from the society witnessed the exchange of vows and rings and gathered in the vestry for a celebratory Cyprus sherry. A few grains of rice still lodged in Amalia's hat and Mr Braithwaite's breast pocket when the groom led his bride to a Chinese restaurant in nearby Balham, where he ordered crab and ginger for two, the appearance of which surprised him, the negotiation of which defeated him.

Amalia attended Horace's every need. Indeed, Horace had to admit her attentions actually exceeded his mother's. And Amalia was reassured by the security his pension provided. But it was the lovely bunches of flowers he brought her every Wednesday and Saturday that touched her heart. It had not escaped Amalia's attention, of course, that these gifts followed inexorably upon her husband's bi-weekly visits to his club. But Horace was a creature of routine. And the subject of the club, had, soon after their wedding, been easily despatched between them.

'Amalia dear, I hope you'll understand,' Horace had said. 'I go to the club on Tuesday and Friday evenings. It was Mother's wish that when I retired I should keep in touch with male company. . . .'

'Of course, Horace,' Amalia had agreed, pleased by the prospect of two evenings a week without it.

It was Amalia's secretary, Mrs Willis, who cast the first shadow.

'And who d'you think we saw in Piccadilly on Tuesday evening?' she enquired of Amalia, who did not even hazard a guess.

'Why, Mr B!'

'What a small world!' replied Amalia. But her seeming unconcern masked surprise. What was it that took Horace to the West End when his club was in Balham?

It seems that Mrs Willis and her husband went 'up west' to the cinema every Tuesday and Friday evening when Mr Willis was not 'on the road'. Like Mr Braithwaite (now retired), Mr Willis travelled in stationery. They spotted Mr B. on four occasions and Mrs Willis, anxious to exploit the opportunity to make inroads into her superior's private life, told Amalia so. Meanwhile, Horace reported to his bride the substance of his evenings at the club, in Balham. At first Amalia half-seriously entertained the possibility that her husband had a double. But on the fifth sighting of Mr B. she became alarmed.

Mr Willis was 'on the road' the following week – so Amalia asked Mrs Willis if she might accompany her to the cinema in the Haymarket on the Friday evening. At 10.45 when the two women waited at the bus stop to return home, Amalia saw Horace walking towards Piccadilly with a young woman on his arm.

Over the pale toast and Golden Shred Amalia enquired next morning whether Horace had enjoyed his night at the club.

'Topping time m'dear. Old Jarvis turned up and we took a jaunt down memory lane together. Good times the old times ... God bless me! Yes!' Amalia searched her husband's face; was he taking pride in the craft of deception? Would he concoct his tales with care? Coyly she suggested Horace might take her along to his club one evening.

'Commercial travellers are not the sort of company for ladies, m'dear. I'm afraid our memories would thoroughly shock you!'

Amalia stared at the tulips Horace had brought home on Wednesday. Their bowed stalks and lowered heads hung in guilty confusion. Horace looked out of the window and forecast rain. Amalia followed his gaze.

'We could do with a bit of colour in those beds now the frosts are over,' she observed.

'If it's colour the lady wants it's colour she shall have! I'll drive down to Potters on Monday when you're at work. Would you like a range of petunias? Or would you rather geraniums and cherry pie?'

Giving evidence in the coroner's court six weeks later PC Wagstaff described seeing the off-side front wheel of the Austin Seven detach itself: it flew off to the left and sent the car crashing into a ditch on the right.

'We never found the missing bolts. I had three men searching for them but we never found them.' And under cross-examination the forensic scientist regretfully admitted that it had been impossible to say for certain whether the driver's heart attack had been the cause or the result of the accident. An open verdict was returned on the death of Mr Horace Braithwaite, aged seventy-one.

Like Father Like Son

In an immaculate five-storey house in an exclusive Kensington square there lived in solitary splendour a barrister who received sometime visits from his only son.

Sir Oliver Grant QC – rich, elegant, aloof – had taken silk at thirty-five; at thirty-seven had married, suitably, Georgina Templeton-Farr, a 'gal' renowned for her seat on a horse and her expertise at the dinner table. At thirty-eight an act of innocent incompetence had led to Georgina's pregnancy, and by thirty-nine Sir Oliver had a son. This event, arising so unexpectedly for Sir Oliver, hurtling him downstream on an emotional tide whose rapids had been hitherto unexplored by him, and down which fate had thrust him blindfold, might have expanded and deepened his emotional life. But the initial surge of joy occasioned by the doctor's announcement 'You have a son!' was quickly shattered by his quieter notification that he had lost a wife.

Sir Oliver's hostility to self-examination was inborn and fostered by his education. It did not cross his mind that the act he had regarded as ludicrous, that had resulted in James's conception, would breed guilt in himself. Yet had he not been responsible for Georgina's death? His unconscious certainly judged so. And so it was that the suffocating guilt transferred itself to the son who had survived Sir Oliver's crime.

Sir Oliver declared war on James. The battles he conducted he won and in victory he restored to himself the trophy of an image with which he was well-satisfied. In the future, when James was old enough to score a century or top the examination lists published in *The Times*, the boy would gather laurels for his father's luxuriant crown and, in the autumn of his life, lead him to the edge of the pool to gaze with him at its reflection.

James passed his first eight years on the fourth floor of number 19 Palmeston Square presided over by a Norland Nanny until he was five and thereafter by a governess. He attended church with his father on Sunday mornings and took afternoon tea with him in the drawing-room on Sunday afternoons. At eight he was packed off to a boarding preparatory school; at thirteen he was installed at his father's alma mater; and at eighteen was up at Oxford reading English.

When questioned by his contemporaries regarding his family James concealed both his circumstances and his feelings, and took refuge in describing the architecture and appurtenances of 19 Palmeston Square.

The building had been erected in livid red brick at the turn of the century, by an architect possessed of a passion for the Italian *palazzo*. The reception rooms had lofty ceilings, tiled floors and vast stone fireplaces, and their walls had been stacked by Sir Oliver, from waist level to their ornate cornices, with elaborately framed, highly varnished eighteenth-century Italian oil paintings. But it was with a shudder that James would add that the most striking impression left by the house was its unnatural quiet and order, reminiscent of an under-attended provincial museum. A sense of breathless expectation of an imminent, possibly momentous event pervaded the spotless silence. James felt that he was destined to participate in the fulfilment of a promise held out by the house.

He was expected to follow his father to the Bar. However, having spent his youth emotionally and geographically remote from the neglect and indifference of his father, no filial inclination for proximity stirred in him. Politely but firmly he declined an invitation to be introduced into chambers; James had made up his mind to write and would find a none-too-demanding job in publishing to support himself.

His father's treatment of him had produced in James an almost pathological antipathy to material baubles, in particular to those of an antique character: early musical instruments that lay about the library, study and drawing-room in Palmeston Square like stuffed masks; Sèvres too fragile to eat off and too gaudy to look at; and paintings by the 'School of Tiepolo', which only served to illustrate that the essential quality of genius that resides in a master cannot be passed on to his students. And it was as well that Sir Oliver's example had had the effect upon his son of regarding material belongings as an impediment to a happy, creative life for he had certainly not provided James with the means to acquire them.

It was not only that Sir Oliver was tight-fisted; like so many mean men he was envious. His despised son was popular. This fact not only called in question Sir Oliver's response to the boy but contrasted strikingly with his own social neglect.

'I shall be having a few *intimate* friends in for drinks on the 30th!' And as he testified to his butler the gift of one hundred *intimate* friends, Sir Oliver acknowledged to himself he lied. He had no friends. The guests upon whom he would lavish *foie gras*, caviar and vintage champagne were solicitors and journalists he despised but upon whom he relied for briefs and a good press. When James spoke of a friend his father knew he legitimately dignified his contemporaries and their parents by the term.

James joined a firm of educational publishers and when he had been with them for two months acquired two well-proportioned rooms, kitchen and bathroom in a tree-lined street of Regency houses within walking distance of his office in Bedford Square.

It is a fact of modern life that the amount of a man's salary is calculated in inverse proportion to the satisfaction his job affords him, and its social relevance. Thus it was James found himself as short of money as always. He went no more than once a week to a theatre, cinema or concert, and rarely ate in a restaurant. He confined his drinking to a pint at his local when his writing stint was done and might have survived contentedly on take-away *puris, papa dosa* and *biryanis* had it not been that a single, good-looking, literate male of a retiring disposition has throughout history been unable to avoid the attentions of society hostesses. James was neither surprised nor displeased that the life he made for himself lacked glamour. He regarded himself as colourless, when he regarded himself at all, and welcomed anonymity. It came, therefore, as something of a shock to discover that he aroused interest in women, the bored wives of rich men who were 'something in the City'. He was fought over to accompany them to the *Ring* – something their husbands avoided like the noose. He was fought over to attend their dinner parties, there always being need of an unaccompanied male.

Yet it was neither from a sense of economy nor the need to protect himself from the tireless attentions of society hostesses that decided James against installing a telephone. He was childishly devoted to the post. He did not know for what he was waiting to change his life but was confident that it would arrive through the letter-box, if at all.

However, it was not with pleasurable anticipation that he spotted the confident hand of Sir Oliver on the expensive envelope that lay blanched and inert on the doormat. And there being no enjoyment to be extracted from mulling over a communication from his father over coffee, James opened the envelope at once, before mounting the stairs. Sir Oliver, for reasons of economy and convenience, had decided to sell number 19 Palmeston Square and move into the Barbican. He demanded that James present himself on Saturday to pack up such as remained of his personal belongings, failing which they would be put on the pile destined for the scouts' jumble sale.

For the first time that James could remember, 19 Palmeston Square was in chaos: tea-chests, dust sheets, all the paraphernalia of Pickfords had transformed the house. In the basement cook was wrapping the tools of her trade in newspaper, in the pantry the butler was wrapping the silver in green baize. Upstairs, the housemaid was attaching scented sachets to pristine, conjugal sheets for wrapping them in linen bags. Every piece of furniture bore a label: Barbican, Sotheby's, Jumble, Cook. For what Sir Oliver did not want, and could not be otherwise disposed of, the servants had been instructed to take to their families in the depressed valleys. James studied the contents of his cupboard that had been emptied on to the floor of his old bedroom. He trampled the teddy bear and picked out six books from the pile and joined his father in the study.

'It can all go to the jumble sale!' he said.

'Ah! Yes ... jumble...' and muttering, Sir Oliver pointed to a pile of unframed pictures that had accumulated from parts of lots for which he had bid at auction. In a carefully constructed sentence or two, nicely balancing his contempt for his son and the make-weight paintings, Sir Oliver informed James that since he could not bring himself to let the scouts have them (and since cook had turned them down) perhaps James would like the pictures.

'Look through them! Take what you want and chuck out the rest. Since our tastes in all things are so different, you might even find something you like!' Sir Oliver's tone implied he imagined he had expressed his contempt with humour.

It was on the Tuesday following this visit that James read the report in *The Times*. A fire had gutted the Kensington residence of Sir Oliver Grant QC. The report stated that the house had been unoccupied, its furniture and effects ready to be packed by the removal men expected on Wednesday. Foul play was not suspected, the cause probably electrical: exposed naked wires, resulting from the dismantling of chandeliers, had possibly come into contact with one another. James picked up the telephone but his father was not in chambers and his secretary had instructions not to disclose his whereabouts. It would be a year before James discovered that the house had been insured for its purchase price twenty-five years ago, and that the furniture and pictures had not been insured at all.

Three months after receiving the pile of unwanted art, Lucinda Lawtry, a society hostess anxious to make herself indispensable, found herself 'just passing' James's flat at 7 p.m. and thought she would 'just see' if James were by any chance at home. He was; he had settled to work in front of the gas fire and had a mug of Heinz tomato soup at his elbow. He was obliged to answer the bell and invite Lucinda in; obliged to offer her sherry and to enquire after Jerry Lawtry. No, Lucinda insisted, she was not the least busy that evening: she had been invited to drinks in the neighbourhood and thought how very much more to her taste drinks with James would be. And what was there in the portfolio? Might she peek?

'Good Heavens, darling, what lovely things! And why are they not on your walls?' James shyly admitted he did not have the 'readies' to mount and frame them.

'Dear boy, just leave all that to Lucinda! And we must find some pretty curtaining and lay a few Kelims...' Lucinda drew a tape measure from her bag.

James judged that so long as he gave Lucinda a free hand with his environmental needs she might be distracted from attempts to minister to his more personal needs. It was therefore willingly that he hung over the portfolio with her.

'It was frightfully generous of your old man....'

'D'you think they're worth anything?'

'Worth anything! Darling, they're worth a small fortune! We must get them properly valued. I'll take them round to Georgie-Porgy at Christies, myself.'

In the event, the pictures fetched two hundred and fifty thousand pounds in Christies' spring sale of Important Continental Drawings and Watercolours.

James's altered financial situation radically changed his life. He gave up his nine-to-five job to devote himself full-time to writing. He lost contact with his friends in publishing and found himself unable to apply himself all day to his writing. He was dropped by the society hostesses. Lucinda had accompanied him to the Christie's sale and relayed the news of his financial *coup* to the others in the set. Being no longer a deserving candidate for their patronage, they all expected James to return their hospitality. This he did not think to do.

The shock of his losses robbed Sir Oliver of the clear-mindedness required by his profession. Within two years of the fire he was reduced to a service flat in Crouch End. He addressed several begging letters to his son; the first of these James read with a modicum of concern, although he did not reply to it; the second and third he read without concern and the fourth envelope in his father's hand that landed on his doormat he threw away, unopened.

Myra's Marilyn

It was November 1954. By the time Myra Varney returned home from work it had been dark for two hours. They were quite accommodating at W. J. Farmer and Sons. If you got in at 8 a.m. you were free to leave at 5 p.m.; that way you could avoid the rush, get to the bus stop before the queue started to form, and almost certainly get a seat. The older members of the typing pool always liked to get in early and leave early; the younger ones preferred to get in later and leave late – but then they went out of an evening. Myra did not; she had no one to go out with. She had had her opportunity in the war, and she had not taken it, not like so many others. She often thought of Captain Burge when she was on the bus, travelling to and from work. Typing for him on the American base outside Norwich had been a real pleasure, a privilege, really. But she couldn't agree to . . . and he had a wife. Back in Idaho.

Myra got off the number 13 bus at Swiss Cottage, crossed the Finchley Road and made her way straight to Winchester Road, where she rented a basement bedsit opposite the paper shop. She paid £4.10.0. a week, rather a lot out of her wages but worth it, she thought, to have her own front door. At the back of the bedsit, down a windowless corridor, was a scullery, and by the scullery door another that led out to a tiny yard and a WC. The greatest single disadvantage Myra had to put up with was damp; mould grew on the walls of the corridor and the scullery was only warm when the oven was alight. 'It's like crossing the Siberian steppes, going from my bedsit to my scullery,' she would say. She kept an electric kettle by her bed in order not to have to broach the steppes when all she wanted was a cup of tea. She feared for Tibs, the cat, her not being able to afford to keep the gas fire going all day when she was out, and having to leave the door into the corridor open for him to come and go through the scullery window as he chose. . . .

As Myra rounded the corner of Winchester Road a little surge of pleasure arose in her breast. It was nothing dramatic but it was reassuring; only a few more yards and her eyes would stop running and her ears stop throbbing, and she would shut out the wind and penetrating damp for the night. What would the Captain think of her having her own accommodation, she wondered?

She picked up the milk bottle from the top of the basement steps, descended the steps, fumbled in her bag for her key, opened the door, picked up a circular from the mat, stroked the cat who rubbed against her legs, switched on the light, lit the gas fire, put on the kettle, turned on the wireless and drew the curtains. The routine was the same every evening, except that during the summer months she did not have to put on the light or draw the curtains until after she had had her supper. But summer or winter it was only after half an hour, when the cat was fed and she had had a cup of tea, that the room was warm enough for her to take off her overcoat and hang it on the wire coat-hanger behind the door, and take off her pull-on felt and put it on top of the cupboard. Then she would exchange her Lotus walking shoes for slippers, and sink into the armchair. This was a sign for Tibs to settle on her lap, while she read the *Evening Standard* from 'shock horror' to goals scored. She might have read it on the bus – she bought it at the bus stop in Oxford Street, just outside W. J. Farmer – but she never did; she saved it to enjoy at home. On the bus she unwound, that was how she put it to herself. 'I need to unwind,' she would murmur, twitching at the neck and shoulders. And more often than not, she allowed herself a few moments to remember the Captain, Hank Burge.

On this particular evening Myra read and reread an account of a rape on the last train from London Bridge to Haywards Heath. The account was lurid; Myra read it twice. Perfectly horrid ... she probably asked for it ... like those wicked girls on the base ... They weren't respected and respect's what you want. Discipline, that's what they need.... A good thrashing never did anyone any harm. As she pondered over details left out of the *Standard*'s account and thought back to the goings-on at the base, Myra carefully cut the page out of the paper and put it between the covers of her scrap book. And then she put her overcoat back on again and made for the scullery where she grilled two pieces of toast, opened a tin of baked beans and heated them, and a tin of rice pudding. She placed the beans on the toast and put the plate on a tin tray with the rice pudding in a small Pyrex bowl. She took the tray back into the bedsit and ate it all, very quickly, by the fire. The sound of her eating was accompanied by the continuous hiss from the gas flame.

The Monday Play was well into its stride before Myra felt ready to remove her coat. She listened to the play with the cat on her lap and only when the nine o'clock news headlines had been read, and the details were being filled in, did she rise, spilling the cat on to the floor as she did so.

'It's my bath night, Tibs!'

The bathroom at number 28 Winchester Road was sited on the half-landing above the ground floor, and shared by all the tenants. A notice board by the telephone where messages were left listed tenants and the days and times each might occupy the bathroom. It was understood that in the event of a tenant wishing to change his or her night it must be negotiated strictly by arrangement. There was a meter for the gas but the water took so long to fill the ancient tub that by the time it was full the water was tepid, however much the meter had been fed. Myra often took up a kettle of boiling water, but this did not help much; it was icy on the stairs and the tub was exceptionally deep.

Having twice addressed the cat as to her intentions, Myra Varney put her candlewick dressing-gown over her underclothes, draped her bath towel and her wincyette nightdress over her arm and tucked her sponge bag under her arm. Just as the newsreader closed the bulletin she opened the door at the top of the basement stairs and listened out. Reassured that she would not bump into any of the tenants, she switched on the landing light and shot into the bathroom like a frightened rabbit, shutting the door soundlessly behind her.

Captain Burge would be sixty-five by now. She wondered whether he ever divorced his wife.... She wouldn't have cared to live in Idaho, anyhow....

A sixty-watt bulb in the bathroom concealed the worst of the peeling paint on the walls and the wear in the enamel on the tub. Myra dropped a few crystals of *Mon Âme* into the bath, her clothes on to the wicker chair and a shilling into the meter. She turned on the water; as the water ran into the tub the crystals foamed on the surface and their scent rose on the steam. The bathroom had been made from a back bedroom; it was a sizeable room and draughty. It was fitted with a full-length looking-glass, an old one with a nicely carved oak frame. Myra often wondered why it had been installed here; she could not imagine who would want a full-length image of themselves naked, and always hung her bath towel over the corner of the frame. As she bent over the bath and swished the few remaining crystals that had obstinately not dissolved, she noticed a razor lying on the bath tidy, its handle red with carbolic soap. She handled it with distaste, regarded it closely and washed it under the tap. When she was satisfied it was clean she tried the blade on her arm and found that it was sharp. She wondered to which of the tenants it belonged. She turned off the bath water and peeled off her underclothes. As she turned to place them neatly on the chair in the corner of the room, she caught sight of herself in the looking-glass. Unaccountably, in an action of spontaneity which took her by surprise, Myra Varney pulled her bath towel off the corner of the glass, flung it on to the chair and took a long look at the reflection of her naked body.

She was tall, she was thin, and on her last birthday she had been fifty-five. Confrontation was shocking; her neck appeared unnecessarily long and her shoulders dreadfully round. Her breasts hung gloomily, like those of starving black women. She put her hands where her hips would have been if she had had any, and she saw her belly was concave. Her pubic hair was sparse; it looked moth-eaten; Myra Varney wondered whether it would not be better to do away with it altogether. She raised her arms high above her head. She was always very fussy in summer to keep her armpits nice – she used Veet, despite its smell – so that when she wore cap sleeves it would be perfectly obvious to everyone that she was an English woman – and not French or Italian . . . quite disgusting they were. . . . But in winter she let the hair have its own way, like a gardener who allows nettles to overrun a corner in which he has lost interest. Myra Varney looked at the reflection of her legs and ran her hands up from the ankles. She could see and she could feel bristles. She drew herself up and examined her head and face. Her bistre hair was arranged in a sausage of curl that swung from one ear round to the other. Her face was pale; she had grey eyes, a straight nose and a rose-bud mouth. She could pass unnoticed, anywhere. And did.

But Hank had appreciated her. He had made her feel . . . good. She hadn't minded how late he kept her filing and typing and running little errands for him. And what other mother and daughter had nylons throughout the war?

Myra was cold; goose pimples rose all over her body as she submerged herself in a bath that seemed to her unusually hot. It was not the only unusual circumstance, she thought; she could not remember ever having examined and considered her body before. And she wondered where decisions form themselves and why it was that she had in mind to have her hair shingled tomorrow, and how it was she had decided to shave her armpits, her legs and her pudenda, *right away*. There was no doubt in her mind; she had decided, and that was that. She fished in her sponge bag and placed flannel and soap (*Mon Âme*) by the side of the razor she had found, and the piece of broken mirror that lay permanently on the ledge by the bath, probably, she thought, because the other tenants were so forgetful. . . . She hated the wood bath-tidy that straddled the bath and carried tell-tale remnants of soaps other than her own. She particularly disliked the carbolic soap used by Mr Deeds and the Cuticura used by the girl in the attic with the acne. Myra resolved that tonight she would use the body lotion (that went with the soap and bath crystals the girls at the office had given her for her birthday) as the manufacturers recommended: all over. She would pamper herself. If she didn't no one else would, not again, she thought bitterly. She soaped herself attentively and lay back thinking of the transformation she was about to perform. She decided to start at her ankles and work up. The hair on her legs grew no more enthusiastically than that on her pudenda and in the pits of her arms and it was hard to make out under the suds whether she was successfully removing whatever fuzz existed. She ran her hands over her legs and found that they had shaved smooth; she stood up and shaved off her pubic growth. Looking down on her handiwork she was surprised to observe that, hairless, her pudenda were not flush with her stomach but swelled out a little, making her stomach appear particularly starved. She got out of the bath and faced the full-length glass; she wiped a corner free from steam and shaved her armpits. She dried herself, and with cupped hands filled with *Mon Âme* body lotion she worked the fragrant liquid over her body from neck to toes. In some way, in some indefinable way, Myra Varney felt herself to be performing a ritual the significance of which lay too deep for the likes of her to fathom.

He had called her his English rose. Imagine! And he'd had experience of women. Before the war, he'd visited Paris. . . .

Myra sat in bed feeding her face with Pond's cold cream. She had put her hair in curlers and set the alarm, and now she took up a copy of *Woman* and read an article on matching accessories. She studied the advertisements with attention and marked items with a red pencil. Myra had faith in advertisements – particularly when they appeared in her favourite magazine. She did not have the money to take the advice proffered by the manufacturers of hygiene and beauty products, but she knew that if she had, and if she followed their counsel, she would be a more appetizing, more attractive woman.

'I'm going to get in extra early, tomorrow,' she informed Tibs as she settled him at the foot of the bed, 'I must see Mr Farmer before the girls get in.'

The caretaker was in, taking covers off machines, flicking the filing cabinets with his feather duster.

'Good morning, Mr Horace!'

'Morning.'

Mr Horace was a man of few words, inseparable from his tobacco-brown overall and an expression of chronic indigestion. Myra pushed past him and, standing by her desk, took up a file and examined it. From where she had stationed herself, she could see through the glass panes into Mr Farmer's office. Once she was seated at her typewriter she could no longer see into his private sanctum and so she remained standing; and as soon as she saw him arrive, as soon as his coat was off, his spectacles on and his chair pulled out ready for him to sit down at his desk, Myra closed in.

'You're early this morning, Miss Varney!'

'Well, no, Mr Farmer. I'm always in at this time. But I'm pleased to have caught you alone.'

Mr Farmer looked up from a letter he was reading, astonished. Miss Varney was not the type to wish to see him alone. She was the type whose reputation is built on punctuality, reliability and general unobtrusiveness, the type one is better pleased to find at her machine than at the office party. Miss Varney was taking in breath for what Mr Farmer feared and forecast would be a lengthy speech. He did not want to lose her.

She started by reminding him of her six years uninterrupted service. He was certain it was the prelude to a favour. And sure enough, it was. Miss Varney wanted the morrow off.

'My best girl, Evelyn, will cover for me!' Observing Mr Farmer was not preparing himself to answer her request, Myra added, by way of explanation, 'It's a personal matter, Mr Farmer.'

'Nothing distressing, I hope.' Mr Farmer's formal tone trailed into indifference. It was obvious that only illness or death could have prompted Miss Varney to make her request.

'No,' Myra answered tonelessly, 'nothing distressing'. But Mr Farmer was not convinced. It was only because he was wholly uninterested that he did not pursue the subject.

'Well, I imagine we can just about survive one day without your valuable services,' he said in tones barely the right side of sarcasm. 'Will you now please take dictation. Mosketh Pearson, 2 Ludgate Hill, etc. etc. Dear Mr Pearson . . .' And as he dictated, Mr Farmer regretted that only very plain women were very reliable.

When Myra got back to her desk the typing pool was awash with young women and the sound of rustling paper and tap-tapping. The morning proceeded along the lines of every other morning. Girls approached Myra's desk from the two rows of four desks that faced hers for work she was responsible for apportioning. When the hands of the clock above her desk drew themselves together in a clap, the back row of girls rose in mid-sentence, even mid-word, to go to lunch. When, punctually at one o'clock, they returned and were seated, row two rose as enthusiastically as row one had done. Myra had tried to alter her lunch times so as to get to know the four older girls with whom Evelyn was not so friendly, but somehow it had not worked out; those girls had not welcomed her and she had reluctantly faced the fact that she had no choice but to take her lunch with those who tolerated her. Evelyn and her set – Marge, Flo and Betty – patronized the Express Dairy, where they ate either poached eggs on toast or welsh rarebit, washed down with strong tea from the huge brown china pot the café provided for groups. When Myra was not being addressed personally, when she herself was not speaking, she listened with alternate fascination and embarrassment to the girls' conversation. It was worse than the conversations she had overheard at the base.... She flushed when she contemplated that her typists' intimacies might be overheard by the men – tellers from the National Provincial Bank – who regularly ate their lunch at the adjacent table, or Mr Horace, who ate alone in the corner. Myra's anxiety led her to receive the girls' conversation as a series of disjointed revelations more suited to the confines of the bathroom or bedroom than the public arena.

'Look at my spots, will you? I always get spots this time of the month. I can't bear it!'

'Have you tried Valderma?'

'Does it work?' Marge asks, incredulous, as she packs rhubarb pie into her mouth.

'Oh! Yes!' and turning to Evelyn: 'Pass your cup, dear!' and when Myra ignores Betty's instruction: 'Myra! Wakey-wakey!'

'Sorry, dear. Thank you!'

'Stan and me went dancing last night. I wore that dress, Marge, you know the one I got in the sale at Swan's.'

'Did 'e like it?'

'He said he could see right down to my navel! Saucy boy!' There were giggles all round. 'I really like him,' said Betty sadly, 'but I suppose he's a bit common.'

'Sounds common as dirt to me, my girl,' said Evelyn roundly. The girls bantered noisily. Their conversation was exclusively concerned with clothes, with men, with their marriage prospects. Myra felt excluded. It did not enter her head that the reason why the girls did not draw her in, did not question her, was due not to their disregard for her feelings but rather for their regard for them: she was dowdy and she was a spinster and she was fifty-five. She was unknown to experiences such as theirs. In deference to her position on the boundaries of human experience Evelyn would sometimes introduce the subject of parents, nephews, nieces and the local vicar, in an effort to find common ground on which all five might stomp.

'Have you heard from that nephew of yours in Hastings, Myra?'

'No, dear, I only hear from him twice a year. He writes in January and June to thank me for the savings certificate I send him at Christmas and on his birthday!'

'The ungrateful so and so!'

'Well, you know, it's the way these days!'

And having tried Evelyn would give in and answer Marge's question regarding her newly acquired lipstick. 'It *is* a lovely colour, I'll give you that, but I can't see why they call it orange banana. Bananas aren't orange ever, are they?'

'Evelyn, did you read that report in the *Standard* last evening, about that girl being raped? They say he's got bright orange hair and those cold green eyes.'

'I know what I'd have done to rapists!' Evelyn said darkly.

'Oh, no! Even so! You can't do that; they're sick men.' Marge objected.

'Sick or not that's what I'd do. And in some countries, in the East, that's what they do do.'

'How d'you know?'

'Well, it's obvious, isn't it. Stands to reason. They cut off their hands for stealing. . . .' Betty offered.

Myra listened. Betty's interjection had given rise to a great deal of interest. She pressed her views on the subject through narrowed lips and clenched teeth. 'I think it's just as much the girl's fault. Some girls ask for it.' Her head twitched as she spoke.

'Why should they ask for it? You don't have to get raped to have sex, you know!' An uneasy silence followed Marge's observation.

'Well,' said Myra, unable to bear the implied criticism any longer, 'I still say she probably got what was coming to her.'

Ever so many girls on the base gave in to the men but Hank was a gentleman. He never insisted. He said he respected her.

Anyone watching Myra Varney leave home on Wednesday morning would have to have had an unusual measure of intuition to suspect she was preparing to spend her day in a markedly different way from any other day in the six years she had worked at W. J. Farmer. She left home at the usual time, wearing her usual outfit. She carried her usual zipped bag and she caught the 8.26 number 13 bus – the one she always caught. She even got off the bus at her usual stop. But instead of entering W. J. Farmer Myra Varney turned and walked back twenty yards along Oxford Street, crossed, and walked down Bond Street. And as she walked she stopped and looked in the shop windows. She knew the shops; that is to say, she knew they existed; she passed them daily on her way to lunch. But in the past she had never imagined they were there to serve her needs. She had thought of them as the prerogative of women so different from herself that they were, in her mind, of another species. They looked unlike herself, they were not of modest means. Their lives were not circumscribed by two bus journeys, an office and a basement bedsit, and their relationships confined to a single four-legged creature. They were the women of the *Standard* and *Woman*. And, of course, the very much grander variety in *Vogue*. Even the girls in the typing pool would not have dreamed of entering Rayne and trying on shoes, or Smythsons and looking at diaries. They kept their shopping to Oxford Street: Bourne's or Selfridges.

Myra was not yet ready to enter the shops in whose windows she examined her reflection with distaste. That would come. Nor was she equipped to make purchases from them. She would need to go, first, to the Post Office and withdraw a sizeable sum from her savings book. No, before embarking upon the adventure of new clothes, Myra Varney would need to modify her appearance. She was aware of the fact and grateful her close reading of the *Standard* had made known to her the most stylish hairdresser in London: Colmar, of Bond Street. Myra had read that the tone of a woman was established by the cut and set of her hair – and the hat with which it was garnished. Funny, really, to have your hair done expensively only to cover it up with a hat. . . . But 'they' insisted it was the case. She had read an exhaustive article on the Woman's Page of the *Evening Standard* about how it was no good putting a fashionable hat on a head of unfashionably dressed hair. Those in the know could always tell – could see through garnish.

Myra Varney pushed open the plate-glass door of Colmar's salon and was confronted by a sight for which neither the *Standard* nor her imagination had prepared her. It was sumptuous. Behind the pink leather reception desk sat three young women receptionists who had modelled themselves on film stars. There was a Betty Grable, a Lauren Bacall and a Jennifer Jones. Opposite the reception desk stood a line of gilt chairs on which waiting women, in pink capes, sat reading glossy magazines. The noise robbed Myra of all vestiges of composure: voices, hair-dryers, telephones and the barking of a Yorkshire terrier sitting on its owner's lap, taking exception to a Burmese cat on a lead on its owner's lap some four chairs to its west. Myra approached Lauren Bacall; she noticed with a mixture of envy and distaste that Lauren's finger-nails were like talons and redder than letter boxes. Betty Grable and Jennifer Jones, believing Myra to be an applicant for the job of tea-lady for which Colmar was advertising, dropped their heads towards one another and discussed the wording of the advertisement Jennifer, herself, had inserted in the newspaper shop.

'I definitely put to present themselves at the tradesmen's entrance.'

'She's really got a nerve!' But by the time they had opened the sluice-gates of their indignation Myra had found her breath and had presented herself full face to Lauren Bacall.

'I would like to have my hair shingled,' she said, adding quickly, 'and I would like to know, first, how much it will cost.' It had been brave of her to ask and she had done so rather loudly.

'Shingled! My word! Why that's really up to the moment!' Myra does not notice that Lauren Bacall is being patronizing. On the contrary, she welcomes what she takes to be contact and watches as Lauren's talons slip down the very full appointments book, looking for a junior who might be free to execute an outmoded style. As she does so she keeps up non-stop chatter.

'Come full circle, it has, the shingle! Very smart!' Her middle talon has come to rest half-way down the page. 'Oh what luck! Our Mr Gavin, one of our most experienced stylists, could do you in an hour if you would care to come back. Or, if you prefer, you could wait.' She indicates the row of waiting clients.

'You might like to order a cup of coffee and read a magazine. . . .' Myra says that is what she would prefer. And the cost? It will be six pounds because 'Mr Gavin is one of our top stylists.' Myra allows no visible expression to cloud her face.

Someone, she cannot see who, is trying to relieve Myra of her coat by lifting it from her shoulders from behind her. Myra found that disconcerting and wheeled round to find herself facing a nice, elderly woman with a ticket in her hand which she pressed on Myra.

'Suzanne, vill you be zo good? Take modom to a seat and give her a very nice magzine.' The accent was extraordinary, unidentifiable, but the woman was kindly and Myra was grateful and she was not going to have to ask for a chair or something to read; she was going to be provided with both. And nobody could see her beige skirt and jumper because the nice elderly woman had shrouded her in pink, like all the other customers.

'Shall I order you a cup of coffee?' Suzanne asks.

'No thank you. I shan't bother,' Myra replies. She feels she might come a cropper with that. Would she have to pay for it? Would she have to tip Suzanne? How much? Better leave well alone, and anyhow liquids have a habit of running through her ever so quickly, they do. Myra looked at the clock on the wall. It was gilt, shaped like a summer sun, its pointed rays shining down on everyone. Myra had one hour in which to escape into the world of *Vogue*. For three-quarters of an hour she luxuriated in furs, on a yacht, plastered with diamonds. She ate at the Caprice, she floated in a gondola on the Rialto. She dowsed herself in *Femme* and strode along the Champs-Elysées led by a huge Borzoi. . . . As she emerged from her reveries she delved into her zipped bag for her typist's pad and pencil and with constant reference to *Vogue* made notes: black crêpe, diamanté, pearls the size of gulls' eggs, stockings with clocks, patent, ankle-strap shoes, Dr de Fresnay, plastic surgeon – and an address in Harley Street.

Myra Varney was unaccustomed to boys of sixteen looking like the one who presented himself to her as Mr Luke.

'Miss Varney? Would you come this way please? I'm Mr Luke and I shall be shampooing you.' Disorientated by the mincing walk affected by Mr Luke, Myra faced to bend into the backwash. She suddenly realized her error and sat back plum-faced. Luke – she could not bring herself to think of him as 'Mr' – asked her revolving self what shampoo she would 'care for'. She did not know what to answer. Boots?

'I leave that to you,' she tried, and Mr Luke picked up strands of Myra's loam-brown hair between two of his fingers and quickly dropped them as if each hair was infected.

'I think we'll use the medicated,' he sniffed, 'and conditioner.' Myra hoped most fervently that no one had heard this exchange. When Mr Luke had done all he felt possible in the circumstances, he threw a towel over Myra's head and left her stranded. She felt anxious but clean. From a feeling of being condemned for being contaminated she felt refreshed. It occurred to her that she should, rightly, be enjoying herself. How would she achieve that? She looked about her; the other customers were so relaxed. They looked as if they lived at Colmar's. How intimately they chatted with their stylists. Myra was astonished. There was no one with whom she talked that way.

The scent of pine is strong in her nostrils. And there is bracken and nuts. Funny how the past can float back on the scent of conditioner! Myra remembers an event in her childhood that she had not thought of for thirty years. Well, not so much childhood but we didn't have teenagers, then, she remembered. Funny how it all goes by, submerged in London Transport, typing pools, groceries, Suez and all that sort of thing. There had been that boy, not unlike Mr Luke, lived down the lane, in the same village, and took her to the common on nature walks. One day nature had been their own, and he had volunteered to show her the difference between men and women. She hadn't been that keen to be shown but she agreed to lie in the bracken, under the pine tree. She could remember the thud made by the dead cones as they dropped to the ground. The boy had been dead common, but quite nice, in a way. Myra's mouth curled into a half-smile, half-grimace. Well, she thought, that sort of thing goes on when you're young. And we didn't go too far; in those days you didn't or you got landed with a kid. Of course, the girls on the base knew how to take care of that. . . . Myra looked about her. All these women, she thought, they'd know about precautions. They went as far as they liked, and back again for more. Disgusting, it was. Of course, if she'd let Hank Burge go as far as he would've liked, she'd probably not got left on the shelf. . . .

Mr Gavin did not utter a word to Myra while he cut her hair. What a relief! She wouldn't have known what to say. She sat, transfixed, as she observed her head of hair fall to the ground. Suddenly, her face looked much larger than she remembered it.

'Luke! Rollers, please!'

As Mr Luke ushered Myra to the dryer she heard Mr Gavin comment to another stylist:

'I'll be doing water into wine next week!'

Seated under the dryer, Myra returned to the unfamiliar world of luxury, a world bounded by foreign travel, expense account eating, beauty and romance, the passport to which was an obsession with body hygiene, diet, make-up and clothes. She observed that an essential component of the world of luxury was a man on whose arm to lean and on whose cheque book to depend. A man not only conferred social success on a woman but was necessary to achieve it. Myra's purpose might have been undermined had she not had more time to absorb the inferences in the values of *Vogue*. In the event Mr Luke appeared, threw up the hood on the dryer, unfurled a roller and satisfied himself Myra's hair was at least bone dry.

'Would you like to come this way?' Not much alternative, Myra found herself thinking.

Mr Gavin combed out Myra's hair in silence and dabbed a kiss curl either side of her forehead. Taking a hand mirror he showed her the back of her head. The cut was superb! Myra observed the other customers would say as much. She could not bring herself to do likewise and just nodded.

'Yes, that's very nice, thank you!' she managed. Ignorant of the fact that she was expected to tip the cloakroom attendant, the girl who had shown her to her seat, Mr Luke and Mr Gavin, she paid her £6 at the cash desk and was subsequently pursued by four pairs of eyes staring, in contempt, at her back as she pushed open the plate-glass door and let herself out into Bond Street.

Myra stopped every fifty yards to examine her reflection in shop windows. She was astonished by her changed appearance. Her head seemed not only larger but lighter. The last time she had thought seriously of her appearance was when she worked at the base and compared her own looks with those of the 'fast' girls.... She would need to change her clothes. She would change them from head to foot. The flat brown shoes would have to go; she would need to learn to walk in high heels, however uncomfortable they were. The lisle stockings would have to be replaced by nylons and the nappa bag that had been her mother's she would put in the dustbin.... She would buy dramatic clothes! Things with a swirl, things that would draw attention to herself! Myra thrilled and shuddered at the thought. Apart from everything else, it cost money to be dramatic and in fashion. How, she wondered, could she stretch her ten pounds a week to encompass the world of high fashion? Where could she make economies? For a start, she would stop sending saving certificates to her nephew in Hastings.... Wretched boy! Never telephoned or visited. And she would go in the 1/9s rather than the 2/3s, even if the rough gang was in. She must speak to the manager of the Odeon and get him to control those boys.... Perhaps if she went on a Friday rather than a Saturday evening she could avoid that gang.

Thoughts of change, of economies that could lead to other expenditure, so dominated Myra's thoughts she was hardly aware that she had boarded her bus in Oxford Street and alighted at Swiss Cottage and crossed the Finchley Road. It was only when she rounded the corner of Eton Avenue and Winchester Road that she came to and noticed that the workmen, who had started that morning on a gas leak that involved taking up the road in front of her house, had made considerable progress. There was their tent! She could see, from one of the flaps drawn back, that a man was sitting having a cup of tea. A deep hole had been excavated outside her own house and a plank laid across from the road to the steps leading down to her basement. There was mud on the plank. She would need to take care negotiating it. The road was forever having something done to it ... war damage.

If only he'd answered her letter. If only he'd explained why he'd left without saying goodbye.

Myra carried on down the west side of Winchester Road until she reached Preston's, the papershop. Her relationship with Mrs P. was important for being one of the very few she had outside work. It was not entirely satisfactory because Myra felt that Mrs P. expected her to buy more from her than Myra did. She did not take a daily paper, like everyone else in the road, and she picked up her *Standard* in Oxford Street because she could be sure that way of getting the late edition.... But she did buy for Tibs at Preston's, and she bought sweets for herself from time to time, and Mrs P. put *Woman* and the *Radio Times* to one side for her.... Mrs P. knew better than to try and get he customers to make purchases for which they might be sorry. Better to let them make their own choices and not risk losing their custom, however exiguous it might be. ('Exiguous' was a word Mrs P. had taken on board only recently. It was a word loaned to her by the neighbourhood writer, Carson Churchill who, rumour had it, was not a Churchill at all....) And Myra needed Preston's as much for gossip as for the odd box of Black Magic, tin of Kit-e-Kat and battery for her torch. Mrs P. knew everything there was to know about everyone in the neighbourhood, and if you were prepared to stand in the shop long enough she would share the information with you. Of course, Myra did not always have the time but on

Saturdays she tried to make time; it was nice to be in the know.

'Oh, Miss Varney, dear, it's ever so smart!'

'Do you think so? I'm certainly pleased, very pleased. But I'll have to do something with my clothes, shan't I? They don't go at all ... I'll need heels for one thing,' she said looking down sadly at her shoes. 'I see from *Vogue* it's all black diamanté, crêpe and pearls for evening wear. . . .'

'We don't all 'ave to be fashionable to look nice,' Mrs P. said firmly, pulling her pink hand-knitted cardigan as far as it would stretch over her forty-eight-inch bust. 'Myself, I like to be comfortable.'

'Yes, well, that's what I've always thought but I must say I'm beginning to think clothes can make a real difference to life. I've noticed that in fashionable circles sensible and comfortable clothes don't seem to be worn at all.'

'Fashionable! My word! What would the likes of us know about fashionable circles? And what with the rents going up, you'll not be courting extra expenses!'

'My rent's *not* going up!' Myra said tartly, wondering how it was Mrs P.'s information was not correct in every detail, for Mrs P. knew her landlord.

'Is that so! Well, then that's a good thing if you're planning a wardrobe for fashionable circles.' Mrs Preston relied upon a world without change. It was the first time Myra had noticed this because since the end of the war and her disappointment, she too had relied upon such a world.

'They've got on with it, I see,' Myra observed, pointing to the open gash in the road.

'I don't know how they've found the time, though. They've 'ad more cups of tea than I've 'ad hot dinners this twelve month! Did you see this?' Mrs P. pointed to the front of the *Standard*. 'They've caught that rapist!'

'Filthy beast. I hope they doctor him!'

Myra took her leave of Mrs P., and with her paper still rolled, and her brown felt pull-on rolled in the same hand, she walked carefully across the plank to her basement steps. As she did so she thought she heard one of the flaps on the workmen's tent snap to.

The girls in the typing pool were agog next morning. Myra walked into the officer, her shoulders rather less rounded, her head held slightly higher.

'It suits you lovely!' The girls crowded round Myra and noticed that in addition to her new hair-style she was wearing a little powder on her nose, and pink lipstick.

'No need to ask what you're up to!' Evelyn whispered to Myra, knowingly.

'What do you mean?' Myra was mystified.

'Who is he? No, don't answer. No time. Tell me all about him at lunch!'

'There isn't anyone, silly. I'd tell you if there were, you know I would. . . .' Myra insisted, almost sadly. 'And by the way, dear, I won't be joining you for lunch for the rest of the week. I've got business to attend to!' she quickly added.

'Up to you!' Evelyn turned to go back to her desk. She was hurt. She was not convinced that Myra was telling her the truth. And Myra had not even enquired how things went yesterday, when Evelyn had taken charge. . . . Evelyn rated Myra her friend. Of course Myra was years older than she, and if she wanted to keep her affair secret it was her privilege to do so, but in that case Evelyn would not be so forthcoming with *her* in the future. No, she certainly would not. And that was for sure.

'I can't invent someone for you, dear.' Myra addressed Evelyn's turned back.

The trouble was the girls – Marge and Betty and Flo, in particular – would expect Evelyn to offer an explanation for Myra's appearance, and her absence.

'Where's Myra?'

'She says she's got business to attend to.'

'I bet she has! Come on Evy, you're her friend, what's she up to?'

'I don't know, honest I don't. She wouldn't tell me. I suppose if she wants to keep herself to herself that's her affair. And from now on, I can tell you, I'll be doing the same.'

'D'you think it's Mr Horace?' Marge suggested. The girls giggled uproariously at the suggestion, and turned their heads towards Mr Horace who was seated alone, at a corner table for one, eating his beans on toast.

It took Myra until the following Wednesday to settle on purchases. She had window-shopped and tried on; she had fumbled in necklaces and agonized over stockings; she had been overwhelmed by the quantity of cosmetics to enlarge the eyes, lengthen the eyelashes, colour the cheeks. The whole experience had been both exciting and humiliating. The sales assistants could be very tart in the shops in Bond Street, quite unlike those in the suburban shops, where Myra normally bought her jumpers and skirts. And in the chain stores they were understanding of her sort. But if she was to change her image she would have to put up with barbs, Myra told herself firmly. And she did. And then there was all that business of leaving a deposit to be sure the article would be there next day.... That was a risk.... In the event, Myra bought nothing for a week and found the dress, the shoes, the necklace and the stockings were all available when she returned for them. Knowing the dress and shoes fitted, the necklace became her, and the stockings were both sheer and durable, she felt confident they were what she wanted. She totted up the sum she would need to withdraw from her post office book, acclimatized herself to the ravages the withdrawal would make in her savings, and on Friday took the plunge. She paid for what she had chosen and concealed her purchases in her zipped bag. For the entire Friday afternoon, while she typed the company's report, Myra kept the handles of her bag wound round her left foot under her desk.

On Saturday mornings Myra always rose as early as she rose on weekday mornings. She found it impossible to adapt her internal clock to the less arduous demands of Saturday and Sunday and so she gave in to it, allowed it to tick as it chose, and she adjusted to it. But this Saturday she did not resent the fact; she leapt from her bed with expectations. She braved the below-zero temperature in the outside lavatory without discomfort; she braved the Siberian scullery without irritation. She washed her face and hands in icy water at the sink and as she listened to the wind tear at the tiles on the roof of the lean-to addition, she rejoiced that it was not she who was responsible for external repairs. With a towel pressed against her wet face she looked out of the window. She observed that during the night the elm, whose foliage obscured her from the backs of houses in summer, had finally been shaken barren of its every leaf. Now she and her neighbours faced one another in winter candour, back to back. Plain. Barren. Cold.

Myra dressed in her M&S skirt, beige jumper, ancient brown tweed coat and flat Lotus shoes. She covered her hair with a scarf tied in the manner favoured by the young Queen. She went up the Finchley Road to Sainsbury's, where she had been one of the first customers to arrive on Saturday mornings ever since she had started work at W. J. Farmer and come to live in Winchester Road. In all these years the manager had been the same: Mr Frederick Potts. In all these years he had not once acknowledged Myra as she sped from the cheese counter to the bacon counter, from the butter slab to the tinned meat and fish, buying her week's supplies. Myra's back had not been good for many years. Before she had started work at W. J. Farmer she had had a spell nursing her aunt who had had an attack of pleurisy from which she eventually died. It had done Myra's back in, all that lifting. Myra had taken over Aunt Dorothy's basket on wheels, known by her aunt affectionately as 'Wheely'. She packed all she purchased at Sainsbury's into 'Wheely' and pulled it resolutely back to Winchester Road, against the bitter wind.

Waste-paper and dead leaves in the gutter whooshed round and up in a series of little maelstroms along the way. Clouds scudded overhead. Myra was cold; she was glad of her headscarf and woollen gloves.

Preston's was full of neighbours paying their paper bills.

'Good morning, Miss Varney! Oh, you got that lovely hair-do all covered up! What a pity to hide it – and spoil it!'

'It's cold, Mrs P. What a wind! I'm glad I'm not responsible for the repairs on my place; ever so many tiles got ripped off last night. The war damage – it was never done properly.'

'That's what he needs more rent for!' Mrs P. observed, darkly. 'I'm surprised he's not put yours up, what with your extensions and outside lav....' Mrs P. held out *Radio Times* knowing Myra would be wanting it.

'And I'll have some liquorice comforts, if you please!'

'They've taken their time,' Mrs P. remarked, pointing to the road-works. 'Workmen, these days...' and she sighed as if the matter were tragic and hers alone to remedy. Mr Carson Churchill pushed open the door and as soon as Mrs P. saw him she became wreathed in smiles.

'And what have you been up to this week, Mr Churchill?' she asked, savouring the word 'Churchill', and handing him the *TLS* and *Encounter*. 'Finding me some nice new words?' Myra was embarrassed by the way in which Mrs P. flirted with the neighbourhood author, and astonished that he led her on.

'Charismatic! Mrs P. Try that for size!'

'Whatever does it mean? I hope it's not one of your rude words, Mr Churchill.' And as the author got down to a definition Myra pushed open the door and, pulling 'Wheely' behind her, left the shop.

Myra stood on the pavement waiting to cross the road, wondering how she'd get herself and 'Wheely' across the plank, now that 'Wheely' was filled with groceries. As she considered the matter, and was in the process of working out a plan, a burly man of indeterminate age emerged from the ochre trench by the side of the workman's tent.

'Here, lady, let me have that!' He jumped deftly out of the pit and heaved Myra's basket into the air, above his head, walked down the plank, down the basement steps, and deposited 'Wheely' outside Myra's front door.

'Thank you ever so much. I'm most grateful; I don't know how I'd've managed.' Myra wondered whether she owed him anything for his help.

'It's that windy, Tibs,' Myra told the cat who, had he understood, would have rejoiced in the news and left the fireside, for cats hear things in gustings. 'I've got a nice bit of fish for you,' she added, quite unnecessarily for the cat's whiskers were already rising and falling: he had located the smell that foretold of great promise. His excitement was apparent, the same as it was every Saturday morning. It warmed the cockles of Myra's heart – she often said as much.

Myra went straightaway and got the whiting on the boil and then she gave the bedsit a very good going over. Anyone watching would have thought Myra had all day to turn out her room; she piled chairs, table and oddments on to the bed and took the rugs into the corridor and brushed and polished the linoleum before replacing the swept rugs. She polished the table and chairs, took the books out of the bookcase and dusted them. It was as if she were filling up time by dusting, polishing, sweeping and rearranging. And then, when all was done to her satisfaction, she lit the gas fire and drew the curtains fast over the window. There were two sets of curtains, nets and cretonne. And nets let in enough light for Myra's purposes and too clear a view of the dustbins and she did not trust their keeping the sight of herself from prying eyes. She carefully arranged the cretonne curtains so that not a chink of window remained unprotected. She turned on the bedside lamp. And then she removed her jumper, skirt, stockings and shoes.

Because there was no suitable place in which to put her new acquisitions, Myra had left them in the zipped bag. With all the excitement and anticipation of a child on Christmas morning she unzipped the bag and took out her wrapped purchases. Carefully, ironing out the tissue paper with the back of her hand (she put the paper to one side, the paper bags to another), she laid out the dress, shoes, stockings and pearls on the bed. She sat down in front of the mirror behind the bookcase and, with her pots, her eye pencil, her mascara and lipstick, Myra made up her face for the first time in her life. The girl who had advised her in Fenwicks had persuaded her into a lipstick labelled Fuchsia. The mauve colour created an effect so strange Myra could not judge whether it was strangely pretty or strangely ugly. She applied blue eye-shadow from under her brows to the roots of her lashes and mascara – black and thick – and rouge. She had forgotten the foundation cream and powder and, remembering it at the last minute, dabbed a touch of powder on her nose and chin. And then she stood and pulled on the nylon stockings and slipped into the black crêpe dress. The dress bloused where her hips might have been, and fell to mid-calf; the sleeves were quite full and came to a tight cuff at the wrist. Myra would have liked to pin the label at the neck of the dress on to the front. She knew all about BAZAAR. All the girls in the typing pool were saving for a dress with such a label ... it was exquisite ... expensive, but worth every penny, every line of typing, every irritation, every journey to work in every mood of weather

– wet, cold, blistering, dusty – every insult. And then Myra threw a rope of imitation pearls over her head – Docker sized! The assistant in Fenwicks said she had seen Lady Docker wearing just such a rope – but hers had been real, of course. Still, you couldn't tell, not from a distance. Myra fumbled in one of her drawers and from way at the back pulled out a gardenia, made in wax and cambric, and she pinned the flower at the level of her collar bone. Finally, she put on the Dolcis ankle-strap shoes. She stood up. The heels were horribly high and she had difficulty walking. She hobbled towards the door and back towards the fire. Three steps in all. Back and forth. She was getting used to the shoes. She stopped, combed her shingle and applied *Mon Âme* scent from an atomizer. She peered at her reflection; she could only see herself to the waist. She was astonished. She stared. She did not know what to think. She looked so different! And then she wondered what Hank Burge would think. Did she look more American now? And what should she do? She couldn't go *out* looking like this! She picked up her beige jumper and held it in front of her. She couldn't go out with all that stuff on her face, even! Her legs felt naked. She'd not worn nylons since.... She ran her hands over her body; the dry fabric was lined with something slippery – artificial silk, she supposed. It felt really luxurious!

Myra was both enjoying the sensation of the new image her purchases were lending her, and anxiously wondering what to do with it, when she heard a loud knock on the basement door. Without thinking, she responded to the knock immediately and found she could not stride to the door as she was inclined to do but only mince. She remembered that the milkman usually called on Saturday – and then dismissed that as being a possible explanation because he had called when she was cooking Tibs's whiting, before she started on the cleaning.... She opened the door. There, on the last step but one of the basement flight, stood the workman who had helped her with 'Wheely'.

'Excuse me, lady, ever so sorry to bother you, may I use your toilet?' He was clearly ill at ease. 'Caught short!' he offered, as if an explanation were due.

'Oh!' blurted Myra, 'yes, of course, come this way, please!' She turned and led him to the door that opened on the yard. She pointed in the direction of the lavatory. As the man passed her Myra smelt the combined odours of ferrous metal, gas and mud. Disgusting! She put on the kettle. She would make tea. It was mid-morning and she could do with a cup. She was edgy; she did not like to be disturbed. She did not like strangers in her quarters. It was quite a problem getting the tea and the pot and the milk together when someone else was around and your heels uncomfortably high ... As soon as she was seated with her hands clasped round the mug of strong tea, Myra felt better. She heard the metallic noise the lavatory chain made and then the sound of water emptying from the cistern. And then the door to her room was pushed ajar.

'Thank you, lady; thank you kindly,' the man said. But he did not leave. Indeed, he actually pushed open the door a little further, hesitatingly, and said more cheerfully, 'Elevenses?'

'Yes, I suppose they are – or it is!; They laughed together uneasily. Tibs fled.

'Would you care for a cup?'

'Indeed I would. Ta!' It was not a cup that Myra handed him but an ample mug, like the one she had been nursing. He was glad of it. A tin of biscuits lay open on the table. The man stood with his back to the fire, absorbing most of the heat, his thick, black jacket steaming like a horse in the rain. Myra took in that the man was tall, thick-set and a lot younger than she. Maybe no more than forty.

'That's a pretty dress you're wearing,' the man said, looking down on her. 'You know something? When I carried your basket for you, I was doing my good turn for the day; helping an old lady. But now I see I was helping a young lady – doing *myself* a good turn!'

'It's new,' Myra explained, 'the dress, I mean. You're the first person to see it on!'

'Am I now? Well, I *am* honoured. New for Christmas?'

Myra was extremely grateful for the idea. 'Yes, for the office party.' She had not thought of the office party. She hated office parties. She was obliged to attend, of course, but she would hardly dare wear this. Or would she? Give them all something to talk about, it would ...

'Stand up!' the man ordered, but encouragingly, 'walk to the door then turn round, like mannequins do!' Myra found herself doing as she was bid. As she turned at the door the man drew in a tide of tea on his tongue, swilled it round his mouth and down his throat. Then he breathed out contentedly.

'You look lovely, lady!' he said. Myra could hear he meant it.

'Have a digestive!' she said holding out the tin. Her hand was shaking.

'May I take off my jacket?' he asked.

'Hand it here!' She took the heavy, foul-smelling jacket and hung it behind the door.

'It's filthy out,' the man said. 'Nice in here, though,' he added, 'like evening with the weather shut out behind the curtains. Nice and quiet, too.' He looked about the room.

'Saturdays and Sundays most of them go to their families – the tenants, I mean.'

'Haven't you got no family?'

'Just a sister in Shropshire and a nephew in Hastings, but we're not close. No, not close!' And Myra remembers how remote they are and the thought produces a funereal silence. 'I was close to my parents, though. But I was a disappointment to them. Sad, really.' And there followed a long pause in which to give sadness its due. 'But they had one another. . . .'

'May I sit down?' the man asked, and Myra gave her silent consent. She stared at the man sitting opposite her. She has never had a man friend sit in that chair. Come to think of it, no man has ever been in this flat – not if you don't count the gas man, come to read the meter, and the milkman come to be paid. . . .

'Got a boyfriend?' the man asked. Myra wondered if he could thought-read. It was uncanny.

'What would I be doing with a boyfriend at my age?' she chided. There was a mite of coquetry in her tone as her thoughts returned to Captain Hank Burge.

'No one courting you?' the man tried.

'I've put all that behind me!' Myra said firmly and she sniffed. And then the man rose and poured himself another mug of tea, added water to the pot from the kettle, and took a biscuit from the tin before sitting down again.

The presumption inherent in his actions altered the atmosphere and Myra felt threatened: she was no longer in control. She smoothed her skirt, unnecessarily, and fingered her rope of pearls. She patted her hair and examined her finger-nails. She wished, deeply, that the man would go, but he had a full mug of tea to drink. The man is not sure that the silence is doing much for his chances. He attempts to make conversation.

'What d'you do Saturdays?'

'Just the shopping and the housework. I go to the library, sometimes. And in the evening I go to the Odeon. Saturday's my day of rest. I work very hard all week, you understand. And Sundays I do my charity work.'

'What work d'you do very hard?'

'I'm in charge of the typing pool at W. J. Farmer in Oxford Street. It's quite a good job, I've been there six years. I'm responsible for all the typing, see it's correct in every detail; see it gets signed on time and posted. I've got eight girls under me and some of them can't spell so I have to keep both eyes open.' Myra would have liked the man to go or to speak, but he did neither and so unable to bear a silence she went on. 'It's very convenient, the number 13 bus puts me down at the office door and brings me right back to Swiss Cottage Station. . . .' Her voice raced. 'I don't do a lot else, really. Just the cinema, I like films ever so much.' The man continued to send tea down his throat with the noise of a river in full spate. If only he would say something, Myra thought. Her anxiety led her to fill the silence not only with short bursts of words but with gestures unfamiliar to her. And then she noticed that the man's eyes had fallen on her scrapbook. She did not, at any cost, want him to open that.

'What's your work?' she asked quickly and stupidly, because she knew very well – and he knew she knew.

'I work for the gas. Trace leaks, mend 'em, that sort of caper. And there's lots to mend – war damage, you know. I like it; it's interesting. I get to meet all sorts, and no one job's like the next.' Another pause. And then the man went on.

'I've a gang of four under me. Nice blokes ... but they're not reliable, you know. Not reliable at all. That's the problem these days.'

'Oh, I quite agree!' Myra was delighted to have found common ground, something solid on which to join the man in agreement. 'I have the same thing with my girls. Can't rely on them!' Myra and the man took all the steam out of that topic they could. And then, once again, they fell silent. Myra started to fidget.

'Do we have a leak?'

'Not now, you don't!' The man gulped down tea, 'mended it.' He gulped again. 'We'll fill in the road Monday and clean it up all nice for you. By the time you get back from work, you won't know we've been 'ere at all.' The man was picking up objects from her shelf in the bookcase and replacing them, having carefully examined each. Myra could not be sure whether he liked or disliked what he examined. She did so hope you would'nt drop the china Spanish lady ...

'We might 'ave finished today but my lads like to knock off early Saturdays, and I don't like to stop 'em; they've got families to get back to....' He moved to the window and peered through a gap in the curtains. 'Yes, they've all gone 'ome.' He put down his mug on the table and started on a systematic round of everything in her room. He picked up her knick-knacks, studied each, put each back just where he had taken it from. He seemed particularly taken with her mugs, the ones with 'Present From X' – usually a seaside resort – written in fancy lettering across them.

'Get these on your 'olidays?' Myra nodded in assent. 'Do a lot of sewing?' he enquired, picking up a basket. Myra nodded again. 'I have my mending ...' she added, and then the man passed to a photograph. She knew he'd ask: 'These your Mum and Dad, then?'

'Yes. That picture was taken just before they died – killed on a coach holiday. In the West Country.'

'My Mum and Dad's dead, too. I miss 'em.' The man took in a deep breath, clearly moved by the memory of his parents and his own deprivation. Turning to face Myra he asked her:

'What's your name?'

'Myra!'

'That's an unusual name!'

'I don't know about unusual. It's a horrible name. I do know that. I've never understood how my Mum and Dad could have saddled me with such an ugly name. They were such beautiful people. You can see they were,' and she pointed to the photograph. 'Myra! Ugh! Every time someone calls me by my name I think of mud. The mire, in fact.' There was a pause. Then, with the same passion one imagines Archimedes felt on the occasion of his celebrated bath, Myra announced, 'I shall call myself Marilyn from now on.'

'As in Monroe?' the man offered, adding, 'What a lovely idea! May I be the first to call you Marilyn, then? And you call me Ted!'

Myra did not know when it was that she rose to her feet and how it was that she found herself standing by the side of Ted looking with him at the photograph of her parents. Suddenly, however, she was aware of being dangerously near the strange man, and she took a step back. There was no room for her to make this move in her small room, and her leg hit the chair. Myra was conscious that Ted was staring at her, closely; she was embarrassed and looked down at her feet encased in patent leather.

'Marilyn!' Ted murmured, enjoying savouring the name, 'when was the last time a man made a fuss of you?' His question was said kindly and Myra's thoughts almost returned to Hank but not waiting for a reply to his question, Ted had taken Myra in his arms and was covering her mouth with his own. Myra, as unbending as a stick insect, was terrified, and mistaking her paralysis for acquiescence Ted prolonged his assault. When he released her he saw the fuchsia lipstick had smudged over her top lip and her chin.

Myra was in a state of utter confusion; the man filled her room to capacity and she wanted him out of it. Could she ask him to go and if she did would he leave? Should she scream? There was no one to hear her and in any case, what about? Thoughts crashed against one another in her mind and left chaos. She heard the man say, 'We don't want to muss up that nice new frock, do we?' as he deftly unfastened the zip that ran from neck to thigh down the centre back.

The dress fell to Myra's feet: she found herself standing in a pool of black stillness. She did not know what to do; her feet were trapped. She raised her hands to hide her cotton brassière and petticoat and breasts. None must meet his inspection. She kicked herself free from the dress

and noticed the man stoop, pick it up and fling it over the table. This gesture frightened Myra; the man was in control, he had been in control
from the moment he served himself to digestive biscuits and a second
mug of tea.... That was the trouble: give an inch.... The fragments of
the afternoon were shattered. The hair, the clothes – what an idea!

'And now my gorgeous Marilyn-the-new, you and I are going to
get to know one another....' Ted picked up Myra, drew back the bed
cover, then the bedclothes, and laid her on the bed. In doing this he
knocked over a bottle of eau de Cologne that had been standing on the
bedside table. Myra, who was already frigid with fear, jerked at the
sound. She kept her eyes tightly closed and drew the bedclothes up to
her ears while Ted undressed to his underpants and socks and got into
the bed beside her. And then he drew off her petticoat and unfastened
her brassière and passed his hands over her naked, hairless body.

'My! You're a dark one, you are! I bet you've 'ad more men than I've
'ad 'ot dinners!' And finding that thought encouraging – a licence –
Ted penetrated Marilyn-the-new, vigorously. So preoccupied was he
with his own satisfaction, he did not observe his partner was inert.

'Was I all right? To your taste?' he asked. Myra did not hear the voice,
that is to say she did not hear it in respect of her life. It was a far-off voice,
speaking to another, having nothing to do with her.... Ted repeated
his enquiry, but did not wait for an answer. He jumped out of bed, still
wearing his socks. He whistled while he dressed. He snapped his braces
victoriously. And although the noise he made was loud and shocking,
Myra was a million miles removed from its significance.

'Well, goodbye Marilyn!' Ted said cheerfully, walking to the side of
the bed and peering at the motionless form.

'You all right?'

'I'm all right,' Myra managed.

'Good. Then that's all right: if you're all right, I'm all right!' He
laughed. 'I'll fill in the other 'ole Monday.' And he roared with laughter
at his obscenity. Once more the noise he made as he opened the door,
laughing, and slammed the door, laughing, paralysed Myra. She lay
comatose.

It was many moments, perhaps as much as half an hour, before Myra
moved, and then she merely shifted in the bedclothes, trying to find a
dry, unsoiled patch on which to lie. The bed smelt of metal and sweat
and fish. Myra rubbed her upper arm against her nose. She smelt. She
retched. It was only because Myra felt that she was going to be sick, and
did not have to think to rush to hold her head over the lavatory pan,
but did so automatically, that she got our of bed. She had no wish for
anything – unless to wish for nothing, to be unconscious. Although she

felt herself profoundly soiled she did not think to go upstairs to the bath-room. It was not her day or hour for that, and someone might return un-expectedly. She filled the scullery sink with hot water from the kettle and washed herself from head to toe, over and over. She wailed as she washed, chief mourner at her own last rites. Drained, she wrapped her-self in her dressing-gown and sat down before the fire in her armchair. She took from her sewing basket a pair of dressmaker's shears and she cut the black crêpe dress into two-inch pieces, carefully, measuring one piece against the previous piece. And all the time she wept. She tore the straps from the patent shoes, cut up the stockings and pulled the pearls from their rope. And then she dressed in her beige skirt and jumper, put on her overcoat and went out to the dustbins. There she consigned her dress, shoes, stockings and pearls to the company of rotting vegetable and fruit scrapings and peelings, old tin cans, empty boxes of washing power and other assorted garbage.

Myra sat silently in the darkened room. The purity she had saved for Hank gone.... She could not bring herself to talk to Tibs, or to allow the cat on her knee. Eventually, she changed the sheets on her bed and got into the clean warmth with a hot water bottle. She did not eat that day. She took two aspirins. She slept.

She rose as usual next day. It was Sunday. She went to church and found some solace in the murmur of prayer. She kept her eyes closed for most of the service – it was as if being unable to see the other congregants she went unseen herself. The sermon took as its theme preparation for salvation. Christmas was not far off. In the afternoon Myra went to the Royal Free Hospital to comfort the dying. Her remoteness was not something the patients would register. She went through her routine – obliging, consoling, sympathizing – without difficulty.

On Monday morning Myra left for work at the usual time in her usual outfit. Her shingled hair was concealed under her pull-on felt hat. She did not wear so much as a dab of powder. As she stood at her desk, arranging the typists' work in piles for Marge, Flo, and the others, Eve-lyn arrived in the office and greeted her.

'Had a nice weekend, Myra?' she asked.

'Just the usual,' Myra replied.

'By the way, I forgot to tell you Marge and Flo won't be in today.' Leaning over and whispering in Myra's ear, Evelyn confided, 'Their young men have been down for the weekend. They told me if they weren't in on time we was to assume they'd found better things to do this Monday morning than sit in a blooming typing pool...' and she giggled. Myra loosened her shoulders and shook her head in a gesture of disgust.

'Where's Marge and Flo?' Betty called out.

'I dunno,' Evelyn lied, winking at her friend, Myra. While Evelyn giggled suggestively Myra examined her lot: she would rather type. But she said nothing. She kept that thought to herself with the dress, the shoes, the pearls and the name Marilyn, to which she would never again respond.

Pillion Riders

It was many years ago. I was twenty. I had been married off to one of my father's business associates. He was a kind man but I couldn't fall in love with him for that. I tried, but all I managed was a sort of gratitude to him for not being *un*kind. He was forty years older than I, and he was ugly. But I was determined, from the start, never to hurt him.

We had been married for two years when the doctor told him, 'Your wife's unwell. She's melancholy. Take her away somewhere! See to it that she enjoys herself!'

And so it was that he took me to Paris, where he had a friend from his student days.

'We shall be staying at the Ritz,' he told me.

'Built by Mansard for Armand-Louis de Gontaut-Biron, duc de Lauzun,' he informed me – as he walked me along the corridors lined with show-cases filled with jewellery and other small works of art – leading me into the restaurant, for dinner.

'Marcel Proust used to dine here. He used the Ritz as his corner shop. In the middle of the night he would send his chauffeur here for iced beer.' I didn't admit to my husband that I didn't know who this Mr Proust might be. Nor did I tell him that, whoever he was, I thought him inconsiderate to wake his chauffeur over such a trivial matter.

On our first morning in Paris my husband led me across the Place Vendôme, to Schiaparelli.

'I would like to see you in bright, geranium pink silk,' he said.

I wept.

'Please,' I begged, 'let me wear what I like. I feel most comfortable in black.'

He did not insist.

We drifted across the Tuileries to Notre-Dame. While my husband drank coffee and an *eau de vie* in a café in the *Place*, I went into the cathedral to pray.

'And now I shall take you to the Louvre!'

My feet and back ached. I didn't like the pictures by Watteau that my husband preferred.

That evening my husband took me to meet his friend, Otto von Kramitz, at UNESCO. Mr von Kramitz was a key figure at UNESCO, with a particular interest in Central Africa. We were taken from the foyer of the Palais to the door of Mr von Kramitz's office by a uniformed attendant. The office was vast. It must have been forty feet in length and Mr von Kramitz was seated at the far end. I didn't see him immediately because, seated at the nearside of his desk, obstructing my view, with his back to us, was another man. This other man did not so much as turn his head when we entered; nor did he rise. I could see that he was young. He was dressed casually in a khaki military rain jacket. I wondered, had he just arrived? But following on the heels of that query came the weird, absolute certainty that he was going to play some crucial role in my life. I just knew it!

Mr von Kramitz strode across his office and greeted my husband warmly. Turning to me, he took both my hands in his and said that he'd heard a lot about me and did so hope that a visit to Paris would restore me. The young man remained seated, his back to us.

'We're going to dine at La Boîte!' von Kramitz announced.

'Oh, surely not! Couldn't we eat somewhere more traditional?' my husband pleaded.

'La Boîte's all the rage this season!' his host insisted, adding, 'Your young wife will see *le tout Paris!*'

All these years later, I do not remember how it came about that, instead of accompanying my husband and his friend in the Mercedes, I rode to La Boîte on the back of Claude's motorcycle. Wearing my tight, black velvet suit, my pearl choker and earrings, and the little half-veil – fashionable that year – attached to my head with a velvet band, I rode across Paris, my arms tight round a man to whom I had never spoken, hardly looked at, yet felt I loved. When we alighted at the entrance to La Boîte, I discovered that Claude had as few words of English as I had of French.

I was shocked at how irritably Mr von Kramitz addressed us when Claude and I entered the restaurant.

'You will sit *here!*' he roared at Claude, pointing to the seat next to his own. 'You sit *there*, with Opal,' he told my husband, indicating the banquette against the wall, 'You must face into the place so that Opal can see *le monde*'.

My husband took the starched damask napkin that was floating like a boat on my plate, shook it and spread it across my lap. While doing so he whispered to me: 'That's T. S. Eliot!'

I looked to my immediate right and saw a plain middle-aged man seated beside a plain middle-aged woman, and I was not impressed.

Mr von Kramitz, my husband and Claude seemed to have a great many things to discuss, in French. I was left to my own thoughts and observations. Because I was bored, I strained my ears to hear what Mr Eliot was saying:

'Neither of the protagonists is invested with much humanity, either for good or evil,' I heard him say. I expected he was trying out a speech. At the end of his meal, he asked his companion if she would care for 'a fruit'. I thought that he should have asked if she would like 'some fruit' – or just 'fruit'. But I forgot to check this with my husband, later.

'And how are your partridges?' my husband enquired. He was always anxious for me to enjoy what he chose for me.

'Very nice.' I assured him.

'They are the celebrated *perdrix aux truffes*,' he explained. 'I would like you to try the *granité de melon au Champagne*.' But I was hardly listening. I knew that he would decide for me and, anyhow, just at that moment I noticed that Yves Montand was being shown to a table and Juliette Greco was talking to the head waiter.

'Look! Look!' I said, pointing. I was excited.

'Ssh!' my husband hissed, 'you're behaving like a child!'

I felt humiliated, but I knew that he was right.

Claude could not have understood the conversation but he understood the tone in which it was undertaken. He touched my knee lightly under the table. I put my hand under the tablecloth and for a split second we clasped fingers. When I looked up, into his face, we exchanged understanding.

I thought that Mr von Kramitz's behaviour towards Claude was very strange. He kept putting his arm round the back of Claude's chair and sometimes, when Claude said something that made him laugh, he stroked his cheek.

We had finished eating and were drinking coffee when my husband and Mr von Kramitz started to talk in English about what I should see and do in Paris. I was surprised to find myself suggesting that what I'd most enjoy would be to see Paris by night from Claude's motorcycle.

'*Ne sois pas trop tard!* Don't be late!' von Kramitz ordered Claude.

'No!' my husband agreed, 'I don't want Opal getting overtired.'

Claude rode fast to Montmartre and from the steps of the Sacré Cœur we looked over the twinkling lights of the city. Claude did not take me back to the Ritz. He took me to his attic room in the suburbs of Paris, at Fontenay-sous-Bois.

We dismounted in the rue Victoire. Claude pushed his motorcycle through iron gates, into the courtyard, and led me up five flights of stairs to the top of the house. His room was large, divided by screens into three areas, for sleeping, for working and for preparing food. There was cold running water to the sink: no hot water, though.

Nor was there a lavatory. Everyone in the house shared the single WC by the front door. I had to go back down the stairs. It was eerie; I was frightened. When I got back up into the attic, I found that Claude had boiled a kettle and poured hot water into a basin so that I could wash. He left me behind the screen and passed me a pyjama top.

'*Que tu es belle, ma pauvre fille!*' he murmured, when he saw me naked. I understood *belle*: it means beautiful. But was I correct in thinking that *pauvre* means poor? Whatever else, I was actually quite rich.

I had never been with a young man. I had known only my husband. Claude was slim and his skin was silky. He smelled of hay. He found ways of pleasing me that I had never imagined. But I didn't understand then – and I don't understand now – why it was that we wept so much.

We didn't sleep at all. I thought it would be a waste of time and he must have thought the same. He made love to me again and again.

Between making love and resting to regain strength to make love anew, Claude ground coffee beans and made coffee and we sat in bed drinking, and smoking Gauloises. To this day, the scent of Gauloises mingled with coffee is unbearable to me. I wished then and I wish now that I had understood all that Claude said to me that night. He seemed sorry for me. I couldn't understand why; his life was so much harder than my own. He seemed anxious to protect me; he would fold me in his arms and gently secure my head between his face and shoulder.

The pink half-light of dawn was accompanied by the birds' chorus. Claude rose, drew back the curtain and took down a picture from the wall. He put it in my hands. I saw a hand-tinted photograph of a lovely young woman resembling himself.

'Sister,' he said, and added, 'dead'. And so saying he mimed the awesome truth: she had hanged herself and he had discovered her and cut her down. Too late. He held out his writs; I could just make out the hair-thin bleached scars. And when he saw that I'd understood, he raised his chin and moaned to the ceiling like a tethered dog wails to the moon.

When he had composed himself, he knelt by the side of the bed and drew off my wedding ring. Solemnly, he replaced it – but on the fourth finger of my *right* hand.

'French way!' he explained, and I understood. He was to be my French husband.

'Opal,' he murmured for the first time.

'Claude,' I whispered.

'Man and woman!' he said triumphantly. He took my hands and put them to his face and I felt the tears. And then he put my hands elsewhere on his body.

There was a cast iron stove in the attic. It was a primitive but effective means of heating the large room. During the night, Claude made up

the fire and kept us warm. At dawn he made a blaze. He pulled me out
of bed and sat me down at the table. First, he emptied his pockets on to
the table; he had a bunch of keys, a packet of cigarettes and a lighter,
and the equivalent of about five pounds. Next, he opened his cupboard;
he had two shirts, a pair of trousers, two sweaters, a pair of shoes and
some socks. Then, from his desk, he took a handful of notebooks, two
bottles of ink and some pens and pencils. Finally, with his arm round my
shoulder, he drew me into the kitchen area and pointed to the shelves
above the sink; there was sugar, salt, coffee, rice and noodles. And having
shown me all he had, he looked at me hard and said '*C'est tout!*'

I understood. This was all he had. These were his worldly goods.
Was he inviting me to share them?

I looked at my watch. While I washed and dressed, I was thinking:
his sister is dead and he is sad, almost to death. Mr van Kramitz likes him
a lot. He's very poor. But Mr von Kramitz likes him. He's a writer,
but he earns his money as a messenger, for UNESCO. This attic's his
home; his language is French. He's young and he's beautiful and I never
knew that making love could be.... And when I was fully dressed, I
walked round the attic and looked out at the view from the window. I
memorized every detail. It's forty years ago; I can recall the title of the
book on his bedside table: *Tortilla Flat*; the make of his coffee beans: Mo-
karex; and, across the road on a blue washed wall, the white letters that
spelled out: *Exigez le slip Rasurel*.

I didn't let him drive me to the Ritz. I would have been embarrassed
to alight from the pillion seat at the feet of the head porter. Claude hailed
me a taxi from the rank in the Place Victoire, a hundred yards from his
house.

My husband was seated in his dressing-gown, enjoying breakfast in
our room. I begged him to forgive me.

'It was wrong of me to make you anxious,' I admitted.

'Dear child! Come! Eat! I wasn't the least anxious! Otto assured me
that Claude is the most cautious of riders.'

'But ... were you not ... I don't know quite how to put it ... a little
suspicious or offended that I was spending the night with a young
man?'

'Not when the young man was Claude, dearest. I know what the situation is between Claude and Otto. *Otto* was offended, not I,' he
laughed. And then he said that Otto had told him that the only woman
Claude had ever loved was his sister: 'He will always remain faithful to
her memory.'

I turned away, confused. I didn't want my husband to notice my
tears.

'And now, dearest, if you've eaten enough – very little it seems to me – go quickly and bathe, and change into something less formal. What would you like to do today?'

My husband did not notice that I didn't reply. He simply set to and mapped out an itinerary for our day's sightseeing. He seemed very happy and, as we left the hotel and were crossing the Place, he drew me to a stop under the Colonne:

'Now that I know what pleasure it gives you to ride pillion, I've decided to buy a motorcycle. The chauffeur will take you out, every day, when we get back to London.'

The Writer and Her Public

'*Hotel du Lac*, Mrs James!' The librarian waved a book over the heads of half a dozen women queuing to have their library books stamped and in a stage whisper added confidently, 'You'll have a really good read over Christmas!' Mrs James thanked Miss Fothsdyke and gazed wistfully at the cover of the book: a balcony with a chair and table overlooking toneless water, backed by mountains, with a palm tree rising to flick its attenuated leaves on the balcony rails. As she packed the book into her basket, between a packet of liver salts and an elastic bandage, and her library ticket into her well-worn but once expensive wallet, Mrs James wished the librarian the season's greetings and dragged herself wearily home.

Home was Marlborough House, an imposing seventeenth-century manor house on the outskirts of Lower Minchampton. It was to Marlborough House her father had brought her mother seventy-five Christmases ago. It was in Marlborough House her parents had raised four children, in spacious rooms and five acres of garden. And it was to Marlborough House that Mrs James had returned, parentless and husbandless, to a three-roomed flat on the ground floor. The rest of the house was let as office accommodation to a perfectly respectable solicitor, and the garden – far too costly to maintain – had been handed over to the parish and was now a public park.

It was to be another quiet Christmas. Adele James had been widowed five years and the two sons of her marriage had long since escaped to Canada. Every year, on Christmas afternoon, with their wives and children gathered together in their shared mountain retreat, they performed a ritual telephone call to their mother. By the time they called, Adele would have consumed both the turkey portion for one, pre-cooked by the WI for all villagers who, like herself, lived alone, and the slice of Christmas pudding, similarly prepared. She would be able to report, honestly, that she was in good health, had attended church and been invited back by the vicar and his wife for a glass of celebratory sherry, and that she was now seated comfortably before the fire, a box of Black Magic on her lap, waiting for the Queen to speak to the Commonwealth.

But when the telephone rang this year Adele's conversation proceeded along less reassuring lines. She complained it was horrible to be old, terrible to be alone. How she envied them Canada! Perhaps next year ... or the year after ... God – and the bank manager – permitting, she

63

would come out and spend Christmas with them. England was slipping yet further downhill; everyone was so selfish these days. Take the miners! Only concerned with themselves, not willing to make the slightest sacrifice for their country.... She thanked her sons for the cashmere shawl that was even now draped round her shoulders, and on being asked how she was spending the public holiday between Christmas and the New Year replied, 'I have borrowed a prize-winning novel from the public library! I shall *submerge* myself in it. Poor old Mother, such are the small pleasures to which I aspire these days!' And stroking her cashmere-clad shoulder affectionately, she replaced the receiver.

Adele James borrowed many more books from the library than she read. She had to talk to someone and if that meant the librarian at the public library, so be it. It was her habit to wait until Miss Fothsdyke was free and then buttonhole her. What would Miss Fothsdyke recommend today as a good read? Miss Fothsdyke would slip noiselessly across the polished library floor and pick nimbly among the fiction titles, and Adele, without so much as glancing at the title, would slip the suggested book into her shopping basket. Regularly she returned to condemn Miss Fothsdyke's choice, and regularly she made up for the slight she felt her superior social position demanded her to inflict by accepting Miss Fothsdyke's subsequent suggestion.

Miss Fothsdyke was no fool. She had come to understand that Mrs James preferred to take away a book by someone she had seen on television that she was not going to read, to taking away a book by someone she had never heard of that she was not going to read. And having made this discovery Miss Fothsdyke took to suggesting the much-vaunted novels short-listed for literary prizes. The result was better than she could have forecast. Mrs James became a reader. With titles sanctioned by literary pundits with whose names and faces she was familiar, she tackled miles of type, applying the dedication runners of her age and sex had recently tackled the London marathon. And she returned to have books renewed as many as half a dozen times, to enable her to finish the course, even if, by the final pages, she found herself breathless and mentally supine.

Miss Fothsdyke was surprised to see Mrs James enter the library on New Year's Eve, *Hotel du Lac* in hand.

'You don't need that book renewed yet!' she informed Mrs James rather curtly.

'Oh, I know! I'm returning it! I've finished it!' There was more than a suggestion of pride in her announcement.

'And did you enjoy it?' Miss Fothsdyke enquired, not without interest.

'Oh, very much!' Mrs James assured her and, unusually for her, did not linger to demolish its subject matter, its moral tone or its literary style. She apparently had no criticism of the paper on which it was printed or its type. She did not regret the illustrated dust-jacket. Miss Fothsdyke raised her eyebrows.

Adele James put purpose in her steps and strode back to Marlborough House. And once home she put purpose in her actions. With the precision of one firing tracer bullets, she switched on the kettle, she stoked the fire, she hung up her coat and took down her shawl. She made tea and took it on a tray to her desk. She sat down before a blotter where a pristine sheet of grass-green blotting paper beckoned and from a box took a sheet of Prussian blue writing-paper. She unscrewed the top of her gold Parker pen. But the ritual was too painful. She remembered Cedric, it was he who always prepared the blotter, who ordered the embossed paper from Smythsons, who had given her the Parker pen. And it was he who had died, so suddenly, leaving her so inadequately provided for. How she hated him for dying! She wriggled her shoulders as if to free them of burs of melancholy. She washed down memories with draughts of tea. And then she took up her pen.

Dear Miss Brooker, she wrote, you don't know me but I feel I know you well. I am one of your readers, probably one of your most appreciative readers. And I have just made a New Year's resolution: to give praise where praise is due, and that's why I'm writing to you! I do congratulate you on Hotel du Lac. It's a very nice book indeed.

Just as soon as Hotel du Lac was short-listed for the Booker Prize I short-listed it for my library list. But I might never have actually got around to it had I not seen you on the television. I thought you came over as such a nice, modest young woman that the very next day I returned to the library and filled out one of those reservations cards that put one on the waiting list – senior citizens only have to pay 5p for this service. And as luck would have it I received my card just before Christmas, and being on my own over the holiday was able to do your book full justice.

You must have been pleased with the fifteen thousand pounds! Money does make such a difference, there's no point in pretending it does not. And of course you have the fame, too. I suppose now you will get to meet all sorts of interesting people. You'll have to take care it doesn't turn your head. But perhaps I should warn you: interesting people are usually a great disappointment! When my dear husband was alive I used to come in contact with all sorts of Masonic and civic dignitaries and found them very ordinary.

But let's get to the matter of your book. What I particularly appreciate about Hotel du Lac is that it is full of people I recognize; indeed, they might all have come from Lower Minchampton! We have those little scandals in our village; nothing terribly serious, of course, but it has happened that someone was left at the altar; and it has happened for a nice young woman to leave the straight and narrow on holiday in sunny climes.

And, of course, I recognize your lakeside town. My dear husband and I used to stay at the 'Beau Rivage' – rather grander than the 'Lac' – but autres temps autres mœurs, and in my reduced circumstances I shall try the Lac on your recommendation. Perhaps you would be so kind as to send me their rates?

And before I forget, there are a couple of queries I would be obliged if you would clear up for me: who are Swann and Aschenbach? Should I know? And, at the risk of your finding me shamefully ignorant, what is the meaning of 'occlude'? I cannot find it in my pocket dictionary, and you use it twice.

You may trust me to be discreet, my dear, but tell me: you are your heroine, Edith Hope, I suppose? I thought so! And although I don't think that long affair with David can be right for you, I am sure the devil you know is better than the devil you don't, and Edward would have proved a disaster. Believe me, it was not because you played hard to get that made him pursue you. It was because you are rich and famous. When my dear husband Cedric and I used to holiday at the Beau Rivage there was invariably a man of the Edward type hovering among the unaccompanied women. In those days such men were identifiable by the suede shoes they wore and the silver-headed canes they carried. Like Edward they tended to the view that a sophisticated rudeness enhanced their appeal. Like Edward they were fortune hunters; I expect by now you have discovered he is in financial difficulty with his farm. I hope he hasn't managed to turn you against your long 'cardy' – such a useful and comforting garment.

Should you ever find yourself in this neighbourhood, dear Miss Brookner, do feel free to drop in. I am sure we would have lots to talk about, and I would so like you to give me a few hints on how to write a novel.

It was with a majestic flourish that Adele James threw her name across the page in purple ink. She dived into her wallet for a first-class stamp. Dragging her coat from the stand in the hall she bounded out of the front door and strode to the post box, two hundred yards down the lane.

A bucket of iced water flung at her, naked, could not have chilled Adele more thoroughly, or made her feel more dejected, than did the sticker on the post box informing the public that the last collection on New Year's Eve had been cancelled, and that there would be no collection on the first day of the year. It was of the utmost importance that Miss Brookner receive her letter without delay. As she plodded her way home, pondering the precise moment her letter would find its recipient, a cruel vagabond of a thought wandered into Adele James' calculations.

Miss Brookner might have spent her prize money on a winter cruise with Edward, and be away until spring.

She had no mind to read. And there was no one to whom she could write so soon after sending off Christmas cards. She could not telephone Daphne, not tonight, not on New Year's Eve; Daphne and that dreadful husband of hers would be dressing for the party at Minchampton Hall. She examined the *Radio* and *TV Times*. She was certainly not going to subject herself to Joan Collins or 'The World of Sport'. Really! Who did the programme planners have in mind when they scheduled such things over the holiday period?

It was dusk; the east wind blew under the door and wainscoting, freezing her ankles. Adele James filled the kettle, boiled the water and took herself to bed with a hot-water bottle and the remains of the Black Magic chocolates. By ten past seven she was rummaging on the bedside table for her tablets, which she took from a small tin with the words 'sweet dreams' picked out in violets. She washed them down with a half-filled tumbler of Cyprus sherry.

'Present fears are less than
horrible imaginings'

Slumped at a table tucked into a corner of the restaurant in the Victoria
& Albert Museum was a man whose expression of misery and despair
contrasted markedly with his elegance of dress and refinement of feature.
No one could fail to notice that every article of his clothing had been selected as much for its quality as its visual effect. No one could fail to observe the arresting blue eyes, the Roman nose, generous mouth and
sleek blond hair; one would be bound to conclude that this man's lineage
was on the noble side. It was because of the discrepancy between his dress
and physical make-up and his ashen complexion, blank stare and bent
form, that he attracted the attention of James Dombey who, tray in
hand, was wandering across the restaurant in search of a vacant seat. At
first it was with foreboding that he pulled out a chair at the slumped
man's table. Then, looking more closely, it was with astonished recognition that he exclaimed: 'Good God! It's you. Paul, old fellow, you look
ghastly! What's up?'

Paul Harrigan barely acknowledged his friend with a glance. Word-
lessly, he pushed his empty cup into the middle of the table. James understood the gesture to mean that his friend would like more coffee.
When he returned to the table Paul had straightened his back and pushed
his hair out of his eyes. He dropped three lumps of sugar into the
demi-tasse James handed him.

'I'll explain,' he muttered, 'but it'll take time. D'you *really* want to
be bothered with my troubles?'

'You're an old friend! Of course I've got the time. Perhaps I can even
be of some help.'

Paul Harrigan shifted about on his chair before starting. 'It all goes
back fourteen months. D'you remember how, in late December, '87,
you rang Pippa to invite us to your New Year's Eve party? You were
rather hurt that Pippa declined your invitation. You didn't believe the
reason she gave you. But it was truly the case. We were determined not
to risk drinking and driving and, instead of coming right over to you
in Chelsea, we had accepted an invitation to a local Islington thrash –
one from which we'd be able to lollop back more or less on foot.

'You don't know the Stewarts. You wouldn't want to know the
Stewarts and their friends. I spent the whole of that New Year's Eve
pinned against a modern pine Welsh dresser listening to brokers describ-

ing, to the last pence, how much they'd lost on Black Monday, and property speculators telling me how much they'd made on their bricks and mortar. Pippa who, in the course of the year, had successfully circumvented the attentions of the local Lotharios, was chased to a capacious sofa and run to ground by the most insistent of their breed. In the event, the only way either of us could defend ourselves was to drink, and the more we drank the less able we were to escape: we got legless.

'We had tottered over to the Stewarts at about ten, hoping to grab some food there but, by the time we arrived, all that was left of the buffet supper was a handful of peanuts and some crisp dust. After much Bulgarian champagne and kissing at the stroke of midnight, we were optimistic that Fiona Stewart would serve breakfast, so we stayed on, drinking up the champagne. By 3 a.m. we realized that even if Fiona had had breakfast in mind, she was in no condition to prepare it. I made for the master bedroom where our coats were heaped Oxfam-fashion and, somehow, Pippa and I dragged ourselves home.

'We woke on the first day of the new year around two in the afternoon, hung-over and half-dressed. To our mutual surprise we had both had extraordinary and memorable dreams. As a rule, neither of us remembers our dreams and so we always spare the other from the waking ritual of recounting them. This afternoon, in order to prolong pronetime, Pippa described to me her terrifying sojourn in the rain forests of South America, pursued by every sort of insect, bird and animal known and unknown to the natural world. She'd been bitten, she'd been stung, she'd been mauled and she'd been ravaged.... and I told her how I'd been to the end of the pier at Brighton and had my fortune told. I didn't divulge to her the details of what the fortuneteller revealed to me. I thought it prudent to pretend that, although I had been and was unnerved by the dream, I had forgotten the details.

'What the fortuneteller had to tell me might not have had the peculiar effects it had, had I not been strangely attracted to her. She appeared to me first in the guise of an old hag peering into a crystal ball, but as she started to recount the disasters that were to befall, her black cloak fell from her shoulders to reveal the most exquisite naked flesh. With every threat she posed, my desire increased. I asked her her name:

'"Lamorte" she replied.

'"Where do you come from?"

'"Lamorte!" she repeated.

'"How can you foretell the future?"

'"I cannot and do not foretell the future. I reveal the past. You are going to experience the effects of causes that you have already set in motion. My role is to forewarn you of them. Once you know that the worst is pre-ordained, you will find each situation easier to confront."

'She told me that in the course of 1988 I would lose my job, Pippa would leave me and I would be responsible for my mother's death. Mingled with the desire I seemed to feel towards the fortuneteller and the apprehension aroused in me by her revelations, was warm gratitude. I leant forward and tried to take hold of her hand, to kiss it but, as I moved towards her, her form misted and she dissolved.

'From the 1st of January I waited in a mood that blended acute anxiety with chronic powerlessness. The new managing director, Forrester, at Austin Zahler, had his sights set firmly on profits. He was unsympathetic to my insistence that we continue to publish serious new fiction. At an editorial meeting in mid-January, I proposed three exceptionally sensitively written first novels; in each case the author had pushed forward the frontiers of his craft to create something new and authentic. Forrester was adamant. None of the three novels under discussion would attract the ten thousand pounds in paperback rights that he required to balance his books. He reminded me that he was running a business, not some "cultural charity". I had already given my assurance to the authors that their novels would be published; my previous boss always rubber-stamped my editorial decisions. I was feeling increasingly undermined. There ensued a row of major proportions, during the course of which I argued that Austin Zahler had built its considerable reputation and survived for the past seventy-five years only because it published what was excellent; if the firm were to go merely for quick profits – meaning publishing garbage – it would in all probability collapse within five years. Forrester laughed. In five years he wouldn't want the firm. Austin Zahler would have made large enough profits for a flotation ... by June I was shown the door. At first I rather enjoyed *un*employment. Offers from publishers flowed in and I wasn't worried financially. By August I had decided to publish under my own imprint. I would kick off with the authors rejected by Forrester and I would build a list of socially and politically orientated new fiction.

'I took over the spare room, next to Pippa's study, as my office. I installed a word-processor and a part-time secretary. The only eventuality for which I had made no provision was Pippa's response to my presence in the house all day.

'Pippa was finishing her book on the archaeology of animals and, not having to read in the science library, she was writing at home. She resented my presence in the kitchen for lunch, the sound of my word-processor, the scent worn by my secretary and the fact that when the telephone sounded she couldn't be sure that it was ringing for her. We started to row; she confided that for months she had been finding me intolerably irritating. She couldn't stand the smoke from my cigars, she regarded my vocabulary as pretentious, and the way I ate reminded her of a wart-hog.... She was bored writing, longed for more field work and, just as soon as ever her book got to the printers, she was off.

'"Off?" I asked, "where and for how long?" She seemed either not to know or to wish to tell me. I resisted pressing her for an explanation. I was tempted to ask "Are you leaving me?" But I feared her response.

'The irony of the situation was not lost on me. Pippa had developed something of a revulsion to the sort of stylish work on my list at Austin Zahler. She had kept reminding me that, given the times in which we were living, I ought to be commissioning socially relevant material. Then, just as I took it upon myself to get some of our most distinguished novelists to contribute to a series unstitching the damaging effects of Thatcherism, Pippa upped and left to dig in Egypt.

'I became paralysed with fear. I had lost my job. Pippa had left. What could this mean for Mother? Since being widowed ten years past, Mother had sold up and gone to live in a delightful village in Gloucestershire, where a friend of hers ran a herb nursery. Although well into her seventies and taking medication for angina, Mother was active in local affairs – the WI, the gardening club, hospital visiting in Cheltenham, and so on. Every month I would drive down on a Saturday evening, accompany Mother to church on Sunday morning, devour roast beef and all the trimmings with her at midday and, after a browse through *Country Life*, a walk by the river or a visit to Mabel Huntingdon and her herbs, I would drive back to London in time for bed on Sunday evening.

'Since the fortuneteller's warning, I so arranged it that I never *drove* Mother to church. Even when the weather was inclement I insisted we walk. I said that being cooped up all week I needed every ounce of fresh air I could get. Mother, far from being upset, was delighted that I had adopted this practice and, using it to her advantage, would suggest ever longer walks in the afternoons. I was careful to take a well-worn path, away from the river and the field in which the bull grazed. Furthermore, I always took her arm. I became increasingly confident. There seemed no way in which I could put Mother in mortal danger.

'It was in November when Mother's sister, Mary, wrote suggesting that, since Pippa was going to be away over Christmas, Mother and I should fly to Boston and spend the holiday with Mary and her family. Mother said "no", she had commitments around Cheltenham. She urged me to go alone.

'"Won't you be terribly lonely?" I asked.

'"Don't be silly, darling! When I'm not out and about doing my good works, I shall be in feasting at Mabel's!"

'Well, I booked a ticket to Boston for the 23rd of December. On the 22nd, while I was packing, I received a telephone call from Mother's doctor. There was absolutely nothing to worry about, he said, but he would sleep easier over the Christmas and New Year period if he had my telephone number in Boston. Reassuring though he was, he put the wind up me. I cancelled my ticket.

'I waited until the afternoon of the 23rd to telephone Aunt Mary and explain. On reflection, I said, I just couldn't leave Mother over Christmas. Mary roared with laughter down the phone. "What a funny old couple you and your ma make!" Evidently, Mother had rung Mary to say that she hadn't liked the idea of not being with me over Christmas, after all. She'd managed to get a cancellation on a plane leaving later that day.

'What had happened was Mother had got the very seat that I had reserved and then cancelled. What we did not know at that stage was that, somewhere over the Atlantic there had been a brief loss of pressure in the cabin. Mother's oxygen mask was either faulty or she was not quick enough to fit it over her face. She had a heart attack and died before the plane landed. So, you see, the fortuneteller had been right in every detail.'

James Dombey, seeing that Paul's story was told, shifted in his seat. 'I'm so sorry, old fellow,' he said, 'but it was not *your* fault, if anything it was *mine*! If I had only convinced Pippa that I would feed you properly and see to it, myself, that neither of you drank to excess, you wouldn't have gone to the Stewarts and you wouldn't have had your bad dreams. However, I think I should remind you that you had been thinking of giving Austin Zahler the boot ever since Forrester took over. Pippa may well return to the nest once she feels that her batteries have been recharged in Egypt. As for your mother: she had had angina for years and was in her *late* seventies!'

'How then d'you account for the dream – its persuasive attraction?'

'It's as the fortuneteller explained: once the worst has happened, there is nothing more to fear. You needed to absolve yourself of fear to face a new job, Pippa's exacting standards – and, inevitably, life without your elderly mother.'

Let Me Make It Absolutely Clear!

Two women were coming towards her. They were wearing nice tweed coats with little fur collars, felt hats and leather gloves and had their prayer books pressed closely to their chests. She would need to get off the pavement to let them pass. It was a pity the pram wheels had lost their rubber tyres and rattled so. She'd not wrestle up the unmade road to the church; she'd go down to the front. It wasn't possible, anyhow, not on a Sunday, to rest in church. She probably didn't smell too good. Getting a hot bath was her biggest problem. And the newspaper round her waist rustled.

It was nice being back at Weston-on-Sea. Ever since she'd made her first sandcastle, she'd always wanted to live by the sea. They'd talked about it. John said 'perhaps', when he retired.... But it never came to that – not his retirement nor a move from south London. Weston was even nicer now than it had been, what with the factory shutting down and the caravan park gone. There were no young couples living in the area, no children to stare. Not much for the visitors to do, either, she supposed. And now, what with winter approaching, no visitors.

She'd go and sit in the shelter on the front. The glass had gone from the windows but the building itself was solid. The Victorians knew how to build, John used to say. It would give her some protection from the wind and it wasn't raining. Funny, the things people write on the walls of shelters and lavatories! She wondered why they did it?

Who was it? When was it that someone told her that if ever she needed to keep warm it was her head she must remember to keep covered? She wished she could remember who it had been. At any rate, it was good advice and these days she stuck to it. She *was* more fortunate than most, though. She'd started out on the road well prepared: stout boots, oiled socks, thermal underwear and all. *And* the coat she'd made from the duvet. At first it had been difficult, having to carry everything in the old zipped bag and in John's army rucksack. She'd found that very tiring. But things perked up when she found the pram. Someone must have tried to fling it into the duck pond but it'd got stuck in the reeds. There it was, just waiting for her! So useful, you'd call it invaluable. She kept the little army tent under the boards, with the primus and the sleeping bag, and all her bits and pieces in plastic bags covering them. No one would think she had anything worth stealing but just in case she bought a padlock and chain. Pity the poor tramps who had nothing.

She'd sit here until 3.30. If she craned her neck she could just see the clock on the Liverstone Arms. She loved the sea: limitless, filled with infinite possibilities. And then, momentarily, she was reminded of 'those in peril', as she caught sight of ships on the horizon. She used to like to bathe. They'd both liked a paddle and a swim. And having the bathing hut for changing and sheltering when it rained and eating their meals.... Her fingers fumbled in one of the plastic bags and removed a packet of biscuits. She ate automatically, her eyes fastened on the deep.

Good thing she'd been here before and knew about the huts. After she'd done her little errand, she'd stay put in Weston for the winter. The hut she'd found at the far end of the beach was one of the old, cheap type. It'd never had a veranda or a window. To get any light into the place she'd need to keep the top half of the stable door open, but the lock had been wrenched from the bottom half. She'd have to wedge it. She couldn't leave the pram there, not safely, not during the day. But she could sleep nights. There was just room to lie, corner to corner. No one would find her there, not right at the end of the beach under the cliff, not now it was dark by five. If she took the cliff path when it was dark and left the hut at dawn, no one would suspect. The station was open early and she could have her wash, etcetera, there. Happy in this knowledge, the muscles of her stomach relaxed and she felt a sort of warmth. It was comforting to take a decision.

She got to her feet and slowly pushed along the velvet asphalt on the promenade, automatically stopping at every refuse bin, her eyes automatically scanning every bench. Tomorrow, she'd visit the museum. There was a coffee machine just by the door and she had been allowed to leave the pram in the cycle shed. She'd got ever so interested in animals since she'd taken to the road! Who would have thought it of her? She'd seen foxes and rabbits and moles, all at very close quarters. She'd seen one long creature – something between a rat and a mouse; she must find out what it was. They probably had stuffed ones somewhere in the museum. Not that she was all that keen on stuffed animals – or the curator. That's why she'd go on Monday, when the curator's assistant sat in for him.

Pity she'd not come across a paper but it was still early. Sundays were always a problem for papers, what with the libraries being closed. And when she did come across one, it was never the one she wanted to read. She hadn't lost her marbles being on the road! She still thought like a *Telegraph* reader! But the trouble was, *Telegraph* readers are not the sort to leave their newspapers lying about. They cling to their *Telegraph*, take it home, scour every paragraph and then find a good use for the paper, itself, in the kitchen or at the grate. It's not parsimony, it's being careful; part of a *Telegraph* reader's way of life.

She saw herself on her knees, making up the fire. She saw herself wrapping vegetable peelings in the paper and putting the nicely wrapped packet in the bin. Having somewhere to live that was quiet and warm used to mean a lot to her. Little things had until the big thing went. She had taken good care of the home. John had worked hard to buy the furniture and fittings and she was forever in and out of the market, picking up bits and pieces to make the flat look interesting and cheerful. But once he died, it meant nothing at all. . . . And then she came to positively hate it! It was as if the flat had died with him. A good thing, really – he left no money and she'd nothing to pay the rent and the rates, light, gas and water. Well, she had the widows' pension but that wasn't enough. How *did* other people manage?

And where would she have been without the auction? John always said she'd taste and those boxes covered with shells and glass pictures she'd picked up in the market – had he known they were worth more than she'd paid? Marvellous, it had been! But the rug was the biggest surprise. Just fancy, if Mrs Abdulla, who kept the paper shop, hadn't been rushed to hospital and Mr Abdulla been short of £20 cash, she'd never have bought it. Things happen like that! Naturally, in the circumstances, she hadn't haggled; she'd been pleased to help. She didn't imagine Mr Abdulla realized it was pure silk. Used for their prayers, he said, made somewhere in Iran when it was called Persia. She would have shared the profits with Mr Abdulla if she'd known where he was, but he disappeared when his wife died. And it had been for the best. She needed that £300 to set the record straight.

It would rain before the day was out, she could tell. But why think of that? Stupid to think ahead. Nothing you could do about it. Or the past. She liked to keep her memory empty of the past. But that was more difficult; just as soon as she made up her mind not to think of John, she could think of nothing else.

She had known him since she was eight and he was nine. She couldn't remember a time when she'd not known him; they'd been in the infants together. He'd always been kind – even as a child, he was kind. If he'd known his heart was weak, he would have taken out some sort of insurance for her, she was sure he would have. But he hadn't known – the doctors never told him. He just walked back from work, over London Bridge, as per usual and dropped dead on the pavement! What a wonderful way to go! they all said. Wonderful? What! without saying goodbye? Without having taught her to mend a fuse and deal with the bank and explain about the debt to Aunt Dorothy? Not wonderful at all! Dreadful! She'd far rather have nursed him for a while, talked to him, reminded him of their happy times, spoken of little personal matters and asked him where did he think he was going to when he was dead? She did wish she'd had the opportunity to ask him that. The worst was he'd left in rather a rush that morning, because he'd wanted to repot the cineraria before leaving, and he'd only had time for the one slice and a cup of tea. . . . It is odd he never left a note about Aunt Dorothy's money, just in case anything happened to him. . . . The solicitor was quite sharp in his letter, said Aunt Dorothy was entitled to the immediate repayment of the £300: she needed it for little extra comforts at her time of life. She couldn't have answered that letter, not at the time. And she didn't know who she was up against. The money was much safer in five pound notes sewn into her coat than with the solicitor. It would be quite a pleasant interlude visiting the old lady. She'd not seen her for . . . it must be twenty years. She did hope Aunt Dorothy didn't bear a grudge against John.

There was a plan of Weston on a board just outside the station. She didn't know the area round the railway. She knew Aunt Dorothy's address by heart: Argyll House, Union Street. Aunt Dorothy had moved down here on John's advice. He said that with nothing much to keep the locals employed, they'd be bound to want to take in old people. She'd quite forgotten Aunt D. until the letter came. It was an easy address to remember: John liked the Argyll pattern on his socks, and his billiards club was in Union Street, Walthamstow. It was the coincidences that did the trick.

She wouldn't buy toffees, not for someone of Aunt D.'s age. Nor mints. Soft fruit pastilles would be the best. She'd drop in at about four; the old lady would want a rest before her tea. She wandered into the station, read the headlines standing by the open display and when the man started to shuffle the titles under her nose she bought a packet of sweets. She noticed that the ticket collector had set off down the platform in the opposite direction and took the opportunity to wheel the pram into the Ladies. There was no hot water and no towel. There was a dirty tablet of soap. She peered into the looking glass and pulled her woollen cap deeper over her forehead and ears. She'd almost forgotten what she looked like. If someone asked her the colour of her hair and eyes she'd be at a loss. She dried her hands on her skirt and put back her woollen gloves. She noticed that the hem of her skirt was caked with sand and her boots stained with sea water.

She pushed slowly up Union Street. The identical Victorian terrace houses had their names picked out in white on the glass fanlight over the front door. Carmarthen House, Stirling House, Woburn House. . . . The light was fading and the slope was steep. She did hope Argyll House was not the last, at the top of the hill.

It was; and the front garden caught the full force of the winds. A tangle of sodden Michaelmas daisies, their blue colour turned brown, toppled dejected against low iron railings. Six galvanized dustbins were their only company. She'd chain the pram to the railings.

She dragged herself up the twelve slippery steps, pulling on the handrail. On reaching the front door step and before ringing the bell, she clapped her hands together to rid her gloves of the flakes of rust clinging to them.

A fat woman with yellow hair and garments tightly stretched across rolls of bosom, stomach and thigh, answered the bell.

'Yes?' Oh dear! She's not very friendly!

'I've come to see Miss Hawkins. I'm her niece.'

'Are you now?' looking her up and down, 'And how am I to know that? I've never seen you before!'

'The solicitor sent me!'

'Did he now! And for what, may I ask?' She was so angry....

'I've got some money for her.'

'Oh ... in that case ... all right then! Up the stairs to the top! Number eight. And don't you go upsetting her, she gives us enough trouble as it is!'

There was no answer when Gladyse knocked. She pushed open the door quietly and with difficulty: the knob was loose. She fumbled for the light switch; an unshaded forty-watt bulb revealed an iron bedstead pressed against the wall under the sloping ceiling, in the far corner, and in the middle of the room a table and single hard-backed chair.

'It's me, dear, John's Gladyse!' The little mound under the covers could've been made by a child of six, she thought. The old lady's breathing was peculiar, as if it were coming from under the sea. She bent over her. Aunt Dorothy's eyes were open but unseeing.

'It's me, dear!' she repeated. 'I've come with the money!' There was a faint groan. 'Yes, dear, and some sweeties!' She took a step back and with her scissors she unpicked a few inches of the seam of her coat.

'There you are!' she said, more to herself than to Aunt. 'I've got it here. I've been meaning to get it to you ever since John died. He's dead you know! I got it to you, soon as I could!' She tucked the envelope under Aunt Dorothy's pillow and as she did so, she noticed locks of grey hair detached from the old lady's head.

'Would you like me to turn you, dear? You don't look very comfortable!' She drew back the covers. The smell was dreadful! The bed was wet and soiled. Aunt's nightdress had been cut short; it didn't reach her legs and Gladyse saw that they were covered in bed sores. 'Oh dear! And you're so cold!' She looked around. All she could find was a moth-eaten hearth rug on the frayed lino and this she laid over the threadbare blankets.

She needed to compose herself. She rested against the wall on the first landing. It was unlit and she couldn't see but she had a good view into the landlady's kitchen. A coal fire was burning there and the room was ablaze with light. The table was laid for high tea.

'Bert! Your tea's getting cold!'

'Coming! Put the radio on, luv!'

Gladyse heard a lavatory cistern emptying.

'Let me make it absolutely clear, this government has spent more in real terms on care in the community than any other. I am confident that the most vulnerable in our society have nothing to fear: no one falls through our safety net!'

Gladyse picked her way down the final few stairs and knocked on the open kitchen door.

'Turn that off, Bert! She wants something!' The landlady came to the door and stood too close to Gladyse.

'Would you go and see Miss Hawkins, please, she needs attention: she's wet – and very cold.'

'She gets the attention she pays for!' the landlady sniffed. 'And we don't like busybodies, so you'd better be off!' Gladyse felt a draft of warm air as the door slammed in her face.

It had been raining. She sought the handrail before she dared descend the tiled steps. She looked towards the dustbins and in a split second turned icy cold. All that was left of the pram was one wheel, the one through which she had passed the chain that secured it to the railings with the padlock.

Annie's Story

Father and Uncle Hugo are twins. I know about twins; I was told when I was very little how they have birthdays on the same day and how strangers can't tell them apart because they look like two peas in a pod. That always seemed odd to me because whereas Father was, is and no doubt shall be quiet and sad and stern, Uncle Hugo was – I can't say is or shall be, because I don't know – noisy and happy and forgiving. And although Father had me and didn't seem to like children, Uncle Hugo didn't have children and seemed to like them a lot. Uncle Hugo and father aren't like two peas.

It was the day that I told Father I would rather be Uncle Hugo's daughter than his that must've been the most important day of my summer holidays. Father didn't say anything about it at the time but, since then, everything at home has changed.

It was a lovely sunny morning, warm and bright. Denzil, my dog, was lying on the terrace, too pleased to worry Bo, the cat. Bo had given her face a bit of a wash but didn't have the energy to bother with her coat; she just flopped down with her back against Denzil's and her nose in the Michaelmas daisies. The bees were awfully busy; whenever they're about they seem to have such a lot to do. But no person, except Father, would have worked that day if he hadn't had to.

The day started like other days with breakfast in the kitchen. We always read at breakfast: Father has *Science Survey* and Mother and I have our books. I'd just come to the bit where Alice sees a grin without a cat when I heard Father say something about Uncle Hugo being a 'lay-about'. I knew that a 'lay-about' was not the sort of person Father admired but I thought it was rather a good thing to be and I said that I might actually prefer to be the daughter of a 'lay-about' because they have time to chat and play. Father filled his cup with a *third* helping of coffee and, instead of going out on to the terrace to finish *Science Survey*, or discuss 'lay-abouts' with me, he went straight to his study saying he had a paper to finish.

'What! On a day like this!' Mother sounded really shocked.

'I can't ask *Science Survey* to hold up publication just because the sun's come out.' Father slammed the study door to show that he was cross.

I'm not allowed in Father's study on my own. Anyhow, I don't really like being there. It's a sad place; it's got too much brown in it and it smells of stale tobacco and Vicks. Father's got a weak chest and a *ten-den-cy* to colds. Mother says it's because of all the dust that sticks to his books and papers, and his pipe, and the fact that he never opens his windows. Father says that he hopes that when I'm grown-up I'll want to do research like him. I don't really know what that means. It has something to do with staying indoors, quietly, with lots of reading and not liking interruptions. I don't think it's very good for the temper. I doubt that I shall. But I never say so.

Mother has an even temper. I asked her what she was and she said, 'Just a woman'. She doesn't do *one* thing like Father. And most of the *hundreds* of things she does, she does out of doors, or in the kitchen with the back door wide open. When I needed her, I always looked first in the vegetable garden, second in the potting shed and third in the field with the horses and only fourth somewhere in the house. I think that if there's an opposite to being a researcher, Mother is *that*.

Father slammed the study door and Mother washed up the breakfast things and tidied the kitchen, 'Come Annie, let's walk over Pond Hill.' That meant we were going to visit Uncle Hugo. Just before setting out, Mother opened Father's study door about an inch and poked her nose in. 'Annie and I are walking over to Hugo's. I'll be back to make supper,' she told him.

We picked honeysuckle and red campion along the lane and, at the five-bar gate, we stopped to talk to Magda and her foal. Then, we sat down for a bit to talk. I couldn't help noticing that Mother's face looked sort of tight, and her eyes empty. She'd scraped her hair back and fastened it with a rubber band.

'That's very bad for your hair!' I said, imitating her voice. 'You're always telling me that pulling my hair back in a rubber band ruins it.'

'That's different,' she said, quite sadly I thought. But I didn't insist. I could see that Mother didn't want to talk about herself.

'Where are grandma and grandpa?' I asked.

'In Switzerland. On holiday!' Mother said.

'Why don't *we* have holidays?'

'Aren't you happy at home, doing the things we always do?' Mother sounded rather hurt and I was sorry to have asked the question.

'Father doesn't like change. It doesn't help his work to be stopping and starting, packing and unpacking and being somewhere which might not be quiet. And he'd have to do without many of his books and papers. ...' And then she pulled me to my feet and we marched up the lane in step, hand in hand, singing 'Speed Bonny Boat' loudly.

'No one to disturb out here!' Mother said, and she laughed.

From the top of Pond Hill you can see Uncle Hugo's cottage down in the valley. It looks just like a small head making a dent in a large pillow.

One of the ways in which Uncle Hugo was different from Father was that he looked after himself. He was rather like Mother, he could do *hundreds* of different things. That morning, when we sat down at his kitchen table, we didn't have places laid or napkins or anything that Father insists upon. There was cream cheese that Uncle Hugo had made himself, strawberry jam he'd made from the berries he'd grown, and his freshly baked scones.

'Just lick your fingers!' he told me, when he noticed that I'd got them sticky. And, another thing – Jason, his cat, was allowed on the table; he had his own bowl of cream by the side of Uncle Hugo's place.

'Goodness!' I exploded, 'Father wouldn't allow *that*, would he Mother?'

Mother had loosened her hair. It fell over her face and on to her shoulders. She looked like a girl. Her eyes danced and her cheeks became rosy. Uncle Hugo made a sort of gasping sound and said to me, 'Isn't your mother pretty!'

Whenever I visited Uncle Hugo, I was allowed into the attic to play with his model theatre. He had made it: the stage and the *pro-sce-ni-um* arch, and all the little people and their furniture – even their gardens. There was a stack of boxes labelled 'Peter Pan', 'Othello ', 'Three Sisters', and lots of other titles, and I was allowed to open them and set up any play I liked. And there was a wind-up gramophone to provide music for the audience (me) before the lights went down. It was lovely!

I must have been playing in the attic for quite a long time that morning because I remember I'd started to feel hungry. I climbed down the ladder, on to the landing, and called out for Mother but there was no answer so I went downstairs. Mother wasn't in the kitchen or the sitting-room, but when I opened the front door I saw that she was standing by the wigwam of runner beans with Uncle Hugo.

'Would you want more space for vegetables?' he was asking Mother.

'Much more! And larger soft-fruit cages.'

'They're awfully expensive,' Uncle Hugo was reminding her. Mother and he wandered between the lettuces and radishes and over to the soft fruit. They had their heads down, as if they were worried about their feet, and where to put them.

'Have you spoken to Annie? Have you told her?' Uncle Hugo asked Mother.

I crept over to the hedge where I couldn't be seen.

'Roger's perverse. He hardly knows her! He doesn't even like children but, he insists, she's *his!* And you know what an awe-inspiring regard he has for property.'

'Are you really going to be able to be happy without her?' I could see they'd stopped looking at their feet and were looking into each other's faces.

'The baby will make a difference.' Mother said. What baby? Why was mother going to be without me? If she was going to be without me, that meant I was going to be without her.

'Mother! Mother!' I pushed my way out of the hedge.

'Whatever's the matter, Annie?'

'Nothing!' I lied, 'I love you!'

'And I love you too!' she replied.

When I looked towards Uncle Hugo I thought that he was smiling, but when I looked harder, I could see that he was only screwing up his eyes against the sun.

The whole way home, I clung to Mother. She let her hand rest in mine, like a little mouse. We didn't pick honeysuckle and red campion, Magda and her foal were *not* at the five-bar gate, and I didn't even notice the little moss hummock where we sat to talk. I knew that there was something very wrong happening. It made my throat tight.

Father couldn't have heard us come back because Mother had the supper on the table and had to call out to him, 'Roger! Supper's on the table.'

Father, who insists on meals being on time, always has to be reminded of the time because he's always buried in his books, researching.

'What's this?' he asked, looking down into his soup as if he'd never seen soup before.

'Sorrel soup!'

'Salt!' he demanded.

'Do taste first, Roger!'

'I don't have to – you never put enough salt in the food.' Mother wasn't surprised, neither was I. Father always grumbled about that.

'Salt's not good for your blood pressure,' Mother explained.

'Pity you're not as concerned with my well-being in other respects!'

Father was especially cross. I could tell there was something terribly wrong. It took my appetite away. Everything was crumbling. Inside me I felt cold and empty. I looked round the kitchen, at all the things on the dresser and the vegetables in the crock. Everything looked dead.

'Annie! You've had a long day. Go and run a bath. I'll be up to say goodnight when I've done the dishes.'

I don't know what time it was when I woke, but it was definitely in the middle of the night. My door was ajar and, across a thin column of light that ran from floor to ceiling, I saw shadows pass. And I heard voices. At first I couldn't make out what was being said. Then I distinctly heard Father say:

'You'll break her heart!'

'Hearts!' Mother spat the word out like a cherry pit.

'And how shall *I* cope? *I* don't know how to look after a child.' Father sounded like me when Mother says I'm whining.

'Can't you find *that* information in books? Research it!' My door opened wider and I closed my eyes tight against the column of light that had become a wide shaft. Tight against the shadows, too. As I heard Father's door close softly, I could feel Mother standing close to my bed.

'Annie! Annie! Are you awake?'

I didn't answer.

Mother had gone by the time I got up. Since then I've been helping Father run the house. We've been eating sandwiches most of the time – and raw things. A huge pile of washing against the back door means we have to come in and out by the front door. Father doesn't understand the washing machine. He says Mother will come back but he doesn't know when. I hope he's not saving the washing for her. I'm really sorry I said I'd rather be Uncle Hugo's daughter than Father's. I think I must have put ideas into Mother's head.

When Miss Campbell asked us to write our composition about our summer holidays, I was quite glad. I've not told anyone in *spoken* words what happened. Miss Campbell gave me a red star for my composition, and a 'Very Good'.

The Mechanic of St Loup

Pollarded limes stand in stolid silence around three sides of the square. On the fourth side, iron tables with chairs stacked upon them are randomly distributed. It is eight o'clock; a man in bedroom slippers is dragging himself across the square with a baguette under his arm. A dog of no discernible breed is lifting its leg against one of the tables.

'*Va t'en!* Get away with you!' A waiter is standing at the door of the Café de la Place, flourishing a white cloth. The dog slopes off. The waiter crosses the narrow road between the café and the square and lifts the chairs off the tables and on to the gravel. He arranges everything in military order and then swabs the tables vigorously but joylessly.

'Gaston!' Madame la patronne has the air of an employer who would rather her employee were doing other than he is, whatever that happens to be.

'*J'arrive!*' Gaston calls over his shoulder. But he continues to swab the tables.

I am settled in the warm sun. I am reading the local paper, *Les Temps*. I read that a Monsieur Dubois, from the village of La Chapelle, has been charged with the murder of his wife, Céleste, who is referred to throughout as 'a fat blonde of sixty-five'. For reasons that remain unexplained, Monsieur Dubois carved his wife into small pieces, explaining her absence from the till at the Garage de la Route, St Loup, to everyone's satisfaction, and might well have got away with his crime had it not been that the drains at La Chapelle blocked and their unblocking disclosed Mme Dubois's flesh and bones. I read, with less surprise, that taxes are rising and the nearby Château de Philibert is crumbling. Worldwide, the climate is deteriorating. I read the paper from back to front. When, finally, I arrive at the front page, I see that it is reserved for the greatest tragedy: the defection to the north of the goal-keeper of St Loup's *équipe*.

My train had drawn in to St Loup at a quarter to eight. By five minutes to eight I was seated, reading, having myself removed a chair from one of the tables. My calculations revealed that I had francs enough for a large *café crème* and two croissants before I found a bank and changed my five-pound notes.

The voice of Juliette Greco seeps from the café into the square like the fragrance of roses at dusk. Madame la patronne is leaning against the café door, staring in the direction of the Garage de la Route. She is dreaming. Like me, she is old enough to recall the heady post-war days epitomized by the singer: 'La Vie en Rose'. . . .

French grey: the grey of men's evening gloves. The houses, the gravel, the asphalt, the shutters and all the woodwork of the houses, and the huge ashlar church that presides over the village. Grey, but by no means depressing.

Quiet, though. The road that borders the square is narrow and does not attract traffic. Both the café and the hotel, which occupy positions at opposite corners of the square, receive their deliveries to the side, from roads leading respectively from the station and the cemetery.

St Loup is smaller than I remember.

No one will track me down to this village. I am confident of that. And no stray tourist is likely to come upon me by accident, for there is nothing to attract the tourist: no three-star restaurant, no healing spring, no shrine to an artist. We had found ourselves here by chance, my late husband and I, forty years ago. The guide book did not so much as mention that St Loup was on the road from where we had been to where we were heading. And on our map, it was located with a pin-point.

In the event we had been fortunate to happen upon a village with an hotel. They were rare in the region.

We put up at the Hôtel de la Place. The restaurant – frequented by commercial travellers, who dined between seven and seven-thirty – was closed by the time we arrived, but the patron prepared us an *omelette aux fines herbes*, and provided fresh fruit and local cheeses, which he served in the bar. It was he who showed us to our room. I remember remarking to my husband how little one requires of a room in which one simply sleeps, dresses and undresses, washes and makes love. And our requirements were met by a huge bed, a table and chair at the window overlooking the square, a hook on the back of the door and, behind a screen, a china jug and bowl and a tin bidet that looked like a doll's bath. A pathetically thin chambermaid brought up hot water. It was heavy for her. There was no plumbing upstairs and she was obliged to carry the dirty water downstairs to empty it in the lavatory, in the yard, where the pig was kept.

We slept soundly, incorporating the chimes of the church bells into our dreams. We were woken by the rattle of iron shutters being raised over the windows of the bakery and the grocery.

Edward and I were twenty-five. We had been hiking in England since we were children but this was our first adventure abroad. France, which had suffered so grievously in the war, welcomed us with a warmth and style that were as unfamiliar as they were intoxicating.

The church bells chime nine o'clock and the sun is high. I remove my linen jacket and fold it over the back of my chair. I am glad to have worn this jacket and this skirt; they are among my favourite clothes. However, at my age, I shall not be judged by my appearance. I shall be seen by him for what I was. The others in the village will mark me down a stranger and foreigner, and I shall not be expected to make an impression – only fit in with their expectations.

William, my son, had been adamant: 'You're not strong enough to walk distances! And,' he added, 'these days it's simply not safe for a woman to traipse over Europe, alone. Holly agrees. A package to Paris would be far more suitable at your age than backpacking in the Massif Central. Really, Mother! We'd worry about you!'

William does not know that I am dying. I am often frank with him but seldom truthful. Although I resent emotional blackmail, I know that he and Holly, and the grandchildren, *would* worry about me, and so I lied.

'I've done just as you suggested. I've booked a package to Paris with dear Dorothy Fortescue!'

'Dorothy Who?' It was a bad line and William was calling me in London from Edinburgh.

'Fortescue!' I raised my voice and repeated the name, 'An old friend of your father's.' William was so relieved that he asked for no further details about the friend of his father, whom I had invented.

I've come back to St Loup because there is someone here I have to see before I die. He has been in my heart and on my mind for forty years. I have a single question that I must put to him.

It is, perhaps, all to the good that William never regarded either his father or me as anything but parents. Neither of us appeared to him as a man or a woman in their own right, with independent roles to play, and in the special circumstances of my indifference to Edward, this served to reinforce in William a sense of family solidarity that was, in effect, non-existent.

Now that I am close to death, I feel bitter that I never struck out, never fulfilled myself. For forty years I have been a housewife on a treadmill. I have cooked, cleaned and nursed. I am intimate only with calories, cholesterol, cleaning fluids and childhood illnesses. There has been no honesty in my life, and no passion.

We had entered the café with our rucksacks towards midday. The bar in the Hôtel de la Place was somewhat lugubrious and Edward suggested that it would be more agreeable to pore over our maps in the café opposite. It was too hot to sit in the square. I entered the cool of the café with a sense of well-being. I left the café never to retrieve it.

All the tables were unoccupied and so we were able to spread ourselves across two. Edward ordered white wine and, as the waiter approached, his tray held high above his head, I noticed that instead of making his way direct to our table, he took a slightly circuitous route. There was a large crowd of men at the bar but only one man who stood out from the crowd. He was tall and broad and he was leaning across the counter with his legs extended into the narrow space between the bar and the tables. He made it impossible for the waiter to pass. I detected at once that the man was a mechanic. I could see that his hands bore the traces of dried axle grease and, in any case, he was wearing blue overalls. When the patron put down a *demi* in front of him, he drew himself up to his full height, about six feet and three inches, straightened his shoulders and fished in his top pocket for a packet of tobacco and another of flimsy papers, and he rolled himself a cigarette. My attention was transfixed. I felt that I was participating in a theatrical performance for an audience of one. The man's movements and bearing were hypnotic. It seemed that each of his gestures had been selected with care from a range of possibilities and that he unerringly extracted the most eloquent. The café shrank; the mechanic swelled to occupy both space and time.

'I'm going to get a paper! Order me another glass of wine!' Edward interrupted my reverie.

As soon as the café door swung closed behind Edward, the mechanic, who up to that moment had been offering me his back and his profile, faced me. He lit the cigarette that he had rolled, his huge hands cupped round the flame of his lighter and, as he inhaled deeply, he raised his chin and lowered the corners of his mouth in an unforgettable grimace. He had an arresting face with large, wide-set eyes and a high forehead. As he threw back his head to drain his *demi*, his black curls shook.

'*Encore une!*' His voice was rich and commanding, but his regional accent carried with it hints of intimacy. He turned to face me squarely and he questioned me with his eyes. I felt embarrassed but I did not turn away: I could not. He held my gaze as tightly as if it were a precious gem clutched in his fist. As he put down his empty glass and strode towards the café door, I felt frozen with loss. Panic took hold of me. I followed him with my eyes and saw that he narrowly missed colliding with Edward, who was returning with a copy of *Les Temps* in his hand.

'All I could find!' Edward explained, excusing the local paper. But I could not have cared less. The indifference that has characterized the past forty years was born in the instant that it took for Edward to re-enter the café and the mechanic to leave, for the tide to come in and the tide to go out. As he drank, Edward rocked back on his chair and surveyed the scene.

'Could do with a lick of paint!'

'*I* think it's perfect as it is!' I must have sounded as sour and as irritable as I felt.

'What on earth's got into you, all of a sudden?' But his question was rhetorical and he dropped the front legs of his chair hard and noisily on to the floor, and his head into *Les Temps*.

I peered out of the windows anxiously, hoping to catch a glimpse of the mechanic. He was standing stock still, watching me, leaning against one of the elms across the road.

'We'd best be making tracks. We've only the afternoon and early evening and we've fifteen miles to burn up.' Edward was already on his feet. He gathered the maps together, picked up the heavier of the two rucksacks, paid for our wine, and we left St Loup.

My well-being had been shattered, never to re-form. For forty years I acted out the role of housewife in a marriage whose courtesies were rooted in indifference. A sort of lassitude overcame me; every chore involved effort; no relationship was worth pursuing. My place was in St Loup with the mechanic. It was a fact as immutable as gravity. Yet, I knew that such a claim would be regarded as preposterous and that my circumstances imprisoned me.

Last year, Edward died. I am free at last! But for little time. No doubt the frustration contributed to my illness. They do say that this awesome disease is exacerbated by stress.

The patronne of the Café de la Place wanders over to my table. 'Is madame from abroad? Is madame planning a long *séjour* in St Loup. St Loup is a dull little place, madame. Nothing happens here ... until recently, that is.'

'And what did happen?'

'You have the paper, madame. Terrible, terrible. *Mon Dieu*, it is terrible...' and her eyes misted. 'Le pauvre Michel! A prince among men! He was cut out for better things in life than lying in a pool of oil under a motor car. And he knew it! He was a romantic, le pauvre Michel! Swore he'd never marry until his princess returned. But he fell into debt and married Céleste Forestier – she had money, you understand.' And sighing deeply, her arms folded under her bosom, Madame la patronne confided: 'He'll swing for it, madame.'

As the patronne dragged herself across the square, carrying my used cup and saucer and plate, the sound of Juliette Greco faded. I felt the tide come in and lap my feet.

Shelf Life

John Brown struggled against waking but there was nothing he could do to arrest the surge that was thrusting him into full consciousness. He wondered, were he to lie in this comforting shape long enough, would he freeze in it, never again to have to face the daily round?

For it was the daily round that John Brown, aged seventeen, so heartily disliked. Always had. For as long as he could remember. It consisted of eating the food his mother could afford, going to a job no one in his right mind would do, and living under the same roof as his unremarkable parent, whose lack of imagination had provided him with the same name as half the town in which he had been born, schooled and would probably die.

He had been stacking shelves at the supermarket ever since he left school without qualifications. He and school had somehow flowed along parallel lines, never commingled. His mother, anxious for John's future, had shown an enthusiasm she normally reserved for bingo night when she was told John had been offered a job. It was one the supermarket reserved for young people with special needs.

'You'll be earning!' she said, emphasizing the satisfaction she felt by wiping her hands on her apron several more times than was strictly required.

He did. And what he earned he gave her. There was nothing he wanted for himself.

That was six months ago and still none of the employees spoke to him. The girls on the tills tittered and called him 'dafty'; the managers bellowed orders at him. He would have liked to make a friend if he was to be working there forever. In the event, he felt himself sinking deeper into himself, as if he had swallowed his head so he could not be got at. There was just him and his shelves.

He took the tins of vegetables and soup from the loaded trolley and one by one placed each against the other on the top shelf, seeing to it that the row was dead straight, and all the labels faced out above the prices prominently displayed beneath them. He repeated the same meticulous procedure for the next two shelves. Stepping back, he checked his arrangement. All was as it should be, just as he had been shown. He registered a feeling amounting to a small pleasure. As he rolled the trolley back to the stores, he whistled between his teeth. He loaded up with dry goods in packets and boxes and returned to stack the two lower shelves.

He had pasta in eight shapes and sizes, sugar in six forms and colours, dried fruits in ten varieties and flour in four types. It was the first time he had studied them. Finished stacking, he stepped back, lowered himself on his haunches and in deep draughts drank in the order he had created.

Somewhere, seemingly miles away, a bell was ringing. Someone was shouting, someone was pushing him. And it came to him: in five minutes the store would open and the public would pour in. And then ... His heart sank. His shelves would be plundered. He allowed himself one more glance at the undisturbed pattern of his work, a few seconds in which to consider the different types of lettering that identified objects for those who could read, the different colours for those who could not. And then he raised his hands either side of his face and made a frame through which he isolated his shelves into large pictures and small pictures. While one of the managers took hold of his arm and was hauling John to the back of the store, John found himself rather looking forward to tomorrow.

He had never been excited by the taste of food, only by its appearance, whether raw in the butcher's and fishmonger's, cooked at the take-away or in packets, bottles, tins and jars at the corner shop. As a mere tot in the high chair knocked up by his father, who had been part of the family in those days, he used to fling his dinner across the kitchen when it didn't *look* right. He'd heard his mother tell a neighbour how he had thrown a dish of beetroot over her when she covered the little young, red balls in thick white. It hadn't been the taste of white sauce he particularly disliked – or his mother – it was the fact of her laying a white blanket over beautiful red. What John liked was a feast for his *eyes*. Even now, when his mother filled his plate with meat, dumplings and beans, he would separate the beans from the rest and gaze on green while he downed the brown and white, avoiding the sight of both.

Same with clothes. As a child, unless he had been allowed to choose the shirt or sweater to wear with his pants, he would refuse to go to school. His mother never did understand how he felt about colours, only that he was making her late for work, that he was a difficult child and she wasn't going to risk having another.

Had he not been sacked for his sluggishness ('reverie' was not a word in circulation at the supermarket), John might never have isolated the mysterious pleasure stacking his shelves had given him, and wanted to replicate it. Sitting watching TV alone all day was not only boring but the adverts were a constant reminder of shelves. How he missed his! Someone else would be stacking his rows. He felt a consuming sorrow.

It was half-past seven. The front door slammed behind Mrs Brown hurrying to open the launderette she managed. John got up, threw on blue overalls over a pink blouse of his mother's and made his way out of the house to the crumbling shed where once his father had done his carpentry. He rummaged in a corner, found a sack and went straight down to the refuse depot.

He'd been there before. Before he got his job. Just for somewhere to hang out. The boy who manned the gate had been at his school; being older than John he'd left before him. He was a friendly sort, not a bully like some of the others.

'Yeah! You can look around. But don't touch anything there, there and there!' And he pointed.

John made straight for the pile of tins. At first he set aside only perfect ones. Then picking up a dented tin by mistake, he noticed how it caught the light, he registered that its imperfection made it nicely exceptional and he started looking for others similarly impaired. He gathered tins large and small, some with bits of label adhering, others clean of paper, proudly displaying circular ribs.

John dragged his sack of tins over to the pile where paper was stowed under thick, black plastic. Dropping to his knees, he unfastened a corner of the sheeting and slid himself under, raising his backside to let in a little light. Here he rummaged for boxes, packets, moulded plastic, Cellophane and foil. Having found what he was looking for, he carefully fastened back the sheeting, stood up and scanned the horizon. The place was deserted. Moving as if to leave the depot, John suddenly swerved and concealed himself behind a stack of wood. He put down his sack to examine the planks. Many were damaged, some were thick with brown varnish. He put by a pile. So far as he could see they were all free of knots and such paint as stained them would come off easily. Anyhow, there was no time to go through others. Someone might come along and catch him at it.

He balanced the planks under his right arm and flung his sack over his left shoulder. Standing with his legs well splayed, he distributed his weight evenly and with measured steps made his way to the exit. The gate was unmanned. That was lucky. He couldn't expect his old school fellow to turn a blind eye to good planks of wood.

Back in his father's shed, John unloaded. He filled a bucket from the tap in the alley. He took sheets of sandpaper from a drawer in the work bench and laid them beside paint remover, glue, nails, screws, a screwdriver, hammer and saw. Having assembled all he thought he would need, John sat back to make plans.

He would spend all his waking hours in the shed making shelves. Slowly, he polished, bent and scratched his tins to get effects that pleased him. He swelled out empty packets of rice and sugar with chips of foam rubber. He cut out and coloured cardboard shapes for the biscuit boxes. He filled bottles with coloured waters and jars with large and small stones he had polished. And where he needed an odd letter, a word or patch of colour, he cut them from old magazines.

Once he had his planks sanded, cleaned and polished, he tried his tins, packets, bottles and jars on them this way and that and only when utterly satisfied with his arrangement stuck them fast. Standing back, sitting for long passages of time looking at them, John felt thoroughly satisfied with the result.

When Mrs Brown was approached to donate something ('*anything will do*') to the sale at John's old school, she didn't know where to turn. She was certainly not going to part with the few ornaments that had survived her numberless financial crises. 'Ask John!' she told the boy from the depot, who had been delegated to canvass from anyone in the district whose child had been or was at the school. 'I haven't got anything' John said. 'Yes you have, you've got these!' and the boy pointed to John's shelves. 'Who'd want *them*?' John asked incredulously. 'I dunno, but I've got to find something from this street and I'm not doing too well,' the boy admitted, adding as an afterthought, 'Don't you let on where you get your stuff from!'

It was a matter of pure chance that led Julius Batchi, of Batchi & Batchi, advertising magnate and art promoter, to see John's shelves. His magnificent new car let him down in front of the school on the day of the sale. Being of nervy disposition, unable to sit still for twenty minutes, he had wandered into the school yard to while away the time for the breakdown service to turn up. There were crowds of the sort of people Mr Batchi was unfamiliar with milling around the home-made cake and jam, the second-hand clothes, the books and tapes and the toys. There was not a soul anywhere near John Brown's shelves.

Julius Batchi paid two pounds to a man who said he was the maths master, and that the shelves had been donated by an old pupil who could neither add nor subtract let alone cope with GCE maths. His name: John Brown. Mr Batchi asked for the address of the boy and while he waited for this to be found – and his car to be attended to – he wandered round and round the shelves in a state of euphoria. He's the poor man's Kienholz, he told himself, I'll put him under contract. There's a killing to be made.

It was with Mrs Brown that Julius Batchi would negotiate. She would undertake to see that John produced shelves to given measurement. There were to be series and single examples standing both vertically and horizontally. When each item was completed to her son's satisfaction,

Mrs Brown was to ring Mr Batchi who would have it collected by van. A cheque in Mrs Brown's name would follow.

His exhibition in a celebrated art gallery off Bond Street represented three years of John's work. Julius put on a champagne and caviar opening of lavish proportions. The art world congregated to agonize over the arcane mysteries of the supermarket shelf. Because Julius Batchi would not risk exhibiting his artist and did not provide a photograph of him or a curriculum vitae, far greater publicity resulted for his work than might otherwise have been case.

All could have proceeded along these lines for all time had it not been that John was finding it increasingly hard to bear having his shelves taken from him. The separation was creating a sorrow too deep for words. Where did his shelves go? To whom? Certainly not to anyone who could feel as deeply for them as he felt. Perhaps they died? And so when Mrs Brown asked her son when next he would be ready for Mr Batchi's van, he hedged. 'Not yet' was all he said. He was searching for a solution and he was about to arrive at one.

His solution was to screw his work to the floor, ceiling and walls of the shed. There was no way Mr Batchi's van would be able to lift the shed off its foundations.

Mrs Brown had no intention of hurrying her son. She was already astonished with the sums of money Mr Batchi paid for his work. On the one hand she had never expected *anything* of the boy. On the other, she couldn't understand why anyone would pay good money for his shelves. It was best, she thought, not to try to work it out and just to rejoice in the healthy state of her post office account. She often asked John if there was anything he wanted but the boy always answered that there was nothing. And so it was that Mrs Brown thought it would be quite all right, quite 'fair', if she were to treat herself to the little luxury she had set her heart on.

She answered the advert in the local paper for a small conservatory and arranged with the firm for the men to come when she was at work. It so happened that John was at the refuse depot at the time. Mrs Brown had told the men she would leave it to them to decide where best to erect the conservatory. It was obvious to them. They peered into the crumbling shed, saw it was full of refuse, made a bonfire of everything that would burn and loaded their lorry with the rest. Then they demolished the shed and laid their foundations.

John was not able to tell the doctor what was wrong: he had lost the power of speech. He was kept in a locked dormitory with other young men because it was feared he would harm himself if left alone. The nurses gave him pencil and paper hoping he might write down what he felt.

When he wasn't covering his ears with his hands to keep out the noise and his eyes with a scarf to avoid seeing the colours he disliked, he drew shelves. He lived to seventy-four. During fifty-one years neither his mother nor Mr Batchi visited him and no one thought to provide him with refuse and wood planks.

A Doctor's Daughter

I first met the Coopers socially one Christmas Eve. Prior to that I had never so much as knocked on their front door; the patients' entry to The Briars was to the side of the house.

My indispositions were of a trivial nature but they involved me in confiding intimacies to Dr Cooper, and I regarded these as something of an impediment to socializing. I was quite unprepared to receive a telephone call from Mrs Cooper inviting me to drinks.

Of course, I knew Mrs Cooper by sight. Hamdon is a village – albeit an extended one – and everyone knows everyone else by sight. And what is more, I had not infrequently been inconvenienced by Mrs C., whose most striking attribute was procrastination. At Budd's-the-Bread she positively *agonized* over the choice of wholemeal or barley, mixed grain or Super-white. At Jones-the-Meat I had watched and waited while the patient butcher failed to conclude any sort of deal with the doctor's wife before he had run the length and breadth of his repartee: 'I cannot recommend too highly, Mrs Cooper ... So tasty at this time of year ... You won't beat *that* for price...' But having praised to the skies his lamb, his beef and his pork – even, in recent times, his venison – it was with half a pound of chipolatas that I most often saw Mrs C. quit his premises.

At first glance the doctor's wife looked grubby, but this was only an impression; she was not – she was shabby. She dressed in colours associated with smoky cities rather than opalescent villages on the Welsh border, where the single workshop is devoted to a private press, and the only 'industry' country wines.

Mrs Cooper's mousy hair was streaked with nicotine-stained white strands and her weather-beaten complexion was dependably unpainted. But her skin was smooth and taut, and her deep gentian eyes permanently open wide in an expression of anxious expectation. Beneath the voluminous shrouds she wore, I guessed that Mrs C. was slim.

It was with her back that I was most familiar. Because of her absent-minded way of stationing herself at the counter, procrastinating, she was served before those of us who queued neatly. When I emerged from making my purchases, it was Mrs C.'s back view that I caught, sloping home, weighed down by insubstantial plastic bags in imminent danger of splitting, and depositing their contents in the gutters of the High Street.

Mrs Cooper was a shopper of essentials, not luxuries. She struck me as duty-bound, not pleasure-seeking, a loser, permanently perched on the verge of some disaster. But my pity did not extend to sympathy. Mrs C. lacked inspiration and evoked none in me.

I had registered with Dr Cooper because the alternative was Dr Helvetius, who had a reputation for alcohol dependence. Without being obsessively concerned with my health, I do like to engage with a clear mind when I present my indigestion, my rash and my piles. However, my loyalty to Dr Cooper was due as much to habit as satisfaction with his expertise. Indeed, my suspicion was that because a visit to his consulting room was such a doleful experience, it encouraged in me rude health. I am positively allergic to bottle-green lino, brown leather examination couches of the Edwardian epoch, and the smell of formaldehyde.

Dr Cooper opened the front door and ushered me cordially into a room that might, ordinarily, have done service as a living-room. It was hard to tell, so featureless it was. There were about twenty-five guests standing awkwardly, rehearsing the well-tried topics that are a feature of neighbourhood drinks do's.

I was not surprised to discover that the pleasures of the flesh were neglected at The Briars. The bottles of medium-dry sherry and unknown brand of gin had clearly been bought in for the occasion. The plates of Snax, on which wafers of Danish pork luncheon meat had been sparsely arranged, lacked seasonal good cheer, something that the single branch of holly fixed to the parchment light shade did nothing to mitigate.

I spotted Mrs C. and made my way towards her. She was shifting from one foot to the other, visibly cringing, as Mavis Fanshaw – reputed to be a credit to her husband and the life and soul of the most unpromising social gatherings – was responding to a remark passed by the estate agent that was a little off-colour. I watched Mrs C. melt into the brown velour curtains.

There being no single feature in the room nor any captivating conversational topic upon which to settle my attention, I found my thoughts wandering. How could people live in such environmental wretchedness? How did Mrs C. occupy herself when she was not at the shops? Did the Coopers have a family? Surely, there was a girl. . . .

'May I present my daughter, Dorelia?' It was Dr Cooper awakening me from my reveries. I turned; my glass is empty, I thought, but my cup overfloweth. Dorelia was strikingly beautiful!

'She's just graduated from the Royal College of Art. I was telling her that in our very midst, in Hamdon, we have a neighbour reputed to own a remarkable collection of modern art.'

It was as if lost in the desert I had suddenly come upon an oasis of cool, clear water, fresh dates and scented flowers. Nature is astonishing! How could this exquisite young woman be the progeny of Dr and Mrs Cooper? It was impossible; the stork must have delivered her.

'I would regard it an honour to show you over my collection,' I said, thinking what a pleasure there was in store for me. 'And I hope you will show me your work.'

It is wise to be apprehensive in the face of forthcoming social functions, I mused; the delight that accompanies the unexpected is immeasurable.

The last guest had left when Dorelia fetched my coat and hat. By the light of her torch she led me through the garden wilderness to the shed that had become her studio.

'I painted it green so that it dissolves into the shrubs,' she explained, as she pushed open the door and turned on the lights. Spots focused on pictures and pieces of modern pottery. Books and magazines littered the day-bed and were scattered over the honey-coloured floor boards. At the end of the shed, under the window, was her desk-cum-drawing-board. She was working on a series of pen and ink drawings of men broadcasting seed, tending burgeoning crops, and harvesting.

The indigo curtains had not been drawn across the window. I listened to the furtive tapping of a branch against the side of the shed, and the hoot of an owl. The evidence of night created intimacy. I looked towards Dorelia and saw that she was smiling, and that her smile was lopsided: this exquisite creature had a blemish! She was pleased, it was only the left side of her face that expressed her satisfaction.

'From whom do you derive your talent?' I asked.

'Mummy!' Dorelia said decidedly, 'They're all utterly non-visual on Daddy's side!'

Quite.

'It's really sad – Mummy's a legend at the College; she was an exceptional student. She had her first show before she had me. But when I was about five she just stopped everything – drawing, painting, etching – the lot. And she won't discuss it. But I'm sure she'd be happier if she got back to her own work. . . .' Dorelia's thoughts trailed off on some solitary itinerary.

'She gives me the impression of being an anxious soul,' I said.

'You're right! She is! And she's let herself go. I've tried to get her to spruce up but she always comes back with "Don't be ridiculous, Dorry!", as if I'd suggested something slightly shocking. I believe she's frightened of being desirable.'

❦   ❦   ❦

I have to admit it: I was offended that Helvetius only rang me to invite me to his New Year's Eve party at seven o'clock on the 29th.

'You slipped through my net, dear boy!' He was attempting an excuse and I was tempted to plead a prior invitation. I did not, however, give in to the temptation. I never permit myself to succumb to false pride.

There must have been two hundred guests gathered in the eighteenth-century drawing- and dining-rooms whose inter-communicating doors had been folded back to accommodate the crowd.

'I was determined to bring in the New Year with *all* my friends!' I overheard Helvetius say.

It was the first time that I had been invited to The Grove. My aesthetic taste-buds were galvanized in a state of excitation; I knew that my appetite for the beautiful was to be satisfied. Helvetius was a considerable connoisseur, with the funds to meet his high standards. Ranged round the dining-room was a set of John Linnell chairs with baskets of fruit carved into their backs, and an Adam sideboard. No doubt, beneath the crisp white damask tablecloth – groaning under the weight of exotic foods – there was an Adam table. I was surreptitiously watching Mavis Fanshaw and the estate agent deep in giggles on an Adam 'sofa', reflected in a gilt gesso mirror, when Helvetius approached. Quickly, I gathered my composure.

'James Moore?' I suggested the name as the likely designer of the mirror.

'With John Gumley,' he replied.

'Match' to Helvetius, I thought. But seeing that I was not only genuinely interested but also informed, Helvetius asked if I would care to see the furniture in his study.

'I've had to store the good drawing-room stuff for the night, and I'm not opening the study to my visitors. I don't want to have to pack all my papers away,' he explained. Taking a key from his pocket, and making sure that no one was about to see us enter, he drew me into the room. It was crimson-papered with a good deal of cream and gold ornamentation. The curtains of rich crimson silk were swathed and draped and had lavishly embroidered ties. Helvetius showed me his Chippendale chairs, and the inlay on the sofa table, before pointing to the bureau bookcase.

'I was lucky with that. It was originally made for George II. Evidently it languished for years in some box room belonging to one of the lesser Royals before I picked it up at auction.' And while he spoke, he caressed the walnut. I find these gestures somewhat embarrassing, and averted my eyes. At once they focused on a delightful landscape painting. Because all the furniture and fittings in the study were in period, I was surprised that a picture of an evidently more recent date was included in the decorative scheme. I enquired its provenance.

'Oh that!' Helvetius sounded falsely dismissive, 'It's the work of a non-professional – a young student at the Royal College. It was done some twenty-five years ago.' But he joined me in front of the picture and admitted, 'She had become a legend before she graduated.' I searched for a signature but could only find the letter 'A'.

Helvetius's mood had darkened. Clearly, he wanted to discourage me from making further enquiries about the artist and the picture, and he ushered me out of the study and back into the drawing-room.

David Lomax, the local bookseller, beckoned to me and I joined him and his wife at the buffet, where a waiter was serving bite-size vols-au-vent stuffed with lobster in a cream sauce.

'I found that first of Porter's *Paradise* I was looking for!' Oliver Benson, the dentist, had made his way to David's side, 'I went over to Hay. . . .'

'And paid over the odds, I don't mind betting!'

'Sixty p! It was concealed in newspaper wrapping and was lying on a tray outside the shop.' Oliver was triumphant.

'Never! Some people have all the luck.'

While the two men parried finds and prices, I turned to Angela Lomax. 'It really does seem as if Helvetius has the whole neighbourhood under his roof, tonight. Except the Coopers!' Their absence had only just struck me. I could hardly believe that a New Year's Eve thrash at The Briars was detaining them.

'Surely you know: they don't visit.' I thought Angela said that knowingly, but she went on to say that she had no idea why they did not visit, and assumed it had something to do with professional rivalry. I agreed that the intemperate Helvetius had contrived a very much more agreeable lifestyle than the temperate Cooper.

'The high moral ground,' I observed, 'does not always enjoy the most clement conditions.'

'Discussing the Coopers?' David Lomax butted in. He appeared decidedly lowered by the dentist's good fortune. 'Angela likes people to believe that she knows the whys and wherefores of the Cooper-Helvetius rift. She doesn't. The whole thing remains a mystery.' After a pause, he asked me 'How long have you lived in Hamdon?'

'Nine years.' I replied.

'A newcomer!' Lomax and the dentist chorused.

'Well, I'll give you a run-down of the facts. Angela can give you a run-down of speculation, later, if that's what appeals to you.' And, as if ticking off points of evidence, he continued. 'John Cooper and Lance

Helvetius were students together at Guy's. They were good friends, it's said. As soon as they qualified, Cooper came to The Briars to practise. About five years later, Helvetius bought The Grove. In all the years that the two men have lived in the village, no one has ever seen them speak to one another. Mrs C. fell ill around the time that Helvetius arrived, not physically, mind you, she became agoraphobic. Dorelia had to be sent away to school because Mrs C. couldn't cope. From that time, Dorelia was cared for by one of her grannies – I don't know where.'

'Poor child!' I said.

'Doesn't seem to have done her any harm!' David Lomax observed, smacking his lips, 'She's a real knock-out! And, what's more, she appears to be perfectly well balanced.'

'Makes something of a contrast with her mother,' Oliver Benson remarked.

'Ah! David replied, 'but you didn't know Anne Cooper before she fell ill.'

I yield to no man in my admiration for Helvetius. He really knows how to celebrate the pleasures of the flesh, I thought. Throughout the evening a steady flow of vintage champagne and exotic food flowed from behind the green baize door.

I became aware that a hush was consuming the buzz of conversation, and thought that I detected Big Ben striking midnight. I noticed that Helvetius was climbing to the top of the library steps and, on the final stroke of the old year, holding his glass aloft, he thundered, 'HAPPY NEW YEAR!' As he smiled down on the crowd, I was made suddenly aware that his smile affected only the left side of his face.

Boxes

As usual, at half-past eight precisely, he rang her front doorbell. As usual, he was ushered into the drawing-room where she was seated by the fire, her stick resting against the arm of her chair, a glass of wine on the table at her side.

'Kiss me, dear child!'

As he bent to brush her cheek with his lips, he enquired after her health. It was not too good, she allowed. He took a step back.

'But you look the very picture of health, *Grand-mère!*' he insisted, moving towards the table where the aperitifs were ranged.

However, appearances are unreliable, and in this case particularly so, for Gaston de Rostignac was *not* a child and Mme Forestier was *not* his grandmother.

Gaston – aged twenty-five – would have preferred to have neglected this regular Sunday evening appointment to supper, and to have continued piecing together the intricate mother-of-pearl inlay on the box the local jeweller had commissioned from him. The fruitwood jewel box was the most ambitious he had yet undertaken; it was three-tiered, with exquisite brass filigree hinges, and behind the velvet padding on the inside of the lid he had secreted a vellum envelope for love letters and photographs. But above all, he was proud of the locking device he had contrived. To open the box it was necessary to press the bud of an inlaid rose.

Gaston had been collecting and making boxes since he was five years of age, when he had been abandoned by his mother at the orphanage, told that his new name was Gaston *de Rostignac*, and parted from his few possessions. His tin train had been shunted into a communal toy shed, his three books placed on the shelves of the communal library. It had been only with difficulty and cunning that he had managed to hold on to the photograph of his beautiful mother, attaching it to his person with sticking plaster by day and night and concealing it in his sock when he bathed. There was not a single drawer or cupboard that he could call his own.

The agonizing sense of loss occasioned by his mother's sudden departure for a foreign land never left Gaston. But the matter of being separated from his few possessions was successfully dealt with by an act of imagination on the part of a stranger. A benefactor of the orphanage – called by all the children *Grand-mère* – gave him one of her hat boxes.

Into this box he was encouraged to stash all that was absolutely and sole-
ly his own, those few items with which he had arrived and those that
he would acquire, such as shiny conkers, birds' eggs, used stamps and
pieces of string.

From the first time that she set eyes on him, *Grand-mère* had taken a
special interest in Gaston. She encouraged him to weep in her ample lap
for his mother; she read to him from his own books; and together they
mentally boarded his tin train and voyaged to the land where his mother
now lived. But it was the gift of the hat box that was the source of the
lasting affection between Gaston de Rostignac and Mme Forestier – and
Gaston's eventual livelihood.

It was with pleasure that Gaston discovered that the commissioning
jeweller had been invited to supper at *Grand-mère*'s. He liked the man
personally and respected him professionally. M. Jacob tended to be more
lavish with his praise than with his criticism, he paid his craftsmen well
and promptly , and he dealt only in quality goods.

'My client, Mme Auric, is enchanted with your box!' he told Gaston.
'She has a passion for boxes of all shapes and sizes and insists that your
jewel box is among her favourites.'

Monsieur Jacob spoke admiringly of Mme Auric's taste. 'A natural
taste, seasoned with her experience of the Orient. But –' and he lowered
his voice in concern, 'I fear that the widow's buying days are a thing of
the past. Poor lady, she had a sad and impoverished youth and, I gather,
she had to make great sacrifices. She had a mere eighteen years of ease
and contentment ... but now, once again, she faces loneliness and pov-
erty. She'll be obliged to sell up just to live.' Then, patting Gaston's
sleeve, he added: 'She'll hang on to your box, though. She told me so!'
M. Jacob took a long draught from his glass before lamenting that Mme
Auric, at forty-one, was owed a further thirty years of life, yet admitted
to being world-weary.

On his first meeting with Mme Auric, in M. Jacob's shop, Gaston
was overwhelmed by everything about the woman: her beauty, her graciousness and, more especially, by the melancholy tone of resignation
that accompanied all that she said. She lavished praise on Gaston's taste
and workmanship and insisted to him that she would never be parted
from the box he had made for her.

'You must visit me and I shall show you *all* my children, while I can
still afford to keep them at home!' she said, quickly explaining to the
puzzled young man that she called her boxes her children.

'I would like that,' Gaston said carefully, making sure to absent himself from the shop before any firm arrangement was concluded.

It was a few weeks following this encounter that M. Jacob brought

Mme Auric to Sunday supper at *Grand-mère's*. Throughout the evening, Gaston felt himself to be in the wings of a stage, watching a performance in which his role was confined to a walk-on part. Mme Forestier and M. Jacob exemplified the confidence that comes with age, Mme Auric the confidence that accompanies great beauty. Gaston felt weighed down by gracelessness and inexperience.

It was only at the insistence of M. Jacob that Gaston later kept the appointment with Mme Auric, made provisionally over supper. M. Jacob accompanied him to the widow's large, isolated villa which stood behind tall stone walls in Upper Beaux Arbres. Gaston was never to forget this first visit; the scent of the cut branches of syringa, stood in huge Chinese vases, filled the air with a suggestiveness hitherto wholly unfamiliar to him.

Mme Auric's collection of boxes was large, varied and museum-fine. Every room had its complement. There were porcelain patch boxes, *papier mâché* card cases, silver snuff boxes and vinaigrettes. There were rosewood tea caddies and knife boxes, satinwood sewing and mahogany writing boxes. And on her dressing-table, surrounded by silver-stoppered bottles and silver-backed brushes, his jewel box.

'Yours is the first object of beauty upon which my eyes alight each morning!'

Neither *Grand-mère* nor M. Jacob dreamed of the outcome of bringing together Gaston de Rostignac and Rose Auric. Neither of the ancients' thoughts – embedded as they were in innocence and old-fashioned ways – encompassed anything but the consolations of friendships. *Grand-mère* had always been concerned that Gaston was unsociable, preferring to spend every minute that the good Lord sent at his work bench. M. Jacob had been concerned for Mme Auric ever since she was widowed. Her reduced circumstances, occasioned by her husband's untimely death, would very soon result in her having to sell all the jewels he had bought for her, then the boxes and the furniture and, finally, the house itself. Mme Auric had no friends in Beaux Arbres. She and her husband had only returned from the Orient four years prior to Antoine Auric's death, and such acquaintanceships as the couple had made dissolved when he died.

At Rose's instigation they became lovers. It was she who took Gaston hungrily in her arms, murmured lasciviously 'Come!', and led him upstairs to her bedroom. She had let go his hand at the door of her dressing-room, leaving him to lean against the wall, watching as she unbuttoned her lace blouse, unfastened her taffeta skirt, kicked off her velvet pumps and drew down her silk stockings. He was still standing motionless when she sank down on the bed, only his eyes had followed her and become fastened on the little narrow shoulder straps of her chemise as they slipped, baring her breast.

'Come!' she murmured again, extending her arm towards him. 'Wouldn't you like . . . ? Don't you want . . . ?'

It was dawn when Gaston let himself out of the gate at the end of the garden, and by the time he got back to his workshop the milk of morning was spilled on the fields of Lower Beaux Arbres. The birds were chorusing, and moist air rising from the canal gratified Gaston's nostrils. He fell exhausted on to his narrow bed and slept without stirring until midday.

Quickly, automatically, a routine established itself. Gaston would work at his bench from midday until eight in the evening, when he washed and changed his clothes. At half-past eight, when night had taken possession of Beaux Arbres, and gloom concealed him, he half strode, half ran from Lower to Upper town where his mistress awaited him, her arms outstretched to enfold him.

Three years went by. Gaston de Rostignac and Rose Auric kept their affaire nocturnal and secret. They experienced a constancy neither chilled by absence nor dissolved by familiarity, and it was only when all but valueless beads remained of her jewellery, no boxes, only a few sticks of essential furniture – and the house was up for sale – that Rose visited Gaston's workshop.

It was Sunday. Lower Beaux Arbres was deserted and the barges that plied the canal all week were moored, guarded by dogs. Gaston grilled trout, sautéed potatoes and assembled and tossed a salad. He took lunch on to the narrow balcony that overlooked the water. The couple lingered in the hazy sunlight drinking cool Vouvray. Rose's hands could not resist cupping themselves round the beautifully turned salt box.

'We would buy a box at every port of call, so as never to leave the places we visited completely behind. And I called my boxes my children because each was given to me by my husband.'

'While you were carefully preserving places,' Gaston observed, 'I was preserving time.' And he confided to his mistress details of his collection of boxes – and particularly those about *Grand-mère*'s hat box, which had been the seed of his passion.

Rose expressed a desire to see all Gaston's boxes and the couple moved from the balcony into the living-room. Gaston watched as Rose drifted quietly round the shelves, opening and shutting tin and cardboard boxes that had been made for commonplace things – for gramophone needles, soap, cigars and foodstuffs. Alone of his boxes, *Grand-mère*'s hat box stood under the table by the chair in which Gaston sat to read. The colours of the feathers painted as decoration on the box had faded, the name of the hatters was only just discernible, the ribbons that secured the lid had frayed, but the box itself was in pristine condition. Rose dropped to the floor.

'While you go through my childhood,' Gaston said, 'I'll make us coffee.'

In the time that it took for the water to pass through the freshly ground grains and the aroma of coffee to fill the small kitchen, Gaston experienced the overwhelming contentment of domesticity. Shortly, he would persuade his mistress to share his modest dwelling. Two could live as cheaply as one.... She would soon be penniless.... He looked out of the window on to the backyard. He would clear it. Rose would need the space to hang out the washing.

He returned to the living-room. Something was wrong. From the corner of his eye he could see that the contents of the old hat box lay scattered on the floor. And where was Rose? He put down the tray and quickly fell to his knees and retrieved his train, his books, the fragile birds' eggs and the leaf-dry stamps.

'Rose!' he called out, 'Rose! Where are you?'

It was mystifying. He peered over the banisters: she was not in the workshop and the doors on to the canal were thrown open.

'Rose!' he called – but quietly, for it was not in his nature to shout and, rather than disturb the peace of Sunday with his voice, he would search for her with his eyes. He ran up the towpath, embarrassed by the barking of the barge dogs, and into the fields. He looked up the lane that ran from Lower to Upper Beaux Arbres but Rose was nowhere to be seen. Disconsolate, he wandered home.

He poured himself the lukewarm coffee but before he drank he bent down to replace the lid of *Grand-mère*'s hat box. His blood ran cold. The envelope which for twenty-four years had been attached to the inside of the lid was gone, and with it the photograph of his mother.

His whole body was shaking. He swayed; he felt sick. His head was splitting along the line of his temple. It seemed that a burning nail was being hammered into his skull and slowly turned further and further into the quick of his being. Seized with terror, he shot down the stairs into the workshop and threw open the doors of his cupboards and hurled his materials and his tools to the ground. He swept his arm along the shelves of the workshop and stamped his boxes, large and small, into the earth floor. He wept; he sobbed; he beat his fists against the walls and all the while, in horror, he cried out: 'Oh no! Oh no!'

A faint sunbeam was playing on the scalpel he reserved for his most delicate carving. He picked it off the floor and drew the narrow blade carefully across his left wrist and then his right. He was becalmed, hypnotized by his resolve. He watched the surface of his work bench turn from salt white to vermilion. It was fifteen minutes before he fell forward, unconscious.

The Illustrated Observer

By ten-thirty that Sunday summer's morning the sun was white-hot. There was no movement in the air, and the scent of the honeysuckle that festooned the hedge separating the tea-garden from open meadows hung over the tables. Yellow peaches and misted plums were ripening against the weathered wall of the tea-house. From time to time ripe fruit thudded to the ground and together with the continuous hum and buzz of bees, wasps and blue-bottles produced the peculiar resonance that belongs to the heat and glare of an arid summer. Just below the level surface of the pond goldfish basked, and under the tresses of the overhanging willow a frog sat motionless on cracked mud.

Almost all the tables and chairs had been taken. Londoners, dressed uncharacteristically in bright tropical-weight cotton and linen, had emerged like butterflies from the chrysalis of flat-land to celebrate the peerless summer. Families, couples and single men and women were breakfasting on ice-cold squash and ice-creams. Too hot to talk, they read their papers in the somnolent quiet. Their dogs lay listless beneath their chairs.

Alone untouched by the devouring heat, a little child was darting fawnlike between the tables in pursuit of a cabbage-white. He was naked; his curls were the colour of clotted cream and his skin that of honey. He was oblivious to all but his fervent desire to catch the butterfly. When the insect settled tantalizingly beyond his reach the child waited, gazing patiently until the creature set off again to flutter hither and thither. Then he clapped his tiny hands and made off in pursuit, intoxicated. And then, abruptly, he came to a halt, transfixed.

Into his field of vision came a family – mother, father and twin boys of about seven years of age. Sullenly they approached an unoccupied table. Father was dressed neatly in worsted trousers and a tweed jacket over a striped shirt and cricket-club tie. Mother was dressed negligently in a soiled sleeveless cotton dress and heavy-duty shoes; she was stockingless and her legs showed dough-white and knobbly with varicose veins. The twins wore none-too-white T-shirts and shorts; they dragged their feet in black Wellington boots. Under the right arm each clutched tightly a large model aeroplane. As if on a single command the four members of the family pulled out four iron chairs and sat down. The boys placed their aeroplanes on the table. All the while since the little child had spotted the colourful planes he had stood stock still, his eyes darting from wings to propellers, from under-carriage to fuselage.

Barely sixty seconds after the family had settled itself, the explosion erupted.

'Don't you dare! Don't you dare touch them! They're not yours, they belong to us.' Father's face was puce, his moustache was moist, his fists were clenched. Physical violence threatened but the child, unconcerned, remained preoccupied inches from the table where the planes were grounded. He extended his arm; he pointed his finger.

'Will you go away! This is our table and we don't want you standing over us!' Uncomprehending, the child opened out his hand in a gesture of expectation. Father addressed his sons:

'Now, I want you to listen to me carefully. Those aeroplanes were bought for you. They were not intended for other children. If you don't look after your things greedy children will come along and take them and break them and you'll probably never set eyes on them again!' Relieved of his homily, Father raised his cup to his lips but did not have time to draw a draught. 'Look! Look!' he warned, 'Some children never learn!' And he leant over the table and swept up the aeroplanes and confined them to the protective custody of his feet.

The child's parents were easy to spot. A tall, blond, shirtless Scandinavian and his pretty wife, dressed in the natural dyes associated with wholesomeness. They watched their child attentively, but from a distance, allowing him perfect, protected freedom. They were clearly sane and happy. But the twins' parents were demonstrably unhealthy and miserable. Father: possibly a rent collector. Mother: conceivably a clerk in the pet-food industry. Their home: plastered with texts from Leviticus. Their diet: the gruel of sanctity. All pleasure inimical to their way of life. Such thoughts were enough to obliterate the keen delight of the summer's morning. The family returned me to the concrete, the dust and the fumes of the High Street, they set me down in the smell of fast food and petrol, in the sound of the 2.54 at Towcester leaking from the bookies' corner shop. They had me grappling in the market for tired greens; sitting in the surgery being told that the doctor was held up; waiting for the bus that never comes. . . .

'Don't you dare!' Unable to restrain his desire to look closer, to touch the wonderful toys, the little child had dropped to the ground and was crawling under the table.

'You're not to touch!' In his fury, Father rose, pushed back his chair with the back of his legs and set it toppling onto the grass, narrowly missing the child. The Scandinavian did not rise from his chair but leant over the back of it and from three tables' distance said quietly, in a heavily accented voice, 'I'd rather you didn't speak to my child like that.'

'And' shouted back Father, 'I'd rather you removed your unruly infant and refrained from addressing me!' Slowly, the blond man rose and took two long strides towards the child. Gently, he took him in his arms and, making a game of flying him through the air, deposited him on the table where he and his wife were drinking milk-shakes through straws.

'Did you hear that, Mother? They have the effrontery to come over here and let their children run riot, naked. It's absolutely obscene. It's not difficult to imagine what that child'll be like when he grows up.' And turning to the twins: 'You know, sons, I don't have to remind you it's shameful to go uncovered.'

'I thought only Blacks went about without clothes on, Daddy.'

'You are quite right, child. Now, eat your breakfast.'

To the blusterous malignity was added the smell of bacon fat. Father – a slave to habit – had ordered bacon, egg, tomatoes, sausages and fried bread for the whole family. The twins were reminded not to speak while they ate, and Father took the opportunity of their muteness to repeat his lesson on property and ownership: it belongs to you, you earn it, you care for it, and on no account do you let anyone take it from you. If you lend it to someone they will be bound to break or lose it.

'You'd never get it back! You'd never see it again!' Father allowed a pause for the twins to consider the awesome threat involved in sharing, before adding 'If these lazy and undisciplined foreigners only worked as hard as we do, they too would be able to buy nice things for their children. . . .'

'How can you tell if someone's a foreigner if he's white, Daddy?' As Father defined 'foreigner' to his earnest son it became clear that the term might apply to anyone who did not live on the Frobisher Estate in Crouch End.

'Now, I want you to remember all I've said. If you don't, if you're not vigilant, you'll find yourselves being taken advantage of. Won't they, Mother?' and Mother agreed that they would.

Who could have imagined that the subject of model aircraft ownership was so complex? Father managed to spin it out right through the cooked breakfast, the toast and marmalade, and several cups of tea. 'Remember what the scripture says? "To those who have it shall be given".'

Mother took over, telling her boys that their handwriting was not up to standard and that it didn't matter how clever they were, how much they knew; if the examiners couldn't read their writing they wouldn't pass them.

'I blame Mrs McKenzie. She's too lenient!' Father complained. And

Mother agreed and said she was going to set the boys exercises to do in the mornings, throughout the holidays.

'Oh, Daddy, *must* we?'

'Yes. You must always do as your mother says. You must never question her decisions. And I want no whining.'

'But, it's the *holidays!*'

'Holidays! Holidays from what?' Mother's face had the expression of one whose diet was confined to unsweetened rhubarb.

When the twins had finished breakfast, Father handed them their model aeroplanes and told them to take them into the meadow to fly them. There followed further exhortations. Father did not want them broken or lost – or above all, shared.

'We promise, Daddy, we won't let anyone touch them.'

'Good boys.' And turning to Mother: 'This is a lesson best learnt early in life.'

With the twins out of the way, they could talk freely about the implications of nakedness, the folly of generosity, the value of discipline and the nice, comforting rightness of conformity.

'You can just see where that child's nakedness will lead!' Father said darkly, and Mother passed that sort of knowing look that involves a lowering of the chin into the neck and a pursing of the lips.

'I always make two things absolutely clear to the parents of new boys enrolling at the school: a respect for property and authority is the foundation of our teaching.'

The fragments of the summer's morning were shattered. The ripening fruit was rotting. The pond was stagnant. The smell of heat was cat. A woman at a nearby table was surreptitiously splaying her elbows in an effort to refresh her armpits. Her male companion shifted in his seat, trying to unstick his thighs from his trouser legs. A teenager, evidently irritable, was exhaling vigorously, blowing the breath from her mouth upstream to her nose, no doubt determined that at least two centimetres of her being should be cool. From a table at the far end of the garden came a shout. A woman had been stung by a wasp. Her husband was taking no notice. He was having a hay-fever attack.

Waves of dissatisfaction broke over me and enveloped me. The heat was oppressive, but I was determined to finish the political pages of the *Observer* before going home. I noticed that newsprint had transferred itself to my hands and skirt. I wondered whether my face was dirty, too.

A Letter to My Successor

No doubt you would agree with me that there is no end of scholarship, no unemployment in this field. Just as soon as one man's view has reached a particular conclusion it excites in another man a view to the contrary, or one at a tangent. Just when we confidently assume all available evidence has been amassed, a new document is discovered and all previous scholarship is made redundant and a queue of budding researchers forms to make reassessments. Scholars depend upon publication for their ascent up the academic ladder and publishers depend upon their findings for financial profit. The pleasures of the mind are as liable to corruption as any others.

The general reader of Proust finds it hard to believe that by 1971, the centenary of his birth, over one thousand books and articles relating to his life and work had been published in the English language alone, and is astonished by the suggestion that in all probability this figure would rise to three thousand by the turn of the century. What more could be written about a man who died at the age of fifty-two; a man who did not have the health and time to write more than two novels, and a handful of essays, stories and prefaces? It was a question often put to me; indeed, during my guardianship of the Foundation it ranked as the one most often posed. And if things had not proceeded quite as they did, I have no doubt some other stone flung into the Proust pool would have created other ripples just as disturbing.

In the normal course of events I do not like to speak about myself or about personal matters. During the sixteen years I ran the Proust Foundation I never allowed it to be known that it was the child of my imagination, and that from its infancy to its maturity never a day passed but I assisted with some small detail – an object here, a note in the catalogue there – of its development. I liked it to appear to the public that I was no more than a minor *fonctionnaire*, carrying out orders from an anonymous authority 'above'. Middle-aged spinsters tend to be invisible, and although middle-aged spinster librarians and curators are just noticed by the public they tend to be patronized, even despised. I did not wish to set myself apart from others working at the Foundation. Nor did I wish to have to answer questions. My name, Olga Saul-Dubrovsky, is liability enough: it arouses expectations that I have never found myself able to discharge. As I say, I do not like to speak about myself, but in the light of what has taken place I think I should put you fully in the picture and place the background to the scandal on record. I have to accept it was a scandal, brought up as I was to believe it a greater evil to betray one's friend than one's country, and I still feel that a pledge to a relative must remain inviolate, even when scholarship is at stake.

I was born in London in 1910, the only daughter of an *emigré* antiquarian bookseller. My mother and father settled in a spacious flat in Bloomsbury, to be near the business premises my father occupied before his marriage. He had come to England from Russia via Paris where he had established himself as a dealer in Russian literature and history. He was instrumental in forming some of the most complete university libraries in those fields, on both sides of the Channel. My parents were obsessed by the importance of formal education – having had none themselves – and sent me to a girls' public school in London, and thence to London University. I took the easy option and read French, because that is the language we spoke in the home. Following the post-graduate work I did on Diderot – an author whose work was all but unknown in England – I was invited to join the faculty. I remained a French lecturer at the only college I had known until I was offered the job of setting up and tending the Proust Foundation. I owe this position to the generosity of the late Lord Howard of Bruton, who left his sizeable fortune to create a centre for Proust studies in London, in memory of his daughter Henrietta, who had been my student.

I did not so much fall into this job, but rather was raised for it. Some might detect a chain of coincidences in the events leading to it, the first link being forged in my childhood. It was to prove a weak link. My father had a French cousin, a Hasidic scholar, who had known Proust from the turn of the century until Proust died in 1922. Indeed, he had known not only the writer but the writer's parents and, although not part of Proust's more glamorous *monde*, had been an intimate friend. After the death of Proust, Chaim, my father's cousin, confided details of his relationship with the writer to my father, and because the relationship was regarded in those days as scandalous (not to say illegal in Britain), there was an understanding that no Saul-Dubrovsky would publish anything about it, whatever the inducements offered us. Proust's sexual depravity, which had at its core the defamation of his mother, would be bound to be highlighted by the popular press – regardless of its readers' indifference to his work – and the revelation of the nature of his spiritual quest would open a Pandora's box among his Jewish critics. It transpired that Proust had been an initiate in a sect whose beliefs included the transmigration of souls, the redemption of which was dependent upon sacred sin.

Cousin Chaim died in the early 1930s. He left the letters he received from Marcel Proust and the journal he kept during the years of their friendship to Father. Father and I spent long hours poring over these extraordinary papers, discussing their contents and calculating the extent to which Proust scholarship would have to be modified by their disclosures were they to fall into academic hands. Neither of us at any time entertained the remotest desire of making public what we alone knew: Father had made an agreement with Cousin Chaim and it was his sacred duty to honour it. When Father died the letters and journal came to me, for my safe-keeping. In my will I left instruction for the package to be burnt, unopened.

I do not cleave to the view that there is anything magical at the heart of coincidence: chance plays its part but a greater part, I believe, is played by the individual psyche. We are, each one of us, predisposed to particular tastes and interests and more aware of what pertains to them than to things to which we are indifferent. We cannot see that for which we have not prepared ourselves. It is told that Captain Cook had no trouble invading and conquering a particular island in the South Seas because he arrived there in a large ship. The islanders, never having come into contact with a *large* ship, simply ignored its presence on the horizon. Had the good Captain and his men sailed in small boats the islanders would have picked out their craft at a great distance, armed themselves, slipped into their own canoes and, undoubtedly, spared themselves Western influence to this day. By the same token Father and I regarded it as unlikely that any scholar whose speciality was Proust would take the Hasidic route, particularly one intersected by paths of spectacularly irregular sexual behaviour.

The cultural distance between my own background and that of the students attending my French course at London University could not have been greater, and it was gratifying to me to discover it bridgeable by French literature. Most of my students were ex-servicemen who, for their terrible pains during the previous six years, had been rewarded by higher education. Those who chose to enrol at the University did so, on the whole, for the life London had to offer: theatres, clubs, dance-halls and so on. I found these hard-drinking, self-assured ex-bomber pilots, naval officers and artillery men intelligent and attractive, but a hopeless distraction for the handful of young students for whose moral welfare I was partly responsible. Among these young students was Henrietta Howard: innocent, beautiful and titled. I worried about the effect such cynical men would have on her. When they were not eyeing her lasciviously they were ribbing her unmercifully. But I need not have worried; Henrietta was characterized by a formidable determination to be her own person, to do as she chose irrespective of the attempts of others to influence her. She chose to play the débutante and to do just enough work to gain an indifferent degree.

Henrietta Howard was one of those highly intelligent young women for whom school is anathema, a waste of an otherwise glorious, unrepeatable, sun-soaked childhood. She had been raised with all the equipment to idle in a cultivated manner; her French mother loved nothing better than to see her daughter, prettily dressed and fragrantly scented, lounging on a *chaise longue* reading Flaubert to the strains of a Fauré *chanson*. Lady Howard could see no good reason for the law of her adopted land and the sway it held over her English husband, a law responsible for her daughter's incarceration in an all-girls' public school in the Shires, where the diet was as stodgy as the company. But when Lord Howard submitted to the plea of his wife and purchased a medieval château near Brou, together with one hundred acres of forest and field, a sea-change came over his wife and daughter, and the latter agreed to accept her incarceration graciously during term-time if she and her mother might spend every holiday at the château. Henrietta loved the place for its romantic architecture. It was a thirteenth-century *château fort*, girdled by a moat. And she loved the plain countryside it dominated. The Château de Philibert rose out of an ocean of grain, once the Romans' granary, with beech woodland to one side, providing the only cover for miles for game birds and fallow deer. And Henrietta discovered, quite by chance, that the nearby Friday market town, Illiers, was the model for Marcel Proust's Combray.

It was only when Henrietta came to discuss with me the feasibility of a Proustian subject for her MA thesis that she discovered the author was a particular interest of my own. And when she found that I knew every inch of Illiers and the surrounding countryside, she invited me to join her family and friends at the Château de Philibert for *reveillon* that year. Lord and Lady Howard were most gracious hosts; they responded enthusiastically when on the first of my many visits I introduced them and their guests to the Méséglise and the Guermantes Ways. And they were full of surprise and admiration for my having found a way of getting Henrietta to take exercise. She and I cycled to every church, village and natural site within a twenty-five mile radius of the Château that had inspired Proust's fictional locations.

Until that time Lord Howard had despaired of his only child ever applying herself seriously to anything more demanding than private views and charity balls. Faced with what amounted to an obsession with a French author his wife assured him was *sublime*, he did all in his very considerable power to ease the way for Henrietta to pursue her interest. He augmented her allowance to include a large sum for books; he effected introductions for her among local families with Proustian connections, and he arranged for the Château to be kept open all year round. Lord Howard's generosity to me was rooted in his conviction that without my inspiration and guidance Henrietta would never have glimpsed the ingredients of a worthwhile, creative existence. It was something he felt he had signally failed to point her towards and something his adored wife was unequipped to demonstrate by example.

And so it was all the more terrible when Henrietta died at the age of twenty-eight from a brain tumour. With her death Lord Howard's enthusiasm for life was extinguished; he became inert and silent. Lady Howard – a romantic woman – believed her husband was in the process of dying of a broken heart, and she produced medical evidence to support this view. The shock of Henrietta's death had upset the balance of his adrenalin; so much had flooded into his system that his body had revolted against its presence; subsequently it drained away altogether and he was starved of its efficacy. Lady Howard telephoned me at my office, some five months after Henrietta's death, and spoke at length about her husband's grief. She had noticed he showed a glimmer of the will to live when Henrietta's name was mentioned in connection with her intellectual awakening. This was a birth at which Lady Howard had not assisted, but at which she felt my own contribution qualified me for the title of midwife. I agreed to her suggestion that I call in on Lord Howard and take tea with him at their Kensington house.

Lady Howard received me and ushered me into the drawing-room where her husband was seated, motionless, without so much as a book to engage him, staring vacantly at the elaborate furnishings. He rose and shook my hand and I was made aware that it was physically difficult for him to stir. I was saddened to find this once gregarious man withdrawn into a shuttered, sick-room atmosphere; he was wearing bedroom slippers, as if to insure his noiseless steps would not be required to leave the safety and seclusion of his house. But in spite of his preoccupation, his habitual good manners did not desert him and he greeted me courteously. He spoke in a low, breathless voice, impressing upon me his appreciation for my having transformed the final years of his daughter's life. It had been, he said, a period in which he observed the enjoyable blend seamlessly with the purposeful. He urged me to make use of the Château as if it were my own; he himself could not bear to go there. He suggested I take along other Proustians, there being no suitable hotel in the neighbourhood of Illiers where scholars could stay in peace and tranquillity.

I made a point of visiting Lord Howard once a week. Out of these meetings there emerged the idea of the Proust Foundation as a memorial to his daughter. There would be a Proust Museum, and a Proust Library containing a comprehensive holding of English-language scholarship devoted to Proust. It would be a place to which scholars from all corners of the world would come, and the general public would visit to learn about the author's life. The aim was to create a wider reading public for his work.

Lord Howard mustered just enough adrenalin to finalize the arrangements for his Foundation. And then he died peacefully. He endowed the Foundation lavishly, in perpetuity. It was to rise out of his own house and garden. I was to be in charge of its design and its collections. I was to employ whomsoever deemed appropriate; and I was to run the Foundation until I wished to retire and then install a successor. My annual salary was set at three times that of a French professor, and increments were to be in proportion to those received by professors.

While the legal formalities were being completed I worked out my year's notice in the French Department. In 1955, at the age of forty-five, I embarked on my new life. I should perhaps emphasize that it was not Lord Howard's generous salary that lured me away from academic life. I left the university because I was out of sympathy with my colleagues. They were dry uncreative pedants; they had no passion for their subjects. I dreaded I might crumble to dust with them.

As Director of the Foundation I was also Curator of the Proust Museum. I had almost unlimited funds to make of it what I wished. I was keenly aware that whatever I decided to do the French scholars (who in France, did little for Proust) would find faults. I forecast that the Japanese would fuss over the *genius loci*: could it really be re-created in a garden in Kensington? and did not doubt that the Americans would demand more elaborately fitted 'bathrooms' than I was willing to install. And, of course, every national would be bound to question the usefulness of a library that did not contain copies of its scholars' works. I was prepared for this; I decided that I would not be able to please everyone and that all I had to keep in mind was to create what Lord Howard would have wished to see.

At this juncture I sensed a possible conflict between my two responsibilities: the one Lord Howard had entrusted to me, and the one to Cousin Chaim. The duty I owed to Lord Howard was to facilitate Proust scholarship in England; the duty I owed to Cousin Chaim and my family was to frustrate it by concealing information which, if revealed, would modify all assessments of Proust's psychology and his spiritual orientation. I recognized my position as potentially invidious, and as a way of shedding my unease I threw myself unsparingly into the pressing practical concerns the Foundation presented.

I found an architect familiar with the text of *A la recherche*, and he found a theatre designer with whom he felt he could work on interiors. It took three years to install a replica of Tante Léonie's house in the cavity left by gutting Lord Howard's Kensington mansion and a further two years to reproduce other of the rooms in which Proust had lived and worked. The Museum was so constructed that from a replica of Proust's real and actual environment dark corridors radiated, and in recesses on either side three-quarter life-size *tableaux vivants* of significant fictional rooms were constructed: the ante-room to the salon of the Princess de Guermantes, the Verdurins' drawing-room, some of Odette's rooms in the rue de la Pérouse, and Marcel's hotel bedrooms. The intention of the designer was to disorientate the visitor in the dark corridors and then confront him with not quite life-size rooms that he would recognize from the pages of a book, familiar yet not known, the demonstrably un-enterable – for who can literally enter the pages of a book?

The existence of a vast conservatory at one end of the house, built facing a path with a drop to a sunken garden, proved a boon to the architect, who artfully transformed the glazed construction into the dining-room of the Grand Hôtel, Balbec, and the path into the 'front'. By erecting a weatherproof backdrop behind the path the designer contrived the illusion of a beach, with the sea at low tide in an eternal Normandy summer. He scattered bicycles and golf clubs on the path and concealed recordings of screeching gulls and breaking waves. In those early days I found the effect quite stunning; the associations were so vivid that I myself fancied, when I sat down at one of the tables tricked out in starched damask, I could smell the promise of rich food in preparation in unseen kitchens.

A landscape gardener contrived the Guermantes Way and Swann's Way; the former was reached through an iron gate with a bell at the back of the house, the latter led from the front door. Both 'Ways' were reduced in length but contained every detail of the originals. We wanted visitors to spend at least three hours in the Museum – indoors and out – and to so absorb the Proustian milieu as to be transported into that world.

From the day it was officially opened the Museum attracted an interested public, and scholars flocked to our Library, preferring it greatly to the alternatives – such as the British Museum Reading Room and the London Library, where readers were subject either to noise and delay, or a membership fee. Members of the general reading public who had hurdled *Swann's Way* but not managed to take the second fence, *The Guermantes Way*, revelled in the reconstruction of Marcel's Combray and in the sight of the familiar objects that furnished it. To witness Golo riding towards the castle of Geneviève de Brabant on Marcel's bedroom walls, to see the shadow cast by the replica of Uncle Adolphe handing a child marchpane under a ceiling painted blue in imitation of the sky was to become an initiate in that closed world.

Our financial situation was such that we had no need to make the Museum and Library pay for themselves – and certainly no need of profit. Our aims were to extend Proust's readership and facilitate scholarship. To these ends we constructed a bookstall at the entrance to the Museum from Moriss columns, and from it we sold more volumes of Proust than any other bookshop in London. We bought up editions of scholarship that would otherwise have been remaindered or pulped. Literary journals that published articles relating to Proust's work printed extra copies and we had them bound to be sold as separate items. I commissioned a cartographer and illustrator to design maps of Proust's Balbec, Paris and Combray as they exist in the real and actual Cabourg, Trouville, Paris and Illiers, and these became popular as wall hangings. I also found an author with a particular gift for description to make a new translation of George Sand's *François le Champi*. It became essential reading in Proustian households. We combined with a record company to commission a recording of the music Proust told Jacques de Lacretelle was the source of the 'little phrase', and this sold in its thousands and was frequently requested on the radio. And in a heated greenhouse at the rear of the Pré Catalan we grew Cattleya orchids. They sold astonishingly well. It became a vogue for men and women to send them to one another to alert them of their passion.

The architect sited our picture gallery at the top of the house. Here we hung first-class reproductions of all the original paintings referred to by Proust in his work. And it was here for the first time that we established the link between the American marine painter, Alexander Harrison, and Proust's painter, Elstir.

The importance of scent to Proust involved us in reproducing a range of smells throughout the exhibition and, depending upon the season, we decked the rooms in appropriate flowers – lilacs, chrysanthemums, hawthorns and violets – and showed how each flower had become associated with a particular character. We bathed Combray and the Verdurins' salon in the music associated with each place, and once a month held a Proustian meal round a table in the Combray dining-room, served on plates decorated with scenes from *The Arabian Nights*. Every day we were open visitors were served *petites madeleines* and lime tea.

My life had become so dominated by the physical presence of the world of Proust that I often found myself in a state of confusion outside the Museum, unable to discharge the smallest obligation or contemplate

the smallest action without submitting them to a Proustian considera-
tion. In the real and actual world I felt constrained but in the world of
Proust I could move freely. This led me to feel confident that our visitors
would come under the same spell.

My task as Director of the Museum and Library had also included en-
gaging staff. They were hand-picked; agonized over. Our 'Françoise'
was the most difficult to find. She was required not only to see to the
baking and boxing of the *madeleines* we sold, but to prepare the monthly
dinners we held for the public and oversee the 'Proust dinners' we orga-
nized in the dining-rooms of interested 'Friends'. For by now we had
started a society, 'The Friends of the Proust Museum in London', and a
journal, *Proust Praxis*, in which we published notification of the scholarship being undertaken on our premises, occasional articles by members
of the Foundation staff and others, as well as less rarefied matters of more
social interest to our 'Friends'.

I might have avoided implication in the scandal had the editor of
Proust Praxis, Professor Jardine – a retired Oxford professor of French
who suffered the Museum and its accent on the actual, but who in his
work strove for matters not so much with being as with meaning – not
felt he owed it to me to ask me to contribute to the journal. He specified
he would like my contribution to concern itself with Proust's spiritual
orientation. I told him immediately that I had nothing to add to the
work being done by Dr Blumenthal. What I did not tell him was that
Dr B. was careering off-course, following an altogether false scent in the
direction of Christianity. In order to placate Professor Jardine I offered
him a choice of two other subjects. I could make an informed stab at the
reason why Proust had chosen the name Swann for his 'hero'; it was certainly not, as one biographer held, simply because Proust had seen the
name on a pharmacy in Paris.... Or, if Professor Jardine preferred, I
had a tentative suggestion to make regarding the so-called 'enigmatic
Proustian metaphor', the one concerning the vertebrae on Tante Léonie's
forehead. Professor Jardine was not enthusiastic about either topic. And
so I offered him a third: the reason why Proust had chosen the orris root
and wild currant to invade the *petit cabinet* and associate with Marcel's solitary gratification. Professor Jardine preferred this, and I wrote up the
data.

Proceeding from a lesson learnt from the evidence of his nose, Proust
had stumbled on a scientific fact and subsequently made good use of it.
The smell the boy Marcel created reminded him of orris root and currant, and they of semen and urine, because trimethylamine, which occurs
both in orris root and flowering currant, is present also in semen and urine, together with its characteristic smell. Chemistry, along with every

other subject, could yield reciprocal imagery. It was a nice example of the way in which the creative, rather than the academic, mind works: through the sensual to the cerebral. This was something my former colleagues would never have allowed; it says quite a lot for Professor Jardine that he was enthusiastic about the piece. He published my finding in *Proust Praxis* and was genuinely delighted that I had succeeded in demonstrating Proust's excursion into the scientific world – a subject hitherto neglected by Proust scholarship. It was my misfortune, however, that his enthusiasm led him to pursue his original request with renewed vigour. He was temperamentally more drawn to matters related to the soul than the body; he felt more comfortable in the place of worship than in the place of bodily evacuation.

'Dr Saul-Dubrovsky! Do tell me, where in the religion you share with our illustrious author is there credence given to the idea of transmigration of souls?'

'There is none – in Orthodox Judaism!' I reassured Professor Jardine, adding that Proust had been no more concerned with Jewish belief and liturgy than I.

'His religious affiliation was a burden to him in an anti-Semitic country, a burden to be borne with fortitude because Judaism was the religion of his adored mother. When Proust threw a handful of stones on the grave of his maternal grandmother he made the gesture for his mother. She would have been deeply shocked had she lived to read his single paragraph on metempsychosis. . . .'

'And yet I find its traces throughout his work! Transformed, of course. I suggest we see its trail in the changes – the successive egos – a being acquires in different places and times, up and down the moral scale, up and down the social ladder . . . I suggest there is more influence of metempsychosis in all this than our author was willing to spell out!'

I saw where this conversation was leading us: into a cul-de-sac in which I had no wish to be trapped. The transmigration of the soul had no place in Orthodox Judaism, that was true, but it was central to the belief of the Cabbalists. Perhaps Professor Jardine had noted the hints of Zionism in Proust's work and subconsciously transformed the image of the ingathering of bodies into one of souls? The Professor was disturbed; whilst he did not expect an author of creative literature to propound his beliefs in a doctrinal way, he was vaguely (and justifiably) conscious that Proust continually expressed intellectual views through imagery. As an academic the Professor was programmed to trace beliefs to their source, and in so doing I could see he was poised to desert the tarmac of conventional wisdom for the ley lines of speculation.

About this time, I and my assistants in the Museum and Library, and

Jardine and his small staff in the *Proust Praxis* office, realized that preparations for the centenary year, 1971, would need to be set in motion. It
was three years hence, but there was a great deal to consider and co-
ordinate. There would be the many internal events on our own premises:
concerts, exhibitions, and a special commemorative issue of *Proust Praxis*.
And there would be the external events to which we would be invited
to contribute, or advise upon. Since we would wish to keep a measure of
control over external programmes it was suggested that I make the job
of liaison my particular responsibility.

We closed our premises to the public for a month in November
1968 in order to be free to plan our centenary year programme. It
emerged that the Library staff, and the staff on *Proust Praxis*, were
anxious that our role in scholarship should take precedence over our
promotional function. Remembering the wishes of Lord Howard, I
gave this matter serious thought and eventually found myself able to
agree to this new emphasis because, and only because, for some time
it had become evident that no matter what efforts we made we were
not going to be able to create more than a small, if faithful, readership among the general public. The number had reached a plateau
five years after we opened. This is not a circumstance unique to our
world: 'In New York City, in the year 1955, there were, on the average 75.3 reports per day to the Department of Health of (dogs) biting
people. In 1956, the corresponding number was 73.6. In 1957 it was
73.2. In 1958 and 1959 the figures were 74.5 and 72.6.' And if this
comparison seems odious or far-fetched, you must bear in mind that
there are as many efforts made in New York to dissuade dogs from biting people as there are efforts in London to persuade the public to read
books.

If my memory serves me well, it was June 1970 when I received a telephone call from a Miss Auriol Anders, who was working on a television
arts programme and had been assigned to three programmes on Proust
subjects to be screened during the centenary year. She suggested we
might meet to discuss her ideas; she did not want to duplicate any we
might be considering. Ideally, she thought, the programmes she made
should complement our own.

'I shall want to do programmes to which the serious but not necessa-
rily committed viewer can relate. I think, on the whole, I ought to con-
fine myself to people and places, rather than abstractions. But I know
my boss [and at this point she named a distinguished critic of French Literature, who was to edit the series] will want to do something a bit cerebral for one of the three films – if only for his reputation.'

It transpired that Auriol Anders knew our Museum well but had never eaten in our Combray. She was entranced by an invitation to attend the Combray Saturday luncheon.

'Would you be able to arrive an hour earlier than is customary for luncheon?' I requested. She laughed heartily.

'Of course! I know Françoise will need that extra hour if she is to get to the market at Roussainville-le-Pin!'

'I am so glad you have not revealed yourself a "barbarian"!' I parried, and when I put down the receiver I immediately called Françoise on the internal telephone and asked her if she agreed that 'a nice piece of veal' would be appropriate with the endives. . . .

The BBC decided to devote one of their three films to a subject that could be located on our premises. I was delighted we were to receive this publicity and I worked happily on the project with Auriol Anders. She is a charming person and has a sincere, if amateurish, interest in Proust. Professor Jardine was somewhat impatient with her unscholarly approach, but I pointed out to him, rather firmly, looking back, that the most important thing for our purposes was to encourage visitors to the Museum. The more scholarly part of our work could not be expected to be advanced through the medium of a television programme. Of the two other films the BBC proposed making, one was to be devoted to English cultural influences on Proust's work, and the other to people, still living, who had known him. Auriol intended to gather a very small group of ancients round our Combray dining-table, and film them in unscripted conversation.

I would be involved in more libel cases than I can afford were I to confide in you the names of some of the individuals Auriol unearthed who purported to have known Marcel Proust. Their disclosures would have made front-page headlines. Many of them are well known in fashionable circles, others are members of the lesser nobility; still others were wholly unsavoury. They reminded me of derelict ruins kept standing by the ivy that clings to them. Not only were they all title and no substance, their sole claim to fame in the present was to have curtsied to a Romanian monarch, or overheard a *bon mot* from Proust or Gide in a Turkish bath. They tended to a pattern: the women overflowed their clothes, particularly their décolletages; the men were wraiths, mere adjuncts of their garnished canes and ear-trumpets. It is unlikely that the general public would have spotted the ironies; it was, after all, such company Proust had had to discard in order to write. They might well have come away from the experience of these anachronisms reinforced in their conditioning that Proust was a snob who, throughout his life, enjoyed such company. The women brought along the Fortuny gowns they had worn when young. They caressed them lovingly while they talked, but it was impossible to imagine that these exquisite tubular silks had once covered lithe forms. There was nothing left of these people's elegance; their appearances in old age owed more to the animal than the human kingdom. The women had become bovine, the men hawklike. In voice and gesture they appeared to have fulfilled a Proustian forecast and exchanged sexes.

Auriol was in despair. She placed advertisements in the personal columns of *The Times* asking anyone who had known Marcel Proust to contact her. She received a dozen replies. Of those applicants we interviewed Auriol Anders found only two convincing: the Comte de Y and the Princesse de X. Could I suggest someone else? Not for the first time I explained that Céleste did not speak English, nor did Proust's very frail surviving niece. And the lively, eccentric M. Larcher of Illiers-Combray had never actually met Proust; even though as a child Proust had played in his garden in Illiers, it was with M. Larcher's brother the young Proust had been friends. . . .

It was three months after this exchange I received an excited telephone call from Auriol. She was in Oxford:

'I have had the most wonderful stroke of luck!' she announced. 'I must come and see you tomorrow and discuss it all but in the meantime: does the name Lev Bar-Lev ring any bells? Saul-Dubrovsky certainly does for him. Mr Bar-Lev's about eighty, quite brilliant, eccentric, central European. He lives half-way up a Welsh mountain but is perfectly willing to descend. . . . Well, perfectly persuadable, I should say, to make an appearance on television. He wants to make money, terribly badly! If you saw him you would understand how unlikely that appears. I'll tell you all when I see you.' And she did.

Auriol Anders described to me the channels through which she had passed to find Mr Bar-Lev and how, over a period of days, he had unfolded his life story to her, including his relationship with Marcel Proust. That relationship, pursued rather independently of others, had included one Chaim Saul-Dubrovsky. . . . So this was the Bar-Lev whose intellectual curiosity Cousin Chaim celebrated so generously in his journal! It had never occurred to me that he might be alive and well – let alone living half-way up a Welsh mountain. I had taken it for granted when I read the journal that he – like the majority of French Jews and central European Jews who fled to France – had perished in World War II.

Having agreed to sum up the programme on Proust's extant social contacts before Auriol discovered Mr Bar-Lev, I did not feel justified in refusing to do so because she had found him and succeeded in unleashing information that had been bottled up in him for so long. Before I met the three – the Princesse, the Comte and Mr Bar-Lev – I had agreed to the film being made in the Combray dining-room but as soon as I saw them together, in Auriol's office in Lime Grove, I realized it would be both more appropriate and more dramatic to seat them in the dining-room of the Grand Hôtel, Balbec, facing the 'front', set off by salt-white starched damask and the strains of Fauré's Violin Sonata. Immediately I entered her office Auriol said: 'Here is Dr Saul-Dubrovsky! Welcome!' Mr Bar-Lev rose untidily from his chair, risking to topple it and a vase of flowers on Auriol's desk, and greeted me with unusual warmth.

'Ah! Yes!' he intoned as he took both my hands in one of his and looked deep into my eyes, as if he had discovered a new species of insect life within a flower, or a new constellation. 'The Saul-Dubrovsky eyes! They couldn't belong to any other! Topaz speckled emeralds! They were especially designed for members of your family!' I motioned him to sit down again.

'Did you know Chaim?'

'Only at second-hand,' I replied.

'He was a remarkable man. In his way he was as remarkable as Marcel. He and Marcel were deeply in love.' And as he made this simple statement of the truth it occurred to me that a benefit of being over eighty is that a man may say anything then, if he says it with sincerity and it is true.

The Princesse de X and the Comte de Y were not so much examples of extreme old age as examples of a final stage of existence reserved for those who have overrun the allowance of three score and ten. They had outlived their respective families and were confined, like pet animals in kennels, in an old people's home, south of Dorking. Auriol had gone down in a BBC chauffeur-driven car to collect them and had had difficulty finding the Home, hidden as it was from road by a thick laurel hedge, its wrought iron gates guarded by monkey puzzle trees; it did not exude anything remotely Proustian. And it quickly became evident that the ancients did not normally converse; it seemed as if they did not know, as a permanent part of their daily thinking, that they were linked by Proustian associations.

The presence of Mr Bar-Lev in such company was as inappropriate and astonishing as a bout of croup at a lieder recital. It was not that his shabby clothes stood out; the Comte de Y wore a dinner jacket green with age, and the Princess de X was festooned in paste, having long since pawned her gems. But they bore themselves differently, with an assurance that tomorrow an invitation would arrive to supper at *Le Jockey* with the Prince of Wales. The world that clung to their bearing was Ruritanian, one of applied elegance, romantic love, melodrama and un-questioned ease and privilege. They spoke as if they had enjoyed a single good night's rest since their last engagement on the Boulevard St Germain – not some sixty years of uncomfortable exile. Their memories of sixty years past were vivid for being so utterly to their taste; and they jostled for position in the pecking order that had been disposed of by World War I – together with their titles and their wealth. Mr Bar-Lev, on the other hand, was keenly aware that the world the Comte and the Princesse created for themselves was as unreal as that of Golo and Geneviève de Brabant. He was glad that that was so. Nevertheless, he treated these, his contemporaries, with old-world courtesy. It was his nature so to do.

I do not have to rehearse here the revelations that emerged from the conversation to which Mr Bar-Lev contributed so enthusiastically, but I feel I should point out that the Comte and the Princesse took pleasurable interest in the more scurrilous details Mr Bar-Lev exposed. Their reactions confirmed my long-held conviction that it would not be Proust's beliefs but his practices that would engage the public's imagination. Nor can I criticize Auriol Anders; it is understandable that she should take pride in being the agent who revealed to the world hitherto undisclosed secrets. All that is history. But I do feel I owe it to you, my successor, and to myself for the future of my reputation, to explain why it is I have felt obliged to resign my position as Director of the Foundation. Even if Professor Jardine had been less cordial, if he had been blind to the invidiousness of the position in which I had placed myself, I would have resigned.

The Comte and the Princesse were excited and overextended by the rehearsal of their memories; but they refused all BBC sustenance with the exception of weak tea without milk. The Comte would replace his monocle in his waistcoat pocket when he had finished reading something Auriol or I handed him to jog his memory, and then, for the next five minutes, would hunt for it in every pocket of his jacket and coat. The Princesse knotted and unknotted a piece of old lace, whose purpose, apart from its function as a worry bead, was difficult to fathom. I imagined it might once have done duty as her cuff, or as camouflage for a mole at her neck, when moles once fashionable were deemed unfashionable.

'Le petit Marcel was so generous!' the Comte remembered.

'Generous!' the Princesse hissed. '*Avare comme un juif!*'

The Comte ignored her. 'He would offer the waiter at the Ritz the equivalent of a week's wages just to provide him with iced beer after midnight!'

'Well,' the Princesse allowed, 'he was *terribly* rich!'

'He was not! That is not true! He was *terribly* generous!' The Comte pronounced his 'terribly' just as the Princesse had hers. The rivalry between the octogenarians, whose titles had been won generations ago in less conversational battles, was amusing, but I wondered whether Auriol had misgivings about how she would control them in front of the cameras. Mr Bar-Lev appeared unaware of the sparring. He kept up an intermittent low mumbling in a *macedoine* of languages, deep in thoughts of his own. Then, suddenly, marvelling at my existence, he broke into loud English:

'It is so wonderful to discover a link between those days and these!' And he thrust out his massive hands in an effort to clasp my own.

The Comte indulged in a sort of exaggerated humility designed to give the impression that although he had not been close to Proust, he had been instrumental in getting Proust's work both published and appreciated. Any attempt at deft self-deprecation would have been beyond him. The Princesse insisted she was an intimate of 'le petit Marcel'. She recounted how she had been woken by Proust's valet one winter's morning at 2 a.m. It was in the year 1921. The man had been sent to ask her the colour and design of a hat she had been wearing in the Parc Monceau, on her birthday, in 1913. Proust wanted the details for his book, in which she was portrayed. The Comte interrupted; he recalled a dinner Proust gave in a private room at the Ritz. Some half hour after his guests assembled Proust himself entered with his arm on that of a *clochard*. Proust had observed the man foraging in some garbage in the Place Vendôme and had entered into conversation with him. He had not noticed the passing of time as he enquired of the man how he survived. He settled the evil-smelling *clochard* between the Comte and one of the Bibesco brothers – the Comte could not now remember which of the two brothers it had been.... The tramp was horribly the worse for absinthe but, as 'le petit Marcel' had so characteristically pointed out, if the influence of drink was horribly present in the vagrant, that of food was horribly absent....

Mr Bar-Lev sat through these reminiscences without listening to them. His memories of Proust were of another dimension. They might well have been of another person. When Auriol turned to him and asked: 'When you dined with Proust, did he eat?' – for the Princesse and the Comte agreed that Proust rarely partook of the lavish refreshments he offered his guests – Mr Bar-Lev replied, 'We did not precisely dine together. In the places of amusement we frequented – all male, of course – we picked from trays of aphrodisiacs: lark's tongues in chocolate sauce, hashish fudge and peppered oysters. And yes: Marcel partook...' Mr Bar-Lev's memories seeped from him, as if from the world of dream.

After two hours of preparation, BBC sandwiches refused and weak tea consumed, Auriol arranged for the three participants, herself and her assistant, and me to be driven back to the Foundation. The camera crew and sound technicians had set up their equipment in the dining-room of the Grand Hôtel in the morning, watched over by my dear assistant, Elise, who had been in a state of anxious apprehension all the while. She was convinced that irreparable damage would be done to the set.

The Princesse and the Comte settled round the table most convincingly; they shook out the damask napkins and remarked on the view. I waited for the Comte to click his fingers for the wine waiter. . . . The two old aristocrats talked, quite naturally and fluently about the Hôtel. They remembered it well. They remembered how 'le petit Marcel' spent his summers in Cabourg and Trouville among the *beau monde*. Auriol kept the cameras rolling; she knew it would be easier to edit out material than to stop and start the conversation and at the same time keep it sounding natural. She signed to Mr Bar-Lev who, emerging from a trance, started to describe the places he visited with Proust; they had been in Paris and although members of the *beau monde* were always in attendance they were always in disguise. At first his descriptions of the male brothels of Paris were innocuous enough; the 'swinging sixties' had prepared us all for greater tolerance in these matters. But as he warmed to his memories he described scenes of such depravity that even the camera crew were shocked. The Comte and the Princesse, on the other hand, listened entranced: fairy stories like these were easily assimilable among those for whom the actual world was presently unbelievable. What made the monologue so singular for me and for Auriol was the mismatch between the tales of lurid vice, attached, as they were, to the passions of Proust's heart, and the voice in which the ever innocent Mr Bar-Lev recounted the tales, honeyed with tenderness and longing.

'Ah! Le petit Marcel . . . how keenly he sought the truth! It was his religion.' And with tears coursing down his cheeks and the threat of a sob ready to block his voice, Mr Bar-Lev struggled to describe the depths to which 'le petit Marcel' had been prepared to descend in furtherance of that quest.

'Before the death of *Maman*, in 1905, when he was thirty-four, Proust had become beset with concern for the fate of the human soul after the body's demise; and when his mother died he entered fully into the practices of a mystical sect whose purpose was to facilitate the ingathering of the soul and its ultimate return to the Godhead. You see, he loved his mother so completely, so passionately and so exclusively, that this was the only service he felt was left for him to perform for her.

'Following her death he had to struggle to go on living. Memories of *Maman* stopped him working by day and sleeping by night. We advised him to enter a clinic for neurasthenics on the Ile de Seine, presided over by a physician celebrated for having perfected a technique for memory suppression. It was Proust's aim to train his memory to exclude *Maman* permanently from his thoughts; if he must continue to live – and, however tempting, he rejected suicide as an option – he could only do so dogged by a sense of loss, not by a sense of loss coupled to the memory of what it was he had lost. The physician had some success in teaching Proust his amnesiac technique, but it was not foolproof. I was present on occasions when Proust's whole body would shudder spontaneously, as if stretched on the rack, his eyes would turn up and their lids close down, and he would let out a scream of such penetrating anguish that it pierced my skull and filled me with the knowledge of the whole of human suffering.

'Proust became obsessed with one mission: to assist the process of redemption of the soul of his beloved and uniquely good *Maman*, trapped as it was with all others, unable to complete its journey to the Godhead without a mate. He had only his vices to offer his mother's soul, the very vices he had striven to conceal from her during her lifetime, when he appeared to adhere to the Catholicism of his father, and pretend love for women.'

Auriol Anders resisted the temptation to take a heavy hand in editing the hour-long film. She asked me whether I had known about Proust's descent to the depths of depravity. I told her I had. It was common knowledge. She asked me whether I had known the quest to which his behaviour was attached. I told her I had – but that it was not common knowledge.

'It is an extraordinary coincidence that Mr Bar-Lev should have been involved with a relative of yours,' she remarked. I refrained from expressing my fear that this involvement was going to have far-reaching consequences for me.

I thought it wisest to pre-empt Professor Jardine's approaching me. I rang him at once and made an appointment to see him. I told him my family saga. I told him that Mr Bar-Lev's testimony was on tape and celluloid and that it was an accurate representation of the subject. Professor Jardine was so overjoyed that his tentative steps along the ley lines of speculation had led to the destination he forecast that, whilst showing recognition of and displeasure towards my suppression of the facts, he did not dwell on it. And I made it easy for him by offering, in one and the same breath, my resignation, and the suggestion that he provide an introduction to Cousin Chaim's journal (and the letters between Cousin Chaim and Proust), which I myself would now feel free to prepare for publication.

As a result of our talk Professor Jardine arranged with the BBC for

Mr Bar-Lev to be given a twenty-minute interval slot on the Third Programme in which to elaborate on his reminiscences. In the light of Mr
Bar-Lev's death soon after the showing of the film, Professor Jardine's
initiative proved to have been invaluable, for it resulted in the first coher-
ent explanation of Proust's adherence to the doctrine of sacred sin and
its redemptive purpose. It was to provide the cornerstone in refuting his
biographers' claims that his peculiar behaviour in the male brothels of
Paris had been pursued uniquely for his sexual gratification, making of
him something of a brute.

I shall not quote the full text of Mr Bar-Lev's talk. The full text will
appear in *Proust Praxis*, in the 1972 Autumn issue. But I think you should
have before you his introductory remarks.

'It appealed to Marcel Proust's sense of the ridiculous to share with
certain Jewish mystics the belief that God had been apprehensive at the
Creation, and his apprehension had made him nervous and that this had
led his hands to shake, thereby breaking the vessels in which he was to
manifest himself and letting fall into the realm of the impure world some
of the divine sparks of holiness and good that were himself. It appealed
to Marcel Proust's sense of order and morality that he should offer himself to assist in the reclamation of these sparks and their return to their
source, so that the process of redemption might be made complete. And
if this involved a descent through the gates of impurity to grovel and
grope in the filth of the abyss, so be it! He was to write: "It is only people
who lead really vicious lives who can be tormented by moral
problems."

'To be tormented by moral problems was the condition Proust chose
for the final years of his life. We see from his work that in his younger
years he appeared to accept the conventions of society and in his more
mature years to recreate what he had gone through in the light of experience. But we know that Proust's experience taught him that the actual
world is one of seeming only, that it is not immortal – and that it is de-
formed. His seeming depravity was no more what it appeared than was
his previous apparent adherence to the conventions of society.

'Following the death of his beloved mother Proust allowed his friend,
Chaim Saul-Dubrovsky, to introduce him into a small group of men interested in sacred sin and its redemptive purpose. He was not unduly surprised to discover that among us we claimed that for generations the
Jews had been worshipping the wrong deity – a powerless divinity with
nothing to do with the world, whose purpose was, as Prime Cause,
merely to set all in motion and then retire and provide material for ra-
tional philosophy. This explanation, Proust saw, given the history of the
Jews, accounted for much, including the wrong-minded social and

moral fabric that had woven his own straight-jacket. It accounted for the twin curses laid upon him: being a Jew and a homosexual. And he regarded it as a nice point that these burdens were to lead to his mystical understanding, and prove themselves blessings, for, as he was to write: "In misfortune we become moral". He was to show, at some length, that "the character we manifest in the second part of our life is not always ... our original character developed or dried up, adumbrated or attenuated; frequently it is the very reverse, like a costume turned inside out."

'The image of the costume turned inside out parallels images in our sect, whose followers turned inside out their adherence to the Torah, or Law. Whilst *seeming* to observe it we defiled it; for, in the practice of sacred sin, one must always appear other than one is, and rest utterly silent on spiritual matters.

'It is well known that in his dealings with individuals Proust was unfailingly generous, compassionate, imaginative and loving; there is no evidence of his having behaved towards another with anything but courtesy and understanding. It is this that made his acts of apparent moral nihilism – unknown to all but a handful of us – so convincing; he had sought within himself the spark of divine light and since he had not found it among "society" he sought it in the underworld, amongst other exiles. He laid a trail of eccentric but acceptable social behaviour to distract public attention. As a mystic, however, he passed unnoticed. In his insistence that things are never as they seem to be he was paraphrasing "whosoever is as he appears to be cannot be a true believer", meaning, to the mystic, that the true faith must always be concealed, that even a true act may not be committed publicly for, since all is manifestly false, the true act observed cannot be true.

'And so it was that Proust joined with Chaim Saul-Dubrovsky and me in an exploration of the depraved and the immoral. The intention was to so fill the maw of the abyss with vice that it would burst and thus release the sparks of divinity to join with the Godhead. My own presence in this group was owed to reasons rather different from those that had brought Proust into our midst. I was embarking on my lifelong quest to discover what had attracted my father to such practices, and by taking an active part in the ritual I hoped to achieve this. Proust regarded these sessions not only as his filial duty but also as being part of the process of his spiritual and psychological responsibility; in the performance of his acts of depravity he believed he would be helping the re-forming of the divine, and restoring his own psychological wholeness.'

This brings me back to the beginning of this letter to you, to the question: what more can there be to write about a man who died at the age of fifty-two, whose output was just two, albeit monumental, fictional autobiographies, a few articles and short stories and prefaces to the books of others? With the publication of Mr Bar-Lev's article next year in *Proust Praxis*, the answer is: an incalculable amount. The whole of Proust scholarship will be reassessed and his work re-examined now that his connection with Jewish mysticism is firmly established.

Every reader of *A la recherche* reads that the homosexual Jew belongs to a twice-cursed race. Until Mr Bar-Lev's revelations it had been a matter of contention whether Marcel Proust and the narrator of *A la recherche* were one and the same. With the publication of Cousin Chaim's journal and the letters, corroborated by Mr Bar-Lev's testimony, which includes his eye-witness descriptions of Proust defiling images of *Maman* in the male brothels of Paris, making of his 'beloved . . . the disease and remedy that suspends and aggravates the disease', we know Proust chose the homeopathic way and took, in essence, the cause of the curse to redeem it: the unorthodox Judaism of certain seventeenth-century mystics, for whom sexual licence and the defamation of all that is beloved was the rule.

'Death could drop from the dark
as easily as song'

I had been walking two thousand miles before I entered the silent valley. There had been no warning. Indeed, I had only recently passed through an area of exceptional fertility and noisy, happy villages and was shocked to find myself suddenly in dry, cropless land overseen by hills bereft of tinkling goat bells and sweet bird-song.

The village was steeped in silence. The doors and windows of the little houses slumped on dusty paths were tight shut. No swearing exploded from the tavern, no smoke from mens' pipes rose in curls. Just one or two guard dogs raised their heads and moaned as I passed. As is my custom, I proceeded at once to the market square and sang out my song of arrival. No answer of welcome was forthcoming. None the less, I embarked on my repertoire – songs of wondrous cities, immaculate love and deeds of heroism. I was in no hurry. Travelling and singing are my occupations.

When blue dusk descended, I unfolded my bed roll by the side of the pump. I managed to raise half a cup of water to quench my thirst before lying down to sleep. Just as my eyelids grew heavy, I heard light steps approaching, disturbing the gritty ground.

'Minstrel! Minstrel!' a voice begged, 'Don't stop your singing. We in this village have been waiting an eternity to hear songs sung again!'

I could make out the outline of a man. At once he told me how long ago the village minstrel had been struck dumb and how since then all else had dried up and closed down. He beseeched me to make for the edge of the village and seek out the last house, there to sing my songs.

'Only one songster can muster the power to rekindle songs in another,' he said.

I waited until sunrise and did as I had been asked.

The last house was hidden behind a high wall. I would have to sing lustily if my voice was to be heard within. On the third day, I noticed that the gate in the wall had been left ajar. I approached. Hesitatingly, I pushed open the gate fully to allow myself to pass with my pack and walked up the path and through the half-open door to the house.

Dusk is short-lived in this part of the world. My eyes were slow to accustom themselves to nightfall, to make out what furnished the room: a sackcloth bed, an unlit stove and a stopped clock. Under the broken window pane, by the light of a cautious moon, a shattered crow lay rotting. Under my feet crumbled the little bones of dead mice. The house reeked of mortality. No better than a sty, I thought. As I reflected on the scene I noticed a form stir in the corner, a form draped in black, its face shrouded. I extended my hand but it was not grasped.

I started *sotto voce* with a greeting. I emphasized my pleasure at being where I was, in the presence of a songster. I watched as the veil slipped slowly to expose eyes foaming with grief. I did not stop my singing but continued with a song of reassurance. Useless to enquire how many different songs it took before the woman laid bare her heart to me.

She had been born in the village, daughter of the minstrel. On the death of her father it was she who was called upon to murmur over the new-born, hum to the children and accompany the women at their quilt-making. It was to her the village turned to chant the incantations at marriages, celebrate the pastoral festivities and intone the lessons at death. Hers was the voice in the life of all creation. That was until. . . .

On waking one morning she discovered her tongue folded down its length, fastened with a coarse hair to her back teeth. She took scissors to cut off the hair but as she slid one pointed blade under the strand and brought the other down on to it, the scissors failed to remove the hair – they merely bent it. Moving her face to within inches of a shard of mirror, she saw that if she were to insert her fingers, get them to the back of her mouth, she might be able to unwind the hair from her teeth. In this she was successful and with her tongue loosed a little was able to murmur her relief. With her problem half-solved, she resolved to find a knife to cut off the hair. In the meantime, being a practical soul, she would coil it round and round, as a sailor coils his ropes, and store it under her tongue for she had the hens to feed and the bread to bake.

So accustomed was she to the hair that lay coiled under her tongue, she forgot its existence for days on end. On the one occasion the tip of her tongue found it out, she consoled herself with the thought that her peculiarity must be unique and secret in the midst of a village that was transparent, and villagers cast in the same mould.

The woman had only been wed a year. She was expecting her husband down from the hills with the other men who had driven their flocks to the summer grazing high on the lush mountain slopes. In anticipation of her beloved's return, she swept and cleaned and prepared each of his favourite delicacies: aubergine jam for the goat stew, kumquat schnapps for the curd tarts and a wheat gruel soured with beer for his breakfast.

Her husband was one of the first of the men to gain sight of his house. He was astonished to hear no song of greeting on the air. He started to call out: 'Wife! Wife! I'm on my way!' He burst through the open door inflamed with desire, and gathering his wife into his embrace he carried her up the stairs to bed. So ardent was he – and so much in need of his wife after eight weeks in the hills – he might have been forgiven for a certain hastiness in his approach. But he took his time. He kissed her hands and arms, her bare neck and her sunburnt cheeks and only then pressed his lips to hers. He pressed and pressed, as if on a closed door. How he wished she would welcome his tongue, but she kept her lips tightly sealed. Raising his head from where it lay against hers, he implored 'May I not kiss my wife as a husband should?' 'If you do,' she answered with a laugh in her voice, 'I'll bite it off.' Having been away for eight weeks and having lost touch with his bride's little ways, the husband imagined she must be playing a game the rules of which slipped his mind.

The husband busied himself with the other men making preparations for the winter, fodder for the animals and vegetables for themselves. When he got home at dusk he ate heartily and fell into a deep slumber in the arms of his undemanding wife. But as winter deepened and his work lightened, he felt his sap rise urgently. His wife's coldness was unbearable to him.

She was not nun-hearted but she did not dare allow him an approach which would reveal her secret. And her condition was worsening. Waking one morning she had felt her tongue was oddly rough. Passing it over her upper lip surreptitiously, so that her husband would not notice, she realized that the whole surface had seeded a coating of bristles, like those at the heart of an artichoke.

'Wife!' her husband begged, 'come to me, let me kiss you as a husband should.'

'I'd sooner have this tongue cut from my mouth!' she replied. And so saying, jumped out of bed down into the kitchen where she got busy with the pigs' swill.

The husband had had enough. Driving his flock of goats before him, he left his wife, his house and the village.

It was with her husband's departure that the songster no longer felt moved to sing.

The bristles on her tongue grew thick and long. She drew the rusty old blade her husband had used for his weekly shave across the stubble. The hairs resisted the blade as they had the scissors and knives but made her tongue weep and her mouth sour with blood. She lit a match and tried to burn off the hair but it would not ignite. She took a piece of wire, hammered it flat and bent it into tweezers and tried laboriously to pluck out the hairs one by one. But they were fast-rooted, divided beneath the surface into tiny tentacles honeycombed within her flesh.

The villagers became suspicious: husbands did not forsake their wives in these parts. They might have felt some sympathy for the young bride had she confided in them, offered an explanation. But when asked a question she answered unintelligibly, with her hand in front of her mouth. And worst of all, she no longer sang.

When the bristles lengthened into hair twelve inches long, she packed the strands into the side of her face. If she were to store them on one side only perhaps the villagers would think she had tooth ache. Then when the strands became too thick for one side, she would divide them between right and left. The villagers would think she had mumps and keep their distance.

Increasingly, she withdrew from the village and its people. She no longer tarried in the market place or attended church. She avoided the tavern. And showing herself unwilling to engage in conversation she found herself shunned. Not only was she unfriendly, she was unnatural, for hadn't her husband left her? And wasn't a songster's job for life? Only the children would not leave her be. They ran after her, taunted her and, as her rage mounted, shouted after her 'Keep your hair on witch!' All she could do was raise her broom and sweep them away.

She was finding it messy to eat, even dangerous. Bristles had started to push through the roof of her mouth so that the whole cavity became stuffed with ordure. The matted hair entangled itself in her food and she gagged on the strands she swallowed with her bread.

She caught cold. Unable to breathe through her nose, she took in air through her mouth. But the air could not penetrate the fibrous sieve and she was left gasping. She could think of nothing but her horrible state of being. Time might be passing but her single thought did not. She stopped washing herself, stopped cleaning the house and all but stopped eating. She let her hens and pigs go hungry and the vegetable path become overgrown. Every few minutes she consulted the shard of mirror she kept in her apron pocket, peering into it to see whether the bristles and hair had grown in length and gathered in quantity. Her mouth was so full – 'All ashes to the taste' – she feared her face would burst.

She had another idea: she would draw as much of the hair as she could to one side of her mouth, plait it and let the plait fall from the corner of her lip on to her shoulder. Were anyone to catch sight of her from a distance with her shawl thrown over her head, it would appear that the source of the plait was the hair on her head. But she had not bargained for the children. An ugly witch casting spells that dried the cows' udders, stopped the hens from laying, drove the goats out of the village and made the adults so touchy, needed sorting out. They chased her, lobbed stones at her and stuck out their tongues in contempt of her. She would have liked to give them a lick of the rough side of her tongue, but all she could do was bite it.

She felt degraded and at peril. It was true: the babies *were* dying, the crops *were* failing and the animals were not yielding their produce. She knew the village was feeling unblessed and sensed it had to do with her. What good was a silent songster?

Renounced, she must conceal herself. And so she built a high wall round the house and vegetable patch.

Living out her days of shame in her musty crypt, the echo of her heart continuously rekindled the past, making the present unendurable. The sacred memory of her husband's body throbbed in the void he had bequeathed her. Her hideous deformity consumed her. Her whole head was submerged in hair, her face no longer discernible in the shard of mirror. She was nothing but grief personified. Her outpouring that started as a trickle became an uncontrollable torrent.

The end came in my presence when pain finally released itself in exhaustion. Her garments of concealment loosed themselves and like a snake writhing to shed its skin, she shed them. I watched transfixed as she rose naked from her corner and tantalizingly wound the plait round and round her neck in a gesture both deadly and lively.

A beam of dawn light seized her in its rosy grip and turned her mask of matted hair to dust that settled like the ash from a spent fire to reveal her extraordinary beauty. I felt a sense of impending deliverance – and it came: the plait rotted where it was tied, crumbled to dust and from its imprisoning strands some living thing struggled to emerge. I waited and watched and saw a glorious multicolored butterfly shake free. It settled to rest for a few seconds before testing its moist new wings. And then it flew along the beam of light, through the shattered window pane and out into the land beyond.

I had completed my undertaking and turned to leave. But I found myself restrained by regret. I had no desire to part from such a beautiful young woman and her songs. I had to force myself to go.

I pushed open the door and passed down the path with my pack, through the gate and out into the lane. I could hear the sound of the young woman's voice gathering in strength. As I wandered slowly away from the village, I heard another sound accompanying that of the songs: the splitting of boulders and the tumbling of stones. For sure, the wall about the house was gradually disintegrating. In my mind's ear I heard 'No fears to beat away – no strife to heal, – The past unsighed for, and the future sure.'

The Pink Jug

The old woman carried a dog in her arms and a straw fish basket on a plaited rope slung over her shoulder. She pressed her frail body, from the shoulders to the knees, against the swing doors of The Owl and Mouse and entered the bar.

'How many times have I told you, Biddy? No dogs!' Biddy stood ice-still. She stared unblinking at the landlord. 'You'll not be turning us away, not tonight!' she gasped. It was more of a statement than a query.

The landlord, Stow, sighed to himself, continued polishing beer mugs and watched as the old woman lowered herself on to the wood bench under the bay window. Carefully, in a single movement, she dropped the dog on to the tiled floor and pushed him under the seat.

'Be a good boy! Stay! Mother'll get you something nice.' She cooed to the dog until his body relaxed and he slumped down, his face in his paws, and slept. Biddy shuffled towards the bar and as she shuffled Stow drew her half a pint of ale, without being asked.

'If I've told you once, I've told you as many times as there are frosts in March. No dogs!'

'I can't leave 'im. 'E's too old to be left,' Biddy explained, flatly.

'Like you!' Stow muttered as he rang up Biddy's half pint and threw the coins from her knotted handkerchief into the till.

'I'm not leaving 'im! Never! 'E's coming too. . . .' Biddy talked reassuringly to her herself. She looked up at Stow. 'Where's 'is bone?'

Without turning his head, Stow glanced from the corner of his eye to the end of the bar. 'My wife's too soft,' he grumbled as he pushed the newspaper package towards the old woman.

It was early yet. The Owl and Mouse was empty but for two farmhands playing darts in the corner. The lights were ablaze that end of the bar but where Biddy sat, jugging her mug of ale, just one dim light was switched on.

'I'm not lighting you up,' Stow told the old woman.

'Tight-fisted, that what 'e is,' muttered Biddy. 'Always saving this and saving that. . . .'

'You and your good-for-nothing husband would've done well to do a bit of saving. Look at yourself!' Stow stared at the old woman. Her feet leaked from a pair of laceless plimsolls picked up on the common. Wisps of grey hair escaped from the beret she had pulled down over her head;

a flowered blouse that, years before, had done service as a nightdress, sneaked from her skirt and a child's pullover, sleeveless and fraying, stretched across the flat expanse of her chest but did not reach her waist.

'A right mess you look, Biddy!'

Biddy raised her gnarled hands to her head and made a gesture of smoothing her hair. She passed her hands over her chest and thighs but her fingers were bent and arthritic; they could poke small holes in the ground to set a plant or trace a drill for seeds, but for years they had not served to stroke the dog. Useless though the smoothing gestures were, they spoke volumes to Stow: as a boy in the village of Pied Combe he had been raised on the legend of Bridget Mathews.

Bridget Mathews had been born some seventy springs past on the wrong side of the sheets: the lord of the manor had had his wicked way with the milkmaid. When the pink and white buxom lass was into her seventh month, the gentleman set her up in a cottage in the village of Pied Combe, five miles from the gates of his estate. He saw to the needs of mother and child and, if Bridget had married the man he chose for her, she would have been well provided for for the rest of her life but, when she was just eighteen, she met Seamus. It had been a bad choice from the start.

Seamus was lazy. He had been lazy as a boy and became lazier as a man. Someone gave him a horse and cart and on the side of the cart he painted 'Seamus the Carter'. But, if the weather was unsettled, if the horse was obstinate, if there was promise of rabbit for tea, if he had sneezed five times in a clutch, he didn't cart. Pied Combe was ten miles from the post office and ten miles from the station: he could have made a decent living. When the farmer saw how things were going he jumped right in where Seamus failed to work. He made it known that 'regular' every Monday and Friday *he* would make the ten-mile journey to Carswold, *he* was ready to deliver and collect anything and anybody as was required. Seamus didn't mind; he didn't like to be relied upon. He would drive over to Carswold when *he* felt like it – when it suited him. And only then.

He moved in with Bridget and her mother when he married. From that day Bridget became 'Biddy' and the old lady, Ma. Seamus passed his days pottering with the pigs, the goats, the potatoes and the peas. Four times he got Biddy with child and, somehow or other, husband, wife and children survived. But not Ma; shortly after her second grandchild was delivered, she died. They said in the village that she had died of fear. She had the power of divination; she knew all would turn sour as crabs for Biddy. Anyhow, the girl had married beneath her and no good ever came of that!

'I see the bailiffs 've come,' Stow said with a 'so there' lurking in his voice. Biddy stared towards the bar. 'You've not much as could interest them, have you?' Biddy searched in her ale mug. 'What did they commandeer?'

'Everything!' the old woman whispered.

Stow searched Biddy's face. It was vacant of expression. He watched for a long time. When he stooped, to roll a barrel of cider from the cellar steps to his side, Biddy quickly took the bone from her lap and slipped it under the bench.

'There, my lovely, you'll enjoy that, you will!'

Biddy did not watch the sun set behind the acres of blue-green cabbages. She did not see the men, their forks slung over their shoulders, wander home across the fields. She did not hear the voices of the villagers ring out from open windows as families assembled for high tea, or the delighted cries of the children when Father arrived home.

The farm-hands had finished their game of darts. One of the men knew Biddy and felt sorry for her. He knew that his master's fortune was owed, in part, to Seamus's laziness and he knew that Biddy had a hard time of it. When he could get away with it, he stole butter and cheese and took it along to the old woman. He got her talking about 'the good old days'.

'Your jar empty?' he asked and, without waiting for an answer, he picked it up and took it to the bar and had it filled. 'What happened, to-day, Biddy? I saw they'd come.'

The old woman looked up at the young man. Her brow was furrowed and brown as winter fields. She did not answer; it seemed as if she was trying to reply but could not. 'Where's Seamus?' the young man tried.

'Business,' muttered Biddy, stumbling out of her reverie, ''E's 'ad business. . . .'

'Business? What business would that be?' Stow leant out over the bar accusingly. 'Seamus would have done well to think of business fifty years back. It's too late now!'

You couldn't talk 'private' in The Owl and Mouse. You could be heard from one end of the inn to the other when the place was all but empty.

'Yes, they come,' Biddy said flatly. She looked hard at the young man who had drawn his chair close to the corner of the bench. It seemed she was trying to make out if not who he was, why he was interested. 'Two fat men, ever so fat they was. . . .'

'Bailiffs look to their bellies, bailiffs do,' the young man said knowingly.

'They come in, they looked about, and they *laughed*! I said "What ever are you laughing on?" "You got nothing!" they said.'

'Well, Biddy, it's true: you've not much.'

The old woman's chin sank into her chest. She was silent for a while. She bent down and sought the dog's head.

'I got 'im. I kep' 'im!' And then without warning and with terrible ferocity, Biddy started to shout: 'They took the jug! They got the jug!'

Stow looked up anxiously. 'She's potty!' he muttered.

The farm-hand's mouth fell open and he watched the old woman. Her face was hidden in her hands; her body rocked back and forth. Over and over, she cried out: 'They took the jug!'

'What jug, Biddy?'

Biddy took her hands from her face. Her eyes beseeched the man to know what jug. She watched as he rose from his chair and she made no gesture of recognition when he patted her gently on the shoulder. 'I'd best be getting along, now,' he said kindly, adding 'Seamus'll be here by and by.'

The contours of Biddy's ploughed face were sodden with tears. The small, faded eyes were barren of expression. She sat facing the bar but did not see Stow glance regularly in her direction. The inn was filling; the lights were ablaze; a strong smell of ale, sweat and 'baccy filled the air. Biddy pressed herself flat into the corner of her seat, against the straw fish basket. Under the seat, the dog crunched his bone. Biddy had long since drunk to the dregs of her ale when Seamus burst into the inn.

'Well, now, and how's me Sparrow?' He threw the question at Biddy from the side of his mouth as he toppled headlong towards the bar. Stow put down a pint of ale and eyed Seamus with contempt. He took his money as if it were infected. Seamus lurched unsteadily to his wife's side.

'You bin waiting long?' he asked, without stopping for a reply. 'Meself, I stopped for a jar at The Raven with Tom-boy. I stopped for another at The Crown with Bill-lad,' he offered unnecessarily. He slumped on the bench, half over his wife, drew in draughts of ale, swilled them round his cavernous mouth and swallowed loudly. Then he belched. 'Ah!' he sighed contentedly. 'that's better – a lot better!' He smiled to himself, 'I had a fine day, a right fine day in Carswold!'

'And what about the money? Did you get the money?'

'Well, I wouldn't say as exactly I got the money. No – not precisely. But, mind you Biddy: I got true friends ... and there's promises, promises of loans in good time, me Sparrow!'

'It's *now* we need the money!' the old woman moaned.

'Of course, we need money,' agreed Seamus, reasonably, 'Everyone needs money, that's true enough. There's no argument there! Don't we all need money?' He addressed the bar. 'Me Biddy says we need money! She's right there! Don't we all need money?' The men in the bar turned and stared at the couple, for a split second, and then they turned away and drank. The inn fell silent.

'Don't be downcast, me Sparrow, something'll turn up. It always does. You know that!' And Seamus gathered himself together and attempted to rise. 'We'll be off 'ome, now; we'll 'ave ourselves a nice slice of ham and a glass of your rhubarb wine and then we'll kip and tomorrow I'll come up with something.' Well satisfied with his plan, Seamus stood, balancing himself with one hand on the table.

'We got no 'ome!' muttered Biddy flatly.

'Course we got a 'ome!'

'They took it!'

'Don't be foolish, woman! 'Ow can they took a cot?'

Biddy returned her gnarled hands to her face and rocked her body back and forth.

'They took it! They took it!' she shouted. And then, peculiarly, she stopped rocking and her voice quietened and she leant across the table and, in confiding tones, she told her lurching husband: 'They took the jug, you know. They took the jug, they did! The jug,' she repeated, nodding, making sure her husband got the point. ''Twas the thing I liked the best, Mother's pink jug, very nice, it was.' And so saying, she threw herself back against the bench.

A glazed looked settled on Biddy's face. She mumbled incoherently about the pink jug. Seamus did not listen but tried to turn his face into the bar for support. However, no one was offering him ale or conversation and he turned back towards Biddy, steadying himself with his two hands on the table.

'They come just after you left. They looked everywhere – upstairs, downstairs, in all the cupboards – even under the floor-boards. Ever so thorough, they was. They took the bed to pieces and threw the bits out of the window, "to save time" they said. Yes, that's what they said. Said, too, the mattress wasn't worth much but the brass might fetch a bit. Liked the lamps and the two chairs and your Sunday suit and your pipes. They'll be back tomorrow for the animals.'

'Well, Sparrow, that's not so bad,' Seamus said. Biddy did not hear this assessment. In the same low voice, she continued to relate events from a distant land with customs she did not properly comprehend.

'They liked Mother's sewing machine. They liked the roses and the bindweed and said it would fetch a fair penny. I told 'em, "It gives no trouble, never has done, that machine!" Remember how as Mother sewed for me and the little ones . . . ?' Biddy drew her blouse from her skirt and peered hard at a piece of it. 'Look there! I told them, those were Mother's stitches!'

'I'll just be getting meself a pint!' Seamus said. Rather than follow his progress to the bar, once again Biddy closed her eyes. She settled back into her corner.

'They'll not be making a lot from that sewing machine. Nor the jug, nor the brass bed, come to that,' Seamus said, as he sat down by the side of his wife, clutching his ale.

'Course they won't. That's why they took the cot and the animals,' Biddy leaned towards Seamus, confidingly. 'Cot! That's why they took the cot!' With one gnarled hand she raised her husband's face so that his eyes met hers. 'Understand! They took it: it's theirs! Said it wasn't worth much but that it'd help!'

'Help!' exploded Seamus. 'Not us, it won't.' He was shaking. His shoulders were out of control. He tried to stiffen, tried to compose his irresolute limbs. 'Took it, did they?' he asked, thoughtfully. 'Well, now, I must be thinking of a way out.' But his thoughts bobbed off course. From time to time he managed an expressive sigh. During this speechless lull the dog pushed himself from under the bench, walked into the centre of the bar, where there was now room for him to stretch, and rolled over.

'You kep' the bloody dog, then!' Patches of purple-red anger rose speckled on his cheeks. 'What bloody good is 'e?'

''E's my good, that's what good 'e is. The bailiffs let me keep 'im, said 'e was worthless. I'm used to worthless things, I am,' Biddy added, reassuringly.

Seamus brought his ale mug down hard on the table and clung to it as it swerved to the table's edge. Again he attempted to compose himself.

'Well, now, Biddy me Sparrow, I'd best be thinking for both of us.' And he crossed and recrossed his legs. He wrinkled his forehead into five bold marks such as the tide leaves on the sands. He cupped his face in his right hand. He sought inspiration from the middle distance. Then, in a stage whisper, he enquired anxiously, 'My pistol? Did they take my pistol?'

Biddy did not reply.

'Did they find my pistol, Biddy?'

'I don't rightly know whether they did or they did not.'

'Oh dear me! Now that's serious! We must go right now. It's me pride and joy. And I got no licence.'

'I've told you: the cot's not ours, no more. It's locked and barred. The bailiffs took the key.'

'And where in the world do they expect us to lay our heads?' Seamus's mood had abruptly changed. Ale and self-pity contrived a high-tide of tears, with waves ready to break over seventy years of ineptitude.

'I liked that cot,' he moaned, 'I had plans for it.' Unashamedly, Seamus dwelt on plans both he and Biddy knew would never have materialized.

'You're a silly fool, Seamus, that's what you are!' Seamus sat up straight in astonishment; he could feel his blood thin. 'You know right well as how those men wouldn't wait five year for you to find money to pay their bills. Chandlers and seedsmen don't wait! You bin no good as 'usband, no good at all!' The old woman's head nodded in agreement with her words. She repeated 'no good at all' several times over.

'Now, they're cruel words, me Sparrow. You know I've always thought to do what's best for you.' His tone was set to wheedle. 'Don't you worry your pretty 'ead. Leave it all to Seamus: Seamus will think of something. Right now, you and me's slipping back to the cot. We'll fetch into the cart whatever the buggers've left us. But first, we'll down a jar.'

'That we won't,' Biddy said firmly.

Seamus had no more argument in him. He placed both hands, palm down, on the table and pushed himself into a standing position. He walked round the table to Biddy and pulled her gently to her feet.

'Leave me, do! I've got me basket and the dog to manage.' The old woman untied the rope from the basket and pushed it through the dog's collar. She got down on her knees, picked up the pieces of bone left by the dog and packed them into the basket. She found it hard to get to her feet. She dragged herself up, holding on to the table. No one noticed her difficulty. No one noticed the old couple hobble out of The Owl and Mouse.

The moon was full and the air sharp as pins as Seamus and Biddy trundled the half-mile from the inn to the cottage in their horse-drawn cart. As they drew near the cottage gate, the owl that roosted in their elm swooped to catch a mouse. Seamus and Biddy sat in silence looking towards the cottage that had been 'ome for fifty years and more. Seamus took Biddy's hand in his; the gnarled fingers made him think of the green-grey branches of his apple trees. They listened quietly as the pig snorted and the hens shuffled.

'So they've left us the animals!'

''Til tomorrow!'

Seamus climbed down from the cart. Biddy watched as he tried the plank nailed across the downstairs windows, and the padlock fastened to the door. She watched as he disappeared through the elder bush towards the privy. She fastened the dog's rope to the side of the cart.

'Now, you sit there, lovely!' She patted the dog and placed a piece of bone between his paws. 'You like that, you do! Yes, you do!' She cooed happily as she fished again in her basket and took something from right at the bottom. In the country-night silence she could hear her heart marching in her breast like a brave soldier. Minutes passed before Seamus pushed his way back through the elder branches to the gate of the cottage.

''S'no good!' he called to Biddy, as he walked back towards her, 'the windows're barred, the doors' locked....' A shot pierced the night. The horse rose between the shafts of the cart on its back legs; the dog howled; the garden gate flew open and Seamus dropped forward on to the path, by the side of the lane. Biddy saw that his hand was clutched round a posy of colourless daffodils.

At least there'll be flowers for his bier, she reflected, as she threw the pistol into the long grass. As dry metal met sodden earth, she heard the unexpected sound of shattering china. At once, the pig started up his hysterical snorting and the hens fanned their wings against the coop. Biddy lowered herself from the cart. She shuffled to the gate. Ignoring her husband's inert body, she knelt on the ground where the pistol lay. There, shimmering in the colourless light of the full moon, was the shattered pink lustre jug.

As sharply as it had been interrupted, silence returned.

It was Stow who found Biddy's body. He was walking across the common to the farm, to collect the eggs. Half submerged in the water of the duck-pond and half supported by a clump of reeds, lay Biddy's body. Tethered to it was the dog. He was just alive.

That afternoon, the bailiffs returned to Pied Combe. They opened up the cottage and loaded the pig, the hens and the mangle on to their lorry. A single picture remained hanging on the wall of the front room and the two fat men valued it for the frame. As one took it off the wall, the other noticed a loose brick in the wall. Behind the brick was a cavity; in the cavity was a tobacco tin and in the tin there was no tobacco. There were gold sovereigns.

'Well, I never, Mr Hargreaves. More than enough to meet their debts. Funny they never mentioned the money!'

'The trouble with that lot, they're feckless; they never believe we mean business.'

Seamus's debts to the chandler and the seedsman and half a dozen more were settled. The villagers saw to it that the couple had a decent send-off, and space was found for them in the field that lay adjacent to the village churchyard. The cottage was not impounded, and everything

— the sewing machine, the brass bedstead, the picture, the mangle — was returned and put back in place. But no one wanted to buy the cottage; no one wanted to live there. Biddy's dog haunted the cot. He prowled about the garden by day and slept in the privy by night. Every evening, at dusk, he ambled the half mile to The Owl and Mouse where Stow's wife had a plate of food ready for him, and a bone to take home.

The Hermit of Silene

The village of Silene lies in the lap of white stone mountains. From a distance, it is impossible to distinguish the village from the rocky hills that rise around it. The roofs and the walls of the buildings are fashioned from ground stone taken from the quarry in the foothills, and the decoration the villagers paint in broad bands round the doors and windows is made from the colours of rust bracken, emerald herbs, and purple berries that push from the crannies in the rocks and from the ground of the foothills.

The village is substantial in size, but the number of inhabitants is not known. A count was twice attempted and twice failed. When the count was taken during the day the men were at work, the women were at market or in the wash-house, the children were in school or at play. Despite the ringing of all the bells of the village, with the request that every man, woman and child stand still until he had been counted, it was just not in the nature of the villagers to heed bells. One man's animal strayed and he went in search of it; one woman's bread rose in the oven and she went to save it from burning. As for the children, it was torture for any one of them to stay still for five seconds at a time – there was so much to do! And when the count was attempted at night most of the villagers, drunk on the rich mountain air, slept so soundly they did not hear the knock at the door. And so it is that the village of Silene is hidden from view and its numbers unknown.

The people of Silene, like most mountain folk, are independent and proud. They believe their village to be the centre of the world. They know people live elsewhere, and differently from them, for once in a while a stranger with a taste for exploration climbs over the mountain passes and brings news from outside. But the ways of Silene are peculiar to Silene; they were invented by the inhabitants of long ago and have remained unchanged.

One morning, during the first days of autumn, Silene mourned the loss of the good woman Jess and her husband Stavengro, who kept the small grocer's shop in Bean Alley. The shop was not the largest in the village, nor was it the best, for being small it could not stock the variety of goods kept by the larger shop in the square. However, it was the best-loved shop, for Jess and Stavengro held a special place in the affections of the community. When any family was in need it was to Jess and Stavengro that it turned, and Jess would always take the empty basket

146

of a village woman in want and pile it high with food, irrespective of whether the woman had money to pay for the goods.

Every evening at dusk, when Stavengro lowered the shutters over the shop window against the mountain night, Jess packed a basket of food and carried it up Bean Alley, over Pump Square, across the bracken and grass common where the goats grazed, up to the foothills of the great white rock mountains. Whether it was high summer and the land was parched or winter and the land blanketed with snow, whether it was spring and the stream bulged with water or autumn and the hills on fire with colour, Jess wound her way to the cave where the hermit lived. She left the full basket of today at the side of the cave, by the hermit's water butt, and returned home with yesterday's empty basket.

The job of taking food to the hermit belonged traditionally to Jess's family; for generations this family had been appointed by the village 'Provender to the Hermit'. The job passed to the first-born, whether the first-born was a girl or a boy. Special qualities were required for its performance: fastness of spirit – for the weather was often inclement and the journey to the cave and back long in the rain and cold; generosity – for although the villagers contributed items for the hermit when times were good, when times were bad it fell to the family of Jess the Provender to provide all the hermit needed to sustain him.

Jess knew it was the supreme privilege of village life to meet the hermit's needs, and the grocer and his wife performed the rite with zeal and joy. All the inhabitants of Silene agreed that their continuing good fortune and happiness were guaranteed by the existence of the hermit, the all-good, pure man who lived in the highlands that protected their village, who spent his days and his nights in silent communication with the Great Spirit of the Hills.

There is a handful of things of which one may be certain in life: the sky hangs continuously overhead; the water in the lakes lies flat; the sun gives light and the rains bring forth growth – and hermits bring down blessings.

The grocer and his wife lived in contentment. They knew that when the time came for one to leave behind his body and for his soul to join the assembly of souls in the highest peaks of the hills, the other would quickly follow. There would be no pleasure in lingering in Silene separated from his partner's company.

'When your father and I join the souls in the hills, you will work the shop during the hours of the day, and take food to the hermit at dusk!' Thus they instructed their daughter, Mattanya, from her earliest days. 'And when the Black Daisy that grows in the pot by the kitchen door blooms, you must take to wed the young man who is courting you.

And when you bear a child for the first time, the Daisy will bloom again. This is a sign for all the village to witness, to know that your child is destined to be "Provender to the Hermit" when your soul joins ours in the peaks.'

The villagers of Silene never ventured further from the village than the foothills of the mountains where they cultivated the land. Out of respect for the souls of their dead ancestors reposing in the highest peaks, they did not ascend the hills. However, once in each of the four seasons of the year, Jess had taken Mattanya past the cultivated land, as far as the hermit's cave. The girl would need to recognize the place in all its changing aspects.

The time came for the grocer and his wife to leave their bodies to the ground. There was sadness in the village at their departing, but great joy in the knowledge that their souls would be reunited with the souls of all the others who had once lived in Silene.

It was autumn; the beech trees had thrown their bronze leaves to the ground and the foothills of the white stone mountains were thickly covered with brambles carrying fat purple berries from which the wine of Silene was pressed. Mattanya was making her first journey alone to the hermit's cave with a basket of food. She glanced about her and marvelled at the beauty: flocks of birds were feasting on flying insects; the sun was sinking behind a finger of white stone, making a rim of gold round three sides. Mattanya put down the basket of food to the side of the hermit's water butt, picked up the empty basket and immediately turned to walk back down the path towards the village, as swiftly as she had seen her mother do. As she turned she felt a presence. It was as tangible as if a ray of sun had struck her back.

The following evening at dusk she again placed a full basket of food by the side of the hermit's water butt, and again picked up yesterday's empty basket. She was absorbed in watching the birds that feasted on the wing. As she turned to walk down the path she felt the piercing presence for the second time.

Mattanya was beautiful and she was young, but so were many women in the village of Silene. Mattanya was no different from other villagers of her age. When she had been a child in her parents' house she had done as they had instructed her to do. Now that she was grown, and lived alone, she did as she knew would have found favour with her parents, but she did it all in her own way.

In the village of Silene the manner of living had been established in the far distant past; each succeeding generation added something new, or left out something old, but it was part of the intention of the community of Silene to live so consistently with the past that were a soul from the mountain peaks to find a new body and return to the village it would recognize the place and the manner of living.

In the course of her life Mattanya had heard the villagers speculate on the life and appearance of the hermit. But no one – not even her parents – had ever caught sight of him.

'He's very, very old; he's crooked and gnarled. He looks like a poor mountain ash that ekes out an existence from a cranny in a rock, and is daily subjected to the buffeting of the winds.' This Mattanya heard from a woman at the wash-house, who heard it from her mother who had heard it from another.

'His face is like a blackberry, covered in bumps and bosses – an unripe berry at that, part purple, part green; his hair is tangled like brambles and is wound about his waist,' the blacksmith volunteered.

'His nails are two inches long and sharp as needles. He files them on stone and uses them to cut his food.' Such speculations as these were of little interest to Mattanya, for in her family no one spoke of the appearance of the hermit but only of the purpose of his life.

'He speaks to no one but the Great Spirit, that Spirit which gathers the village souls to himself when our bodies are tired with living,' her mother told her. 'Through him the Great Spirit learns of our needs, and through his will we are brought peace and happiness.' And so it was that from her earliest days Mattanya imagined the hermit as she imagined the wind: invisible but purposeful.

Throughout history there had always been a hermit in the hills above Silene. Throughout the life of a hermit in his cave, time does not exist. He does not know time passes; he does not observe his ageing.

The hermit had become accustomed to an occasional glimpse of Jess or Stavengro, when one or other delivered his food, in the half-light of dusk. Standing well back at the entrance to his cave he would catch sight of a solid figure and observe how the once upright man was become a little bent, and how the once nimble-footed woman was now slow. One evening in spring he happened to be looking out over the village, from well back in his cave, when he observed a long, thin shadow cast by the sinking sun. It clearly did not belong to either the bent man or the slow woman who normally brought his food. It was the most exquisite of shadows! He must watch out for it again. And then he became lost in contemplation and forgot about it.

The hermit might well have forgotten the shadow altogether had he not one evening heard the sound of music in the hills. It was a ravishing sound: not that of birds twittering, nor the donkey braying. It was not the sound of goats' bells nor that of the wind in the trees. It was something he could name. At the back of his mind there stirred the memory of song. He tried to lift his voice and imitate the sound. He looked before him; he looked behind him; he had no shadow and he had no voice. One day, when there was time to turn his mind to such things, he must consider why he had no shadow and why he had no voice.

The hermit's existence continued as it had always done. Baskets full of food were regularly delivered at dusk, and the empty basket of yesterday was removed. And then one day he saw the lissome outline of Mattanya descending the path that led from the entrance of the cave, a basket swinging from her hand, her long hair billowing out behind her as she walked, the gentle breeze collecting in her skirt and ballooning it. She appeared to float towards the village on air – not pick her way carefully down the stony path. Her shadow stretched out behind her and she sang. The hermit threw himself out of the cave on to the ground in an effort to catch the shadow in his gnarled hands – but it escaped his grasp and sank feet first down the hill. The hermit, his hands grazed by the stony ground, stumbled into the cave and lost himself in thought. But the damage was done! He reunited himself with the Great Spirit of the hills but his mind and his heart were judged by memories of, and desire for, the sound of song and the sight of shadow. Henceforth the steadfast rhythm of his life was interrupted.

That night the hermit had a dream. He dreamed of a young man and a young girl walking hand in hand by a river and singing; the sun was setting and cast behind the couple two long and beautiful shadows. The hermit fancied he could smell the warm scents that linger in hedgerows after a sunny day. When he woke he observed how differently he felt from the way he felt after a dreamless night. What a glorious thing it would be, he thought, if my dream became a reality. He resolved to speak of earthly matters with the Great Spirit of the hills. For what he had to say he prepared himself at length and then with the voice of his mind he addressed the Spirit thus:

'Great Spirit, you and I are one since far beyond the counting of seasons. Through your guidance I have protected the village of Silene and no harm has befallen any man, woman or child. The beasts of the fields have thrived; the crops have burgeoned. In return the people have cared diligently for me. Your mercy and generosity have never failed. Now I have a personal wish: before my time comes to join the souls in the mountain peaks give me youth for a season! Desire overwhelms me for youth that I may marry the young woman with the long shadow and sweet voice who brings my sustenance.'

The Great Spirit did not reply. It was not his way.

The hermit spent more and more time dreaming of the young woman who delivered his food, and of how it would be to be an ordinary young man married to a beautiful young woman living in Silene. He spent less and less time in contemplation of the Great Spirit; he was restless and disturbed. He paced up and down the cave; at first he paced slowly, his eyes lowered, his feet shuffling over the uneven surface of the ground. Little by little his pace quickened, his neck straightened, his eyes faced the walls of the cave and he found he was filled with unfamiliar energy. He strode out of the cave and into the open and looked about him. He was astounded! The sky was azure blue; the mountains dazzling white, and great pink birds soared above the lofty trees. Down in the valley the village of Silene beckoned to him with curls of smoke rising from chimney pots. He turned his head to look behind him; he fancied he saw a faint shadow.... Reluctantly, he turned back into the cave.

For longer than he could recall, the hermit had been accustomed to using his inward eye and his silent voice in communication with the Great Spirit. He had never had occasion to see himself in a looking glass. He was so used to his way of life that he did not stop to consider whether he was young or old, ugly or handsome, comfortable or uncomfortable. He just 'was'. But his metamorphosis, as dramatic as that from caterpillar to butterfly, made him *feel* as differently as he appeared. He became impatient to see the young woman who brought his food.

When dusk fell the hermit sat at the entrance to his cave. He was waiting for the young woman. When she appeared, when her head was just visible as she climbed the steep path, he stepped back into the cave so as not to be seen by her. She put down the full basket of food by his water butt; she picked up the empty basket of yesterday and as she did so the hermit's heart leapt into his mouth. He watched as she turned, as her shadow spilled behind her and her voice rose in song on the motionless air.

His mind was made up: the hermit ran down the hill behind Mattanya. In Pump Square Mattanya stopped and drank from the village pump. As she raised the mug, one from a collection kept by the pump for all to use, she stood facing the mountains from which she had just descended. She was surprised to see a strong, fine young man walking down the path towards her. She did not recognize him.

'Who are you? I thought only the ancient hermit lived in those hills.'

'I am a stranger, I am seeking lodging in Silene.' The man stood before Mattanya and, as she refreshed herself with the pure cool water from the mountains at the village pump, he refreshed himself with the sight of her flawless beauty.

The arrival of a stranger in Silene was something of an event, and Mattanya was proud and happy to be the first person to greet him.

'I would be happy if you would do me the honour of lodging in my house,' Mattanya told him. Together, in silence, Mattanya and the stranger walked down Bean Alley to the grocer's shop. As Mattanya's hand turned the knob on the shop door she noticed that the stranger stood some distance behind her in the alley. He had turned out his pockets so that they hung sadly empty over his hips:

'I have no money to pay for lodging.'

'I do not need money,' Mattanya replied, 'It is the custom in Silene for a stranger to give a service in return for food and lodging.' The stranger followed Mattanya into the shop.

'You will be quite comfortable here,' Mattanya indicated a space behind the broad, polished counter. She took a rolled palliasse from under a sleeping cat and spread it over the floor boards. Kneeling down on the straw-filled mattress she showed the man how thick and springy it was, and repeated: 'You will be quite comfortable here by the bags of beans and the piles of wax candles. You won't be disturbed until I rise, at dawn, unless it be by the cat: she guards the stores against the greedy mice.'

It was the custom in Silene for men, women and children to rise at dawn and bed at dusk. It was part of their belief that dark was made to obscure the world as light was made to reveal it. Mattanya slept soundly above the shop as she always did. The stranger slept soundly behind the counter as he was most unaccustomed to do. The mice gathered under the floor boards and feasted on shavings of cheese that had slipped through the cracks during the day when the big cheeses were sliced. The cat lay curled by the biscuit bag, half awake on guard, half asleep, dreaming of the chase.

At dawn Mattanya rose. The man, hearing footsteps above his head and not remembering where he was, jumped up. And then he remembered and he rolled the palliasse into a neat shape, placed it on a pile of boxes and waited for Mattanya to descend the creaking stairs.

Mattanya heated goat's milk on the stove. Together the beautiful young woman and the fine young man sat drinking steaming milk from wide earthenware bowls. Mattanya buttered chunks of black bread and these they dipped into the milk and ate when the bread was soft.

'I shall stay a while in Silene, and in return for my food and lodging I shall help you,' the man announced rather solemnly, looking about him and assessing what there would be to do in a grocer's shop. 'I shall weigh the beans and lentils into bags for you, and cut the logs into splinters for fire-wood and decant the wine and...' The stranger listed all the things he would do to help Mattanya and provide for his board and his lodging.

Mattanya could do all these jobs unaided – and many more besides – but it was not in her nature to make objections and the arrangement might well have its uses, for even when one person can manage all the work to be done, if there are two people to share it time is freed for other things. And if that were not sufficient reason it was considered a privilege of village life to shelter a stranger.

Throughout the day the villagers came into the shop, bought their goods, passed the time of day, and took leave of Mattanya. The presence of the stranger intrigued them, but being tactful they did not question him, but simply wished him a long and happy stay among them. But when they left the shop and lingered in Bean Alley the women speculated. From where did he come and why? As the day drew to a close and the sun was poised low in the sky, Mattanya filled a basket with food.

'I have to take food to the hermit who lives in the hills,' she explained as she left the shop. 'You close the shop when Bean Alley is quiet. Take some food to eat and make yourself comfortable. I shall be back when it is dark.

When she reached the cave Mattanya was surprised to find that yesterday's basket was where she had left it, and it was untouched. She hoped the hermit was not ill. But she knew better than to disturb him by calling out and asking questions. Perhaps he had been so absorbed in contemplation that he had not noticed the passing of a sunset and a sunrise. Or perhaps he had climbed into the higher peaks on business of his own. Mattanya put down today's basket by the side of yesterday's and went to the entrance of the cave.

The atmosphere was changed. Mattanya sensed the absence of something indefinable to which she had become accustomed. It made her feel alone and rather frightened. It was as if her guardian angel had taken flight, abandoning her to the mercy of the wolves, the night, and the mountain tempests. She ran down the path and across the common where the goats grazed. She surprised the beasts, who stopped munching and scattered in all directions to avoid her untidy steps; their bells clanged and the noise filled the silence of the near-dark village. One or two villagers who lived in houses fringing the common, and on Pump Square, came to their windows and looked out in an effort to discover what it was that was causing such a commotion. No sooner had they looked right and left and straight ahead than the goats settled to their munching once again and silence filled every corner of Silene.

Mattanya was out of breath when she regained the shop. She had forgotten that the stranger would be there, and when she saw candle light flickering in the kitchen at the back of the shop her heart missed a beat: so many strange, unaccountable things were happening. Then she remembered.

The table was prepared for two; a platter of beans and a salad of dandelion leaves were placed on the scrubbed table, and a bottle of berry wine was open by their side.

'You are pale and out of breath,' the stranger observed.

'I went to take food to the hermit in the hills. But today, unlike any other day, yesterday's basket was just where I had left it, by the water butt. It was still full: untouched. And I did not feel the warm presence of the hermit as I normally do. I thought the hills were hostile and I took fright in the foothills and ran all the way home. I frightened the goats. Did you hear how their bells clanged?'

'I did,' the stranger replied.

Mattanya and the man ate in silence in the glimmering light of candles.

'I am worried about the hermit,' Mattanya said, talking more to herself than to the man; she was not yet accustomed to his being in the kitchen. 'I hope no harm has befallen him. Not only is he the only hermit we have to care for but without his care for us, our safety, our fortune and our happiness in Silene – all are at risk. He intervenes on our behalf with the Great Spirit in the hills,' she explained.

Next day, and every day that followed, the stranger, who called himself Nimmo, helped Mattanya in the shop. At midday when Mattanya drew down the shutters half-way indicating that she was eating her lunch but that the shop was open to anyone who had forgotten an item they needed urgently, the stranger left the shop and went for a walk. As Mattanya threw up the shutters for the afternoon trade the stranger reappeared in Bean Alley to help her. This daily routine of work, of eating, and of sleeping was augmented for Mattanya by the social life of the village. As time went by the stranger started to explore Silene, and strike up conversations with the villagers.

Life proceeded uneventfully except that Nimmo, the stranger, fell deeper in love with Mattanya; Mattanya became increasingly afeared of her journeys to the hermit's cave; and then a series of inexplicable disasters befell the village of Silene.

First, the hens stopped laying. There was not an egg to be had in Silene. Next, a farmer pulled some young carrots and found that whereas their tops were green and full, the root had not developed. There was no long, fat juicy orange vegetable for the pot. And every carrot was the same! More seriously, two babies were attacked by high fever, and came out in a rash of weeping boils that responded to no traditional remedy. The goats on the common became fractious; their milk dried to a trickle, leaving just enough for the children to drink but none for the adults, and certainly not enough to make the cheese normally consumed in large quantities in Silene. And one night there arose a

storm, the like of which could not be compared with any storm the old-
est member of the village could remember. It swept through Silene, rip-
ping thatch from the roofs and hurling chimney-pots into the narrow
streets. The following day the fresh-water stream that ran through the
village, and from which the villagers drew water for all their needs, ran
yellow-green and opaque, and the villagers were frightened to use it.
And they had no other source of supply.

'In our long history,' the villagers complained, 'we have never known
anything like this!' Everyone worried; no one knew what to do. The
children noticed. The villagers spoke of nothing but the disasters; they
stopped one another in the streets and in the shops; they asked what
wrong they had done? Why should the Great Spirit of the hills bring
down this retribution on their heads?

Mattanya's journeys to the hermit's cave were filled with dread. She
picked up the empty basket as usual, but the once friendly hills menaced
her. Round the cave the foothills were crumbling; there was no foothold
for trees. Coarse heather and juniper grew lazily. Adders congregated
in the sun. A buzzard plunged down and gathered a sinuous snake into
its beak. Then a raven swooped and competed with the buzzard for its
share. The animals that made their homes in the undergrowth, in bur-
rows and in lairs, and the scavenger birds that nested in the rock crannies,
eyed Mattanya as she came and as she went. The wind that once played
in her hair and in her skirt, ripped open her blouse and blew so hard
against her legs she found it hard to put down one foot before the other.
Her skin smarted. The noise of the wind was like the thundering of
drums. As Mattanya climbed up and down the hills she could not have
heard the sound of her own voice, had she a mind to sing. The sun gave
out so much heat she thought the blood would boil in her veins – or it
neglected her altogether, so that the pale air was as cold and sharp as ici-
cles, and her body was shaken with shivers.

Late one evening as Mattanya sat by the kitchen table trying to fathom
the changes in life in Silene and in her own life, Nimmo entered and
sat down beside her and took her hand.

'Mattanya, daughter of Jess, I have been in your company for a
goodly time and I have come to love you with all my heart. You are as
good and as wise as you are beautiful. Will you be my wife?'

Mattanya looked into Nimmo's eyes. She looked long and she looked
hard and she believed his words. Then she withdrew her hand from his
and rose from her seat. She went to the door of the kitchen and opened
it. She reached back to the kitchen table and took the candlestick in her
hand and stood with it held over the plant that grew in a pot just outside
the door.

'I cannot marry you, Nimmo. I have instructions I must obey. My mother told me that I must wait until the Black Daisy blooms before I wed. The plant is not even showing signs of bud.'

Nimmo sank thoughtfully and deeply into his chair. Mattanya, her face resting on her arms, leaned on the table. The soft light shed by the candle obscured the face of each from the other. Before rising from her chair to go upstairs to bed Mattanya faced Nimmo: 'I know every one of us has a purpose to serve. Mine is to provide for the hermit and then produce a son or daughter who in turn will be his Provender. Nothing must come between me and that purpose.'

Nimmo listened as Mattanya's feet creaked the wooden stairs and her light body rang the bed springs as she settled to sleep. He continued to sit in the dim light of the guttering candle. He was moved by Mattanya, for she was such a young girl to be unswayed by desires of her own, content to fill a purpose she had inherited.

Life in the village of Silene was becoming increasingly difficult. There were no fresh eggs, no fresh vegetables, no milk, and no one wanted to eat the fish from the yellow-green waters of the stream. Lowering clouds settled overhead and appeared unmovable. The ducks that lived on the banks of the stream took cover in the trees. The dogs and cats crawled on their bellies and sought refuge under furniture. Men and women complained of feeling unwell and restless.

And so it came to pass that a meeting of all the inhabitants of the village was planned. It was hoped that every man, woman and child would attend. Notices were pasted on the walls of every building in Silene. The meeting was convened for eleven o'clock on the next Day of Plenty: the seventh day of the week. It would be held in Pump Square.

Pump Square was vast and cobbled. It was overlooked by tall thin houses the ground floors of which were composed of open arcades. When the weather was fine the band played here and plays were performed; and, whatever the weather, the market was held. It was a curious fact that the population of Silene never outgrew a number that fitted nicely into the Square and under the protection of the arcades.

The village elders conferred together. They made a list of everything that had gone wrong in recent times. The elders were old, and their memories of recent events were not altogether reliable, so they enlisted the aid of twenty young men and women to check their facts and dates. These men and women were to go round all the houses in Silene and collect information about any curious events as yet unreported. And further: they were to list all the strangers that were living in the village. By the Day of Plenty all this information would have been gathered.

Of course, Mattanya knew the enquiries were being made; the

women who came to buy provisions from her told her so. They even hinted that she, Mattanya, was a mite suspect. And so it was that Mattanya was not surprised when, one lunch-time, as she sat behind the half-lowered shutters, a young woman carrying a slate and a piece of chalk tapped lightly on the kitchen door.

'Come in,' Mattanya called out warmly, 'The door is open!'

'Mattanya, daughter of Jess, Provender to the Hermit, is it true that you have a stranger living in your house?'

'It is true. Nimmo from beyond the hills is lodging here and helping in the shop.'

'And when did Nimmo arrive?'

'Just before the berries were ripe enough to gather, when the shadows of evening were longest.'

'Can you tell me about him? What is he like? From where does he come? Who are his family?' And looking about her the woman asked, 'Where is he now?' Mattanya decided to answer the last question first – it was the easiest.

'I cannot tell you where he comes from or anything about his family. But I can assure you that he is all good, all kind and all faithful. He does not know what evil is.'

'Be that as it may,' the woman replied darkly, 'I must mark him on my list.' Her chalk scratched its busy way over the slate. When she left the shop Mattanya shuddered.

Shortly Nimmo returned from his daily walk. As he threw up the shutters for afternoon trade, Mattanya came and stood by his side.

'A young woman came today when you were out walking. She was collecting names for the census of strangers. She asked all manner of questions about you. I told her you came from over the hills. I told her you arrived just before the berries ripened.'

The Day of Plenty dawned a little brighter than previous days. The villagers threw up their windows and looked towards the Square. They were talking excitedly, speculating on what the elders would have to say. Everyone fervently hoped a solution would be found to their problems.

Mattanya and Nimmo set out together. They sat on the rim of the bowl that collected water round the pump at the centre of Pump Square. The water in the bowl had been drained; no one could bear to see thick, yellow-green liquid pouring from the spout of a pump that had once produced a silver stream of mountain purity. Some attempt had been made to brighten the Square; hanging baskets of mountain orchids swung from the lamps that stood sentry-fashion where the lanes met the Square. At eleven o'clock the village bell rang out eleven even notes. As the final note flew towards the hills, the meeting began.

The elders sat on a raised platform facing the crowd.

'We are here to solve the mystery of our declining fortunes. It is the duty of every one of you, man, woman and child, to assist. No event is so insignificant that it will not be considered by us, and added to the pattern of disasters that has submerged Silene in recent times.'

And then all the major disasters that had struck the village were read out: changes in the weather, the new habits of the creatures and of the plants, and the manner in which the children had first been ill and then become uncontrollable. The adults admitted that they too had been quarrelling as they had never quarrelled before.

A sense of relief stole over the villagers as all was freely aired and taken from the secret places of each individual's mind and made the property of the whole community. Towards afternoon, the most senior of the elders stood facing the crowd.

'Mattanya, daughter of Jess,' he called.

'I am here,' answered Mattanya. She stood on the rim of the pump bowl so that she might be seen by the whole crowd.

'Do you perform your duty to the hermit with joy and with zeal?'

'Indeed, I do. Every evening at dusk I did as my mother, Jess, instructed. I take the hermit a basket of food. It is always full to overbrimming. Very often villagers contribute, but when they are unable to do so I make up the weight myself. It is my duty and it is my pleasure.'

'Yet it appears that the hermit no longer protects us. Has he been offended? Has he fled?'

Mattanya took some while to answer.

'There was just one occasion when I wondered. I went to the cave one evening and found that the basket from the day before had not been touched. But this only happened once.' The crowd spoke among themselves.

'Do you have more to say?' asked one of the elders.

'Well, I must confess, since the disasters struck the village I sensed the hills are hostile. I need much courage to make the long haul there and back.'

'Clearly,' said the elder, 'the Great Spirit of the hills is vexed with us, and the hermit is not interceding on our behalf. Why should that be?' He addressed Mattanya.

'I am only a simple girl of Silene. I cannot answer your question. I have thought long and hard. It may be a question to which there is no answer.'

The crowd of villagers talked in whispers. Questions without answers, they were the worst.

Mattanya stepped from the rim of the bowl on to the ground. By her side, where Nimmo had been sitting, was an empty space.

The crowd slowly dispersed. Knots of men and women stood and talked. Their mood lightened; it seemed that chinks were appearing in the dense, black cloud that had hung so long over the village, and the air was sweet-smelling and warmer than it had been of late.

❦   ❦   ❦

No one noticed Nimmo slip away. He strode up Bean Alley, across the common where the goats grazed, into the foothills and up to the hermit's cave. As he walked, he thought it was true, he was not the right man for Mattanya to marry. The Black Daisy could not be fooled. Mattanya's purpose in life was to provide for the hermit. The hermit's purpose was to justify the faith the people of Silene had in him. He would continue to look to their needs and intercede on their behalf with the Great Spirit.

Nimmo entered the cave. Many sunrises and sunsets followed. Nimmo's young body weakened, his hair and nails grew long, he shrank in size and became bent in stature. At dusk, such energy as he could muster drove him to the entrance of the cave; a basket of food was always there, by the water butt. For many seasons he could not steel himself to watch the beautiful young woman who unfailingly served his needs, on whom the sun shone and bestowed a shadow.

As time passed, instead of leaving the basket and rushing back down the hill to the village, Mattanya was inclined to linger by the entrance to the cave, to look about the hills, and to sing. She watched the birds that feasted on the wing. She gloried in the colour and shape of all she saw. She felt at ease.

Mattanya had been surprised that Nimmo had left so suddenly, that Day of Plenty, without saying goodbye, or telling her where he was bound. But she understood he was hurt that she could not become his wife.

Every morning at dawn, when she rose, Mattanya went to look at the plant by the kitchen door. She yearned for the sight of a bud that might blossom into a Black Daisy bloom.

In the village of Silene there were no more disasters. Peace and contentment returned in full measure.

TOMORROW
Elisabeth Russell Taylor

It is August 1960, and a number of ill-assorted guests have gathered at The Tamarisks, a small hotel on the Danish island of Mon. Among them is Miss Elisabeth Danziger, middle aged, plain and unobtrusive. Elisabeth has come back to remember the summers before the war: for the seven days of her holiday she will permit the past to haunt her. Awaiting her on the island are happy memories of growing up in a brilliant and gifted family, but also darker ones, which she struggles to control . . .

'A haunting, beautifully written lament for the isolating power of love
    – *Financial Times*

'Full of precise observations and unexpected lines . . . A melancholy, compelling book with a surprising ending' – *Observer*